CONOR SNEYD was born and ᵣ studied English Literature at Trinity College. After a brief stint teaching English in Japan, he spent several years working as an environmental and animal rights activist. The larger-than-life characters he encountered in this field served as inspiration for his debut novel, *Future Fish*. He currently lives in London with his boyfriend Gordon.

Published in 2023
by Lightning Books
Imprint of Eye Books Ltd
29A Barrow Street
Much Wenlock
Shropshire
TF13 6EN

www.lightning-books.com

ISBN: 9781785633515

Cover by Ifan Bates

Typeset in Adobe Jenson Pro and Ragland

British Library Cataloguing in Publication Data
A catalogue record for this book is available from the British Library.

MIX
Paper | Supporting
responsible forestry
FSC® C171272
FSC
www.fsc.org

Future Fish

Conor Sneyd

Lightning Books

One

The town is even worse than I expected. You hear *west coast of Ireland*, and you know it's going to be the arse end of nowhere, but you figure it will at least be pretty, right? Rugged green hills, pristine blue water and little whitewashed cottages with flowers hanging everywhere?

Not quite.

I step off the sweaty cross-country bus and into a world of grey. Dirty grey shop fronts lining the seawall, their windows shuttered and signs faded. Dull grey waves rolling in from the Atlantic, washing a tide of takeaway containers up and down the beach. Dark grey clouds bearing down on the rooftops, like an omen of some impending disaster. If you saw it in a photo, you might assume it was a regular seaside resort town, going through the inevitable off-season downturn. Except it's the middle of July right now, so the place has no excuses. It's just a massive shithole. I watch as the bus pulls out, getting smaller and smaller before disappearing around a corner, and begin to wonder if I've made a terrible mistake. But there's no turning back now.

An icy wind blows in from the ocean as I go to check the directions on my phone. But of course, there's no signal out here. I glance up and down the road, hoping for a Good Samaritan to point me in the right direction. But the only person in sight is a grizzly old man at the bus stop. He hunches forward on the bench, sharing the seat with an impressive collection of cider cans, and appears to be caught up in an argument with some invisible enemy. I've been avoiding eye contact so far, but it looks like he might be my only option…

'Excuse me,' I say, taking a tentative step forward. 'I'm looking for Atlantic Lane.'

He glares at me for a moment, like I've just insulted the memory of his mother, then launches a hefty glob of phlegm from between his teeth. It sails through the air – a shooting star of mucus – and lands with a *splat* at my feet.

I stumble backwards, mumbling an apology, and nearly trip over my bright purple suitcase. My heart is pounding as I hurry up the road, but I tell myself not to take it personally. He probably spits at everybody. I just need to approach someone slightly less terrifying next time.

After turning off the seafront and wandering down a random side lane, I encounter two teenaged girls perched atop a pair of wheelie bins. They sit cross-legged, dressed in maroon school uniforms, passing a cigarette back and forth between them. The one currently puffing away looks about seven months pregnant.

I take a deep breath, pausing in front of them. They probably qualify as *slightly* less terrifying…

'Sorry to bother you,' I begin. 'I was just wondering if—'

'Fuck off.'

I blink. 'Sorry, what?'

'You heard me,' growls the pregnant girl. 'Fuck off or I'll throw you in the ocean.'

'And I'll break your legs so you can't swim back out,' laughs the other one. 'Get lost, you fat paedo!'

I scramble to the end of the lane, glancing back over my shoulder to make sure they aren't following. It's only when I'm safely around the corner that I pause to check my reflection in a butcher shop window. I'm not *that* fat, am I?

Just as I'm sucking in my stomach and throwing back my shoulders, an elderly nun emerges with a blood-soaked bag of meat. I breathe a sigh of relief when I see her. Nuns wouldn't usually be my favourite class of people, but surely they can be counted on to help a stranger in need? At the very least, calling somebody a *fat paedo* must go against their vows.

'Excuse me,' I say, waving her over. 'I'm looking for 22 Atlantic Lane.'

She looks me slowly up and down, eyes lingering on the flamboyant purple shade of my suitcase. And then her lips purse, like she's sucking on a lemon.

'ATLANTIC. LANE.' I repeat, as clearly as possible. 'Here, look…'

I pull my phone out to show her. But the stupid thing still has no signal. I smack it against my hand, as if that will teach it a lesson, and accidentally open up a video. A scene begins playing on screen – three naked rugby players getting nasty in a bathtub.

The nun shrieks something unintelligible – possibly in Polish – and begins dousing me with a tiny bottle of holy water.

'Stop,' I splutter, covering my eyes. 'Jesus Christ!'

But taking the Lord's name in vain only makes her angrier. She doubles down on her assault, leaving me no other option but to turn around and run.

I scurry up the road, suitcase bouncing over the cracks in the pavement, and don't slow down until I'm totally out of breath. It's only when I lean back against a filthy green post box, gulping down lungfuls of briny ocean air, that I finally spot the sign on the opposite side of the road. *Atlantic Lane*. A wave of relief washes over me. Maybe the nun really did help me after all – working, like the Lord, in mysterious ways. Or maybe there are only five measly roads in this entire town, and I was bound to find the right one eventually.

Twenty-two Atlantic Lane is a long, concrete office block, wedged between a closed-down pound shop and a chipper with zero hygiene stars. The walls are lined with tiny opaque windows, giving the place an unfortunate resemblance to a small prison, or a large public toilet. Next to the door is a shiny brass plaque reading: *WellCat – whole food for the whole family*. I've seen that slogan a million times now, but it still makes me cringe. There's just something so absurd about an entire company devoted to luxury cat food. Cats need to eat, of course, and I support their right to be well fed. But do they really care if their tuna contains *a bouquet of sensuous botanicals?*

Still though, I know I shouldn't complain. A job's a job, and beggars can't be choosers. Especially not when we're in the middle of a never-ending recession.

I pause outside the building to pull myself together. All the articles say a good first impression is key, so I have to make sure not to fuck mine up. I straighten my tie, smooth down my hair, and run through the lines of my introduction one last time. Finally, with my best attempt at a professional smile, I push open the door and step inside.

All of my preparation is instantly forgotten. I'm not sure what I was expecting to find inside, but it sure as hell wasn't this. And I'm not talking about the décor here. The place looks just like any other office I've ever been to – stain-proof blue carpet, featureless off-white walls, and one lonely houseplant drooping in the corner. No, the thing that's sent me reeling – that's made me forget where I am and what I'm supposed to be doing – is the receptionist at the front desk.

He's beautiful. Unearthly. Like an angel descended from heaven to rescue me from the parade of weirdos on the street. His blonde hair shines like a halo under the fluorescent lighting, his thick-framed glasses only accentuating the sharpness of his cheekbones. He must be somewhere in his mid-twenties – just a year or two older than me.

'Hi there,' he says. 'Can I help you?'

'Sorry, yeah…' I clear my throat, feeling my face light up like a blowtorch. 'My name's Mark. Mark McGuire. I have a meeting with Maeve O'Halloran at ten.'

'Ah, you must be the new starter! Welcome to WellCat. I'm Kevin.' He smiles the world's most beautiful smile and reaches out for the phone. I try not to stare at his arm moving around under the sleeve of his shirt, his bicep contracting as he holds the receiver to his ear. He tells the person on the other end that I've arrived, then sets the phone back down and hits me with another smile. 'Maeve will be with you in a minute. Please take a seat.'

A long, L-shaped couch sits next to the potted plant in the corner. It's made of some hairy green material that makes my thighs itch as soon as I sit down.

'So, is this your first time in Ashcross?' he asks, as I cross and uncross my legs.

'It is, yeah. I had my interview over the phone, so I didn't have to come down then. And to be honest, I'd never even heard of the place until I applied for the job.'

'Most people haven't,' he laughs. 'Which is fair enough. It's not exactly on the list of *top ten places to see before you die*. How are you finding it so far anyway?'

I hesitate, sensing a dilemma. Either I say it's great and look like a simpleton, or say it's awful and look like an asshole. Best just to stick to something vague and noncommittal. 'Eh… it's grand, yeah.'

'Some people don't like it,' he shrugs. 'But if you ask me, it's the greatest place in the world. Although I suppose I'm probably biased, since I *was* born and raised here.'

'It does seem like a lovely little town! I guess I just haven't had a chance to look around properly yet…'

'Well, if you're ever in need of a tour guide, just give me a shout. I'd be happy to show you the sights.'

'Really!? I mean…sure, yeah. That'd be cool. If it's not too much trouble.'

'No trouble at all,' he grins. 'It's not every day we have a new arrival in town. Especially not a strapping young lad like yourself.'

I feel my face turning red again and stare down at the floor. Is he just being friendly, or could that last comment have been a little bit flirty? It's hard to tell. Especially without knowing if he's even into guys to begin with. There's nothing he's said or done so far that would sway my assumptions either way. And it's not like I can just straight-up ask him. But luckily for me, this is a problem that can be solved by modern technology.

With a smooth, nonchalant movement, I slide my phone from my pocket and open up Grindr. A single bar of signal has finally shown up, and my heart starts to pound as the app slowly loads. I'm hoping that when the list of nearby guys appears, Kevin's face will be right at the top. *Less than five metres away.* But when the page finally loads, I feel like I've been punched in the stomach. Because not only is there no sign of Kevin, but there's only one guy within range full stop. And he's a serial-killer-looking sixty-nine-year-old called WildAtlanticGay.

I immediately close and reopen the app, praying there's been some sort of error. Maybe the crappy signal cut out again. Maybe the server couldn't connect... But no. WildAtlanticGay is still the only guy in sight. And – Jesus Christ! – he's sent me a message now. I delete it straightaway, without even peeking. The last thing I want to do on my first day is get caught looking at dodgy dick pics.

My body sags down into the couch, disappointment gathering like a cloud over my head. But I tell myself not to read too much into this. Just because Kevin's not on the app doesn't necessarily mean he's a hardcore heterosexual. Maybe he's just too pure for the world of online dating. Or maybe he's on some niche fetish app instead. I'll just have to figure things out the old-fashioned way. Get to know him better. Find out what his interests are. But our little chat has already trailed off, and his eyes are now fixed on the computer screen in front of him.

I gaze around the room, searching for a fresh conversation starter. But the space is distinctly uninspiring. The only magazine on the coffee table is a boring old business journal, the only picture on the wall an inoffensive abstract blob. I guess the dying fern in the corner could be mildly interesting, but that feels like straying into dangerous territory. I don't want him to think I'm casting aspersions on his plant-keeping skills.

And then I spot it. Sitting there on the desk next to Kevin – a battered old paperback. I can't make out the title, but it looks more like a novel than anything work-related. Perfect for a bit of casual small talk.

'So…' I say, trying to sound only mildly interested. 'What are you reading?'

'Oh, this? It's called *Digital Demons*.' He holds it up so I can see the cover – a snarling red monster crawling out of an old-school computer monitor. It looks like some cheesy old sci-fi story from the nineties. Not really my thing, but it's cute that Kevin's into it.

'Looks interesting,' I say. 'What's it about?'

He hesitates, tapping the book against his chiselled chin. 'It's kind of hard to explain. Unless you already know the author?'

I take another look at the cover. Down at the bottom, in no-nonsense block capitals, is the name *LEWIS N. LEWISON*.

'Sounds familiar…' I lie.

'He also wrote *Armies of the Abyss*, if you've heard of that one?'

I shake my head. 'Sorry.'

'Oh.' His smile falters, and I feel like a monster for letting him down. 'How about *My Name is Legion?*' he asks. 'I think that one was his most popular.'

'Eh...' I know I shouldn't. Honesty is the best policy and all that. But when I see the look on his face – brow furrowed in anticipation, dreamy blue eyes glistening from behind their lenses – there's no way I can disappoint him. 'Oh yeah, I love *My Name is Legion!*'

'Really?' His face lights up. 'I've never met another fan. Or at least, none my own age. What did you think of that ending though? I know a lot of people were shocked when it first came out.'

'The ending? Well, eh...'

Shit. I probably should have seen that one coming. But before I can dig myself an even deeper hole, a door at the back of the room suddenly swings open. In strides a formidable-looking woman in an expensive-looking suit. Her stiletto heels cut across the carpet, her ponytail swinging like a pendulum as she beelines towards me with an outstretched hand.

'Marcus, I presume? Lovely to finally meet you.'

I recognise her voice from my interview. Maeve O'Halloran, CEO. She seemed nice enough on the phone, although our conversation was fairly brief – just a few generic questions about my experience, followed by an immediate offer of employment (on the condition that I was available to start the very next week). Her real-life presence is a lot more intimidating. For one thing, she's far younger than I imagined. Mid-thirties at most, and already running an entire company. She radiates the bustling energy of a Very Important Person, and I feel like I'm wasting her time just by existing.

'Lovely to meet you too,' I say, returning the handshake. Now would probably be a good time to point out that my full name is just Mark – not Marcus. But the thought of contradicting her makes me want to vomit.

'You must have had a long journey,' she says, giving me a quick up-and-down. 'Did you drive all the way from Dublin?'

'No, actually. I spent the night at a hostel in Galway, then caught the bus down this morning.'

'Oh.' Her mouth twitches, and I swear I see her wipe the hand I just shook on the back of her trousers. 'No wonder you look so worn out.'

'I am a little tired, I guess. But I'm looking forward to getting stuck in.'

'Well then, let's not waste any more time on chit-chat. Follow me through to the meeting room and we'll get started on your induction.'

She turns towards the door at the back of the room, holding it open for me to wheel my suitcase through. I mumble an awkward *see you later* to Kevin, then step through to a long, windowless corridor. At the far end, descending down towards what must be the basement, is a steep, unlit stairwell. This strikes me as a clear Health and Safety hazard, but Maeve doesn't seem to notice it. She ushers me through a door marked *Small Meeting Room* and into a tiny airless space with a table and two chairs. One entire wall is occupied by a blown-up print of a WellCat ad – a snow-white kitten gazing longingly at a bowl of glistening meat chunks. I set my suitcase underneath its paw and squeeze into one of the chairs.

'So,' says Maeve, sitting down opposite me. 'Allow me to officially welcome you to WellCat.'

'Thank you,' I reply, with all the enthusiasm I can muster. 'I'm delighted to be here.'

'I thought I'd kick things off with a bit of background on the company, to help you understand how we got to be the industry leader we are today. It all started back in '88, when our founder, Emmet Naughton, was searching for something nutritious yet convenient to feed his beloved companion, Dinah…'

And she's off, launching into an epic tale of one man with a dream – a dream of defying the odds and rising to the top of the dog-eat-spam world of pet food production. There's laughter. There's heartbreak. There's even a part where Dinah's ghost appears to Emmet in a dream and tells him not to give up. I get the sense she's given the same speech a million times before, but she's clearly very proud of it, so I do my best to look suitably impressed.

'…and so,' she concludes, twenty minutes later, 'within two decades, Emmet had built the company up into Ireland's second-biggest independent pet food producer.'

'Wow,' I say. 'He must have been very proud of himself.'

'He was,' she sighs. 'And that was his weakness.'

'*Weakness?*'

She nods, leaning in across the table. 'Emmet was a great entrepreneur, but he lacked strategic vision. He was happy to settle for second best. When I took over as leader, I made a promise to the Board that we'd finally claim our rightful place at the top. Of course, the recession has made things difficult, but I wasn't going to let a little global financial crisis get in my way. After a few false starts, we're finally on track, and I've come up with a plan that's going to destroy Miss Meow.'

She drones on and on, waxing lyrical about *cutting labour costs* and *investing in innovation*. I try to think of something intelligent to contribute – something to demonstrate how interested and engaged I am. But I've never had much of a head for business, and eventually I end up zoning out completely.

My eyes wander around the room, searching for a distraction, and come to rest on the giant kitten on the wall. Its little pink tongue sticks out to one side, licking its lips in an oddly humanlike manner. I can't tell if they trained a real kitten to do it, or if it's all a digital manipulation. It's cute enough either way, I suppose. Although I've always been more of a dog person...

Not that I mentioned that particular fact in my cover letter. I said I loved cats, and I was passionate about promoting their health and wellbeing. A little white lie, sure, but you've got to tell them what they want to hear. Just like when I said I'd always dreamed of a career in the fast-moving consumer goods industry. It's not like I could tell the truth – that I was desperate for a job, any job, and the company could have been selling solid-gold toilet seats for all the difference it would make to me.

'... and so, as we enter this critical phase, it's essential that we keep up momentum. That's where you come in.'

'That's where I come in,' I repeat, my mind snapping back to reality.

'Your role as Customer Service Assistant will be vital in building meaningful relationships with customers and helping strengthen brand loyalty. It's a demanding position, but I'm sure you'll find it rewarding. Especially as we gear up to finally take out Miss Meow.'

'Sounds great. I can't wait to get started.'

'Brilliant.' She leans in even further across the table, hitting me with a whiff of flowery perfume. 'You'll find a copy of the Staff Handbook in your inbox. This covers all the main requirements you need to be aware of. Dress code, social media policy, and so on.'

'Got it. I'll read through that right away.'

'There's just one little thing you won't find in the Handbook…' Her expression falters, the mask of cool corporate professionalism slipping for just a second. When she speaks again, her voice is low and deadly serious. '…The laboratory in the basement is strictly off-limits.'

'Laboratory? I didn't even know there was one.'

'It's just a Health and Safety thing,' she says, reverting back to her former manner. 'Nothing to worry about.'

I nod, feeling a bead of sweat trickle down my neck.

'But it's extremely important, nonetheless. No matter what you see, no matter what you hear – even if another staff member tells you otherwise – under no circumstances should you ever set foot inside the laboratory.

'Have I made myself clear?'

Two

It's a relief to get out of that sweaty little room. Things got kind of weird towards the end, but I feel like the meeting was a success overall. Now I just need to make it through the rest of the day without fucking anything up.

I follow Maeve back out into the corridor and down to the right – straight towards the shadowy stairwell. Only the first two or three steps are visible, before they disappear into darkness, but I assume it must lead down to the laboratory. The one Maeve warned me to stay out of. A gust of cool air blows up along the hallway, sending a shiver down my spine. Whatever's down there, it must be incredibly dangerous. I've never seen anybody get that worked up about Health and Safety before.

She stops abruptly in front of another door, and I nearly walk right into her. 'Here we are,' she announces, with a flourish of her manicured hand. 'The heart of the WellCat empire.'

A friendly hum of chatter leaks out into the hallway, but the room falls silent when we enter. Twenty-odd faces stare up at us from the rows of neatly-arranged desks. A few smile vaguely in our direction, but most look immediately back down at their computers, acting like they haven't seen us. I must admit, I was expecting a slightly bigger reaction to my arrival. But I try not to take it personally.

We launch straight into introductions, Maeve leading me around from table to table like a cat on a leash. It's a whirlwind of names and faces, most of which I immediately forget. There are a couple of thirty-something women who seem particularly pally with Maeve, but the majority of people are middle-aged, with thick West coast accents and photos of smiling children on their desks. They all seem friendly enough, in a polite, if slightly distant, sort of way, but none of them exactly scream *future best friend*.

'Last but not least,' says Maeve, as we arrive at a desk in the far corner. 'This is Noelle.'

A shaggy-haired woman hastily closes down her solitaire window. She's dressed all in black, like a fifty-year-old version of the goth girl I was afraid of at school.

'Nice to meet you,' I say, with an awkward wave.

'Same to you,' she replies, lounging back in her chair. Something twinkles behind her eyes, and I get the unpleasant feeling I'm being laughed at.

'Noelle here will be your supervisor,' says Maeve. 'Which means the two of you will be working together very closely.'

'Oh, wow…' I whimper. 'Sounds great.'

'The last few weeks have been hectic, and poor Noelle has been struggling to stay on top of everything, so I'm sure she'll be very glad to have you as an additional resource. Isn't that right, Noelle?'

Noelle glares at her, like she's contemplating various acts of violence, then sighs and rolls her eyes. 'Sure, yeah. That's exactly right.'

'Excellent,' says Maeve. 'I'll leave you to it so. I'm sure you've got a busy onboarding schedule ahead of you.'

Noelle makes a face as soon as Maeve's back is turned. 'Sorry about her,' she mutters. 'She can be a right wagon sometimes.'

I glance back over my shoulder, making sure Maeve hasn't heard, then laugh politely.

'I bet she didn't even offer you a cup of tea, did she?'

'Eh… There wasn't really time for that.'

'Typical. And here's you looking like you've just made a double donation at the blood bank. Hang on a sec and I'll pop to the kitchen.'

She disappears out into the hallway, leaving me to seat myself at the empty desk next to hers. A sprawling mound of printouts covers her workspace, with a stack of empty mugs acting as a paperweight on top. In the one and only tidy corner stands an ornate silver picture frame. But instead of the usual gap-toothed kids in school uniform, this one houses a frowning old woman in a wheelchair, with a nurse in a facemask standing behind her. I lean forward, trying to work out how long ago it was taken, then quickly sit back up when I see Noelle returning.

She moves slowly, balancing two steaming mugs in one hand and a plate of bourbon creams in the other. My mouth begins to water at the sight of the biscuits. I left the hostel too early for breakfast, and I haven't eaten a single morsel all morning.

'So,' she says, setting the tea down. 'Despite what Maeve might like to tell herself, I haven't prepared any *onboarding schedule*. But don't worry, the job is piss-easy. I assume you've worked in customer service before?'

I sit up a little straighter, clearing my throat. This is exactly the sort of question I've been preparing for. 'I don't have any direct experience in customer service, no. But my previous role was in advertising, and I'm confident that the skills I developed there would—'

She cuts me off with a wave of her hand. 'Forget all that bollocks. The only *skill* you need is being able to keep your cool while some eejit is ranting at you down the phoneline.'

'Well, I have worked with challenging clients in the past.'

'Pfft. You'll wish you were back with those clients when you hear the shite we have to deal with. Let me ask you this – have you ever seriously contemplated killing somebody before?'

I shove an entire bourbon cream into my mouth, not sure what to say to this.

Noelle just sips her tea and sighs. 'What age are you, anyway?'

'Twenty-two,' I mumble, from behind a mouthful of crumbs.

'Jesus Christ, you're just a baby. Far too young for a dump like Ashcross. I know there's a recession going on, but could you not have found something back in Dublin?'

I swallow down the biscuit and immediately bite into another. I've rehearsed an answer for this question too, but I can already tell it's not going to impress her. '…There were a few jobs going, but only with the big tech companies and accounting firms. And

I suppose I wanted to work somewhere smaller. Somewhere I could really get involved and make a difference.'

She snorts. 'If small is what you're after, you've come to the right place. It doesn't get much smaller than Ashcross. Doesn't get much duller, either. And I should know. I've lived here for decades.'

'Well, I'm confident I can adapt. I'm a dynamic self-starter who works well independently.'

'I'm sure you are. But why the hell would you *want* to adapt to a place like this?'

I hesitate, not liking where this is headed, and reach out for the last biscuit.

'Mother of God,' laughs Noelle, picking up the empty plate. 'You made short work of those bourbon creams.'

'Sorry. I should have saved you one.'

'Don't worry about it. I already ate half the pack while the kettle was boiling.' She winks, setting the plate aside, and scoots her chair over towards my computer. 'Anyway, we should probably get started on some actual work. Can't put it off all day.'

She begins walking me through the main responsibilities of the role. It seems I'll be spending most of my time replying to emails in our customer service inbox. There's a huge spreadsheet with pre-approved answers to all the most common questions – like *Is WellCat suitable for human consumption?* and *Help! My cat can't stop pooing* – so a good chunk of the work is just copying and pasting. We run through a few examples together, and then she leaves me alone to start working my way through the inbox.

I'm about a quarter of the way down the list when the office starts emptying out for lunch. 'Not bad,' says Noelle, peering over my shoulder. 'You're flying through it.'

'Thanks,' I reply, trying not to sound too smug. 'It took me a while to warm up, but I think I've got the hang of it now.'

'Well, you're definitely a lot faster than Valentina was when she first started. But to be fair, English wasn't her first language.'

'Right…and who's Valentina?'

'The girl who was doing the job before you. She just left a couple weeks ago.'

'I see.' It hadn't even occurred to me that somebody else was in the role before me. Suddenly, I'm extremely curious about this Valentina person – especially her post-WellCat career prospects. 'And what's she doing with herself now?'

Noelle shrugs. 'I'm not sure, to be honest.'

'She didn't tell you what her new job was?'

'No… She left in a bit of a hurry.'

'Oh. Did something happen to her?'

She bites her lip, shifting around in the chair. It's the first sign of discomfort I've seen from her all day. 'What do you mean, *did something happen?*'

'I mean, why did she leave so suddenly? I hope she didn't have a family emergency or anything.'

'No, no. Nothing like that.'

'So why the big hurry?'

'Look,' she says, glancing back over her shoulder. The place is practically empty now, but still her voice drops to a whisper. 'We shouldn't really be talking about this. But basically, what happened was… Valentina got herself fired.'

She says something else after that, but I don't catch it.

Because suddenly I'm not in Ashcross any more…

I'm back in Dublin, on a pale January morning, sitting in a glass-walled meeting room. Outside the window, snow is falling in dreamy slow-motion flurries. The ground is too wet for anything to stick, melting the fluffy white flakes into dirty grey mush, but the sight still fills me with a giddy delight. Across the table, my manager Liam is droning on about the need to make difficult business decisions. He looks even more exhausted than usual, his eyeballs disappearing into a pair of black holes. We're supposed to be having our weekly catch-up, which usually only takes a few minutes, but he's been rambling on for at least a quarter of an hour.

'And you've been with us half a year now, Mark, haven't you?'

'Yeah,' I shrug, staring out the window. 'That sounds about right.'

'In that time, we've been closely monitoring your development. And I'm sure you'll agree we've provided you with an adequate level of support?'

'Sure, yeah. I guess it's been adequate.'

'We're a family here at HiberNox Media, and we always have the best interests of our employees at heart. But in difficult times like these, sometimes even families have to go their own separate ways.'

'Of course. Yeah.' It's just occurred to me that getting home this evening is going to be a nightmare. The entire transport network goes haywire at the slightest hint of ice on the roads.

'With that in mind, I hope you'll understand where I'm coming from when I tell you that you haven't passed your six-month probation.'

I blink, turning away from the window. 'Sorry, my six-month what?'

'*Probation*. You haven't passed it.'

'Oh.' I'd forgotten probation was even a thing. It was mentioned somewhere in my contract, but nobody's brought it up since I started. I assumed it was just a formality. A get-out-of-jail-free card for the company in case it turned out you were completely useless. 'Does that mean it goes on for another six months?'

He drops his gaze, running a hand along the greasy strands of his combover. 'Not exactly. We could technically extend it, but I don't think that would benefit either party.'

'So that means...' I slump down in my chair, the realisation slowly sinking in. It turns out I'm completely useless. '...you're firing me?'

'We don't say *fired*. But yes. We've decided not to extend your contract beyond the probationary period. You're entitled to one additional week's pay, but I'll have to ask you to leave the premises immediately. You'll find the full details in here.' He produces a brown paper envelope and slides it across the table. 'Now, do you have any questions?'

'Eh...'

Maybe I'm just in shock, but my initial reaction is mainly apathy. I never planned on ending up in advertising anyway – it just so happened HiberNox Media were the first company to offer me a job after college – and working here has always bored me senseless. I've never cared about the clients and their stupid campaigns. The pointless products they peddle to the world.

Protein powder. Weight loss pills. Little gummy vitamins to make your baby's hair grow faster. In a way, it might actually be a relief to get out of here.

But then I start thinking about the practicalities. Like, what am I going to do for money? How am I supposed to find a new job in this economy with a black mark on my CV? And worst of all, what are people going to say when they find out? I can already imagine the *not angry, just disappointed* speech from my parents. The *why do you always have to embarrass me?* lecture from my boyfriend, Neil. And I already know the first question they're all going to ask me...

'Did I do something wrong?'

Liam sighs, like he just wants this to be over. 'It's less what you did, and more what you didn't do. Your work itself wasn't bad. When I was filling out your evaluation, I gave you four stars for *always delivers projects on time*, and three and a half for *work is of a consistently high quality*. It's the questions on attitude that really dragged you down. I could only give you one star for *is passionate about providing value to clients*, and I had to give you zero for *gets along well with colleagues*. Your average came out as a two-point-four, but it needed to be at least a three.'

I open my mouth to defend myself, but nothing comes out. How can you argue with a two-point-four?

'Try not to be too hard on yourself,' says Liam. 'Just think of this as a learning opportunity.'

'But what am I supposed to be learning? I still don't understand what you wanted from me.'

He glances at his smartwatch, a frown cracking the eggshell of his forehead. 'Look Mark, we don't have time to get into it. All

I'm saying is that you could have acted like you had a little fire in your engine. Like you actually wanted to be here.'

I bite my lip, resisting the urge for an eyeroll. Who in their right mind would actually want to be here? 'But I showed up on time every day,' I say. 'And you said my work was good. So what else was I supposed to do?'

'You could have contributed more in meetings,' says Liam. 'Or volunteered to take on an additional project or two. Even just showing up for after-work drinks every now and then would have gone a long way.'

'But I did show up for after-work drinks! One time...'

'*One time?*'

'During my first week.'

'And why did you never go back?'

'I don't know...' Because that one time was terrible. We squeezed into some bright, musicless pub, where the only thing anybody would talk about was work. I thought the whole point of going out for drinks was to get away from all that. To talk about our real lives for a change. But it was like work was the only thing we had in common. The only possible pretext for all of us being together. 'I just didn't feel like it, I guess.'

'And I suppose you *just didn't feel like* showing up for the Christmas party either? You were the only person in the entire office who failed to attend.'

'I thought the Christmas party was voluntary?'

'It was voluntary. But why on earth would you not want to attend a party?'

I shrug. 'I didn't think anybody would notice I was missing.'

'Well, people certainly noticed you were missing from the

staff photo. The one that went out in our client Christmas card. Which, by the way, you never bothered to sign.'

'I thought signing the card was voluntary?'

He flares his nostrils, beginning to lose patience. 'You know, you've never been featured in any of the photos on our website either.'

'How is that my fault?'

'Maybe if you wore your complimentary company t-shirt every once in a while, the PR team would want to include you.'

'I thought wearing the t-shirt was voluntary?'

'Jesus Christ, Mark!'

He's getting angry now, face ripening like a plump tomato. I decide it's probably best not to push him any further. Outside the window, the snow is getting heavier, blotting out the Docklands with an empty white void.

'Look,' he says, his face fading back to its usual pallor. 'Discussing this further is only going to make things worse. The decision's been made, and all we can do now is move forward.'

Before I can say anything else, he's standing up and escorting me out of the room. I clutch the brown paper envelope to my chest as I follow him over towards my desk. It feels like everybody in the office is staring at me. Pointing and whispering behind my back. *There he goes, the useless loser. Thank God he won't be around much longer.* My eyes begin to sting, but I hold down the tears. There's no way I'm giving them the satisfaction of seeing me cry.

Liam hovers over my shoulder as I gather up my things, watching like a hawk to make sure I don't run off with any company property. It's humiliating. Like I've gone from trusted employee to unwelcome guest. An object of suspicion and contempt. I hurry as fast as my shaking hands will allow, just wanting to get it over with as quickly as possible. Luckily, there isn't too much to pack. Just a tea-stained old mug, a few notebooks and pens, and a little teddy bear Neil gave me on my first day.

It's the teddy bear that gets me in the end. The adorable little face, peeping out over the top of a *good luck* heart, is just too much to bear. Suddenly I'm bawling, tears flowing down my face in a snotty waterfall. The people at the neighbouring desks do their best to ignore me. There are no sympathetic glances. No words of consolation. Not even a single crumpled tissue passed discreetly in my direction. Liam puts a hand on my shoulder, and for one pathetic moment, I think he's actually trying to comfort me. But it turns out he's only directing me towards the exit. He shakes my hand, wishes me *all the best*, then ejects me out onto the frostbitten street...

'Mark... Mark... Are you alright?'

Noelle's voice reels me back from the murky depths of memory. She's standing over my chair, staring down with a conflicted expression. Like she can't decide whether she should be laughing or calling an ambulance. My entire body is slouched sideways, head resting against the cool plaster of the wall. I have no idea how I ended up like this.

'Sorry,' I mumble, pulling myself upright. 'I'm fine.'

'Are you sure? You were totally out of it for a few seconds there. If you weren't such a young whippersnapper, I would have thought you were having a stroke.'

'I'm grand, yeah.' I wipe at the corner of my mouth, where a sticky slick of drool has been hanging. 'Just a little tired. I haven't eaten much today.'

'Why don't I pop out and grab you a sandwich so? You can stay here and rest in the meantime. And don't even think about answering any more of those emails.'

'*Emails?*' This one simple word brings it all rushing back. My predecessor Valentina... Getting fired from the job... But for what reason? My hand shoots out, gripping hold of Noelle's chair. 'Wait! You still have to tell me the rest of the story!'

'*Story?* What story?'

'Valentina's story. Why she got fired. What she did wrong.'

'Oh.' She bends over to pick up her handbag. 'Forget about that. Let's just focus on getting some food into you.'

'No,' I groan, pulling her chair in closer. I know I must look like a weirdo right now, but I can't help it. I need to find out what Valentina's crime was. I need to make sure I don't repeat it. 'Please. Tell me what happened.'

'Look,' she whispers, glancing back over her shoulder. 'I'll tell you about it some other time. It's not safe to discuss these things here.'

Three

A cloud hangs over my head for the rest of the afternoon. The focus I had this morning is gone, chased away by visions of all the different ways Valentina could have gotten herself fired. Did she show up hungover for a meeting and vomit all over a client? Or accidentally copy in the entire office to an email badmouthing the boss? Did she call in sick, then get caught downing double vodkas at the local pub? Or was she just another useless loser with no fire in her engine?

The hours pass by in an anxious blur, and I've achieved practically nothing by the time half-five rolls around. Luckily, Noelle doesn't come over to check my work again.

'Home time!' she announces, pulling on a long, black coat.'Do you want a lift?'

'Yes, please. Although now that you mention it, I'm not sure where exactly *home* is...' The company was supposed to be sorting out my accommodation in exchange for starting on such short notice, but nobody's brought it up since I arrived.

'Right, yeah. I forgot to tell you... You'll be living with me!'

'Living with you?' I repeat, praying this is some sort of joke.

'Try not to look quite so horrified. I don't mean *with me* with me. Just in the same building.'

'Oh, right.'

'I can tell you're delighted... Anyway, let's get a move on. I want to get home in time for *Ninety Day Milkmaid*.'

'Ninety Day *what?*'

'*Milk. Maid.* It's a reality TV show about six party girls from Dublin trying to make it on a Tipperary dairy farm. You're welcome to come over and watch it with me, if you've got nothing better to do.'

'Eh... I think I should probably do some unpacking tonight. But maybe some other time.'

'Suit yourself,' she shrugs, heading for the door.

I grab my purple suitcase and follow her out into the hallway. Kevin is still sitting at the front desk when we arrive at reception.

'Hi Mark,' he says, looking up from his book. 'How was your first day?'

'Grand, thanks.' Besides my brief lapse in consciousness. But I decide it's probably best not to mention that – I don't want him thinking I'm lacking in stamina.

'I hope Noelle wasn't too hard on you,' he says, shooting her a playful look. 'She's got a bit of a reputation around here, you know.'

'How dare you?' says Noelle, jaw dropping open in mock

outrage. 'I'll have you know I was gentle as a lamb.'

'Somehow I find that hard to believe. Poor Mark looks like he's just wandered out of a warzone.'

'No, no,' I insist. 'Noelle was lovely. So was everybody else. I'm just a little tired from the bus ride this morning.'

'Well, I'm sure you'll feel better after a nice long sleep. Unless you're planning something wild for your first night in Ashcross?'

'Nothing too wild. Probably just unpacking my suitcase and passing out around nine.'

He pauses, clearing his throat, and pushes his glasses up to the top of his nose. 'Well, maybe some other night, once you've had a chance to settle in, the two of us could go out for a few drinks together?'

'Drinks?' My heart starts to pound. Is he talking casual after-work pub *drinks*, or romantic candle-lit dinner *drinks*? Either way… 'I'd love to!'

Noelle lets out a strange gurgling sound, like she's choking on her own tongue.

'Of course, you'd be welcome to join us too,' Kevin tells her.

'Don't be silly. I wouldn't dream of spoiling you kids' fun. And speaking of fun…' She jingles her car keys in front of my face. '*Ninety Day Milkmaid* starts in forty-five minutes.'

'You'd better not keep her waiting,' winks Kevin. 'I'll see you tomorrow.'

I mumble a goodbye, still thinking about those *drinks*, and follow Noelle out into the overcast evening. A light rain is falling, slicking up the concrete and reflecting the yellow glare of passing headlights.

'You and Kevin seem to be getting along well,' she says, as I follow her around to the side of the building.

'He probably gets along well with everybody,' I shrug. 'He seems like a really nice guy.'

'Don't you mean a really nice-*looking* guy?'

'What!?' I groan, nearly tripping over my suitcase. 'I never said that!'

'You didn't have to say it!' she laughs. 'A blind donkey could see what was going on. But don't worry, your secret's safe with me.'

My face is burning up now, despite the chill from the rain. But beneath the embarrassment, a part of me is delighted. Because if Noelle picked up on the flirting too, it can't have been all in my head. Maybe Kevin really does fancy me back…

We walk down a long, concrete ramp to an underground car park. On the left is an emergency exit, leading out from what must be the basement. A row of big plastic bins stands pressed against the wall beside it. Crowded around these bins, like worshippers at a subterranean shrine, is a herd of feral cats. There must be nearly two dozen of them in total, covering the full spectrum of sizes and colours, but all with the same mangy look to them. They forage around in the overflowing bins, climb on top of the metal vent protruding from the wall, and hiss threateningly as they see us approach. Noelle doesn't seem to notice them, but I make sure to leave a wide berth. God only knows what diseases they could be carrying.

'This is us,' says Noelle, stopping in front of a bright red sports car. At first, I think she's joking – the thing looks ridiculously expensive, not to mention totally impractical for Ashcross's roads. But she goes ahead and pops the lock, proving me wrong.

'You can put your bag in the back,' she says, climbing into the driver's seat.

I hoist my suitcase up into both hands as the boot automatically opens. But when I look inside, I find the space already occupied. A wheelchair lays folded on its side – a crisscrossing mass of metal and rubber. I hesitate, the wet material of the suitcase chafing against my chin. Dumping it down on top of the wheelchair feels wrong. But I'm not sure where else it's supposed to go.

'Everything alright back there?' calls Noelle, sticking her head out the window.

'Eh… I don't think there's enough room.'

She hops out of the car and comes around to have a look. 'Oh, that old thing. I'd forgotten all about it. Just toss your bag on top.'

'Are you sure? I don't want to damage it.'

'Yeah, yeah, it's grand. It used to belong to my mother, but she passed away earlier this year. I've been meaning to donate it somewhere.'

She presses the chair down as flat as it will go and strolls back around to the driver's seat. I lay the suitcase gently on top, then close the boot and climb in beside her.

We pull out of the car park and slip smoothly down Atlantic Lane, before hitting a red light on Main Street.

'Sorry about your mother,' I mumble, as we wait behind a white van.

'Thanks, but it's alright. She'd been sick for years, and she was ready to go.'

I fiddle around with the strap of my seatbelt, trying to think of an appropriate response. I've never been very good at the whole death thing.'…Is she the one in the photo on your desk?'

'That's her alright. About a year before the cancer got her.'

'I'm sorry. That must have been difficult.'

'It was, I suppose. We had a nurse looking after her during the day, but it got to the point where she needed twenty-four-hour care. That's when I decided to come back to Ashcross and take up the job at WellCat. So I could be there for her evenings and weekends.'

'She must have appreciated that.'

'It was hard to tell sometimes, but we did our best. No matter how bad things got, I never had the heart to put her in a home. She would have hated that.'

Traffic has started moving again, and I decide it's probably best not to pry any further. Part of me wants to bring up Valentina – to dig for an answer as to why she got fired. But I know now's not the time. Noelle switches on the radio, and I stare out the window at the passing scenery. The rain is lashing down now, turning the decaying buildings an even more depressing shade of grey.

After five minutes of Radio Atlantic's *hits of the eighties*, we arrive at an apartment block on the outskirts of town. The place is far fancier than your average Ashcross building – six storeys tall, made entirely of glass, and not a single boarded-up window in sight. Just imagining the rent rate makes my sphincter start to clench.

'This isn't where I'll be living, is it?'

'It is indeed,' says Noelle, backing into a parking space.

'But don't you think it's a little fancy? Customer Service Assistants aren't exactly raking in cash.'

'Don't worry,' she laughs. 'It's not as expensive as it looks. Some developer with notions put it up during the Boom, but there's never been much demand for luxury apartments in Ashcross. They're desperate for tenants these days.'

We hurry across the car park and into a brightly lit foyer. Despite Noelle's assurances, I feel like an awful impostor. Like a concierge in a little red hat is going to burst through the door and force me back out. The floor is gleaming white, not a speck of dirt in sight, and I lift my suitcase off the ground to avoid leaving a slug trail. One wall is dominated by a row of silver-plated letterboxes, another by a wide wooden staircase. Noelle leads me into a double-doored lift and pushes the button for the top floor.

'Wait till you see the view,' she grins. 'On a clear day, you can see out miles over the ocean. Sometimes you'll even catch a whale breaking the surface. Meanwhile, I'm stuck down on the ground floor; nothing but car exhausts and peeping toms outside my window.'

The lift opens onto a softly lit corridor. Both walls are lined with doors, but the place is silent as a crypt. There are no TVs blaring in the background. No voices arguing or footsteps pacing. No signs of life at all. It's like being in some seedy, soundproofed hotel, where you never know what sort of weird shit could be going on in the next room.

'Is it always this quiet?' I ask, my voice coming out in a whisper.

Noelle nods. 'The rest of the floor is empty. As is the one below. You've got the entire place to yourself!'

She says this like it's a good thing – like I can finally practice my saxophone without annoying the neighbours. But I find it a little alarming. What if I choke on my dinner and nobody's around to give me the Heimlich? Or I slip in the shower and break my back, but nobody can hear me call for help?

'Here we are,' says Noelle, stopping in front of door number 616 and handing me a tiny silver key. 'Home, sweet home.'

After a brief, embarrassing struggle with the lock, the door opens up onto a spacious entry hall. The place looks even more like a hotel on the inside. All the furniture is brand new, and you can tell from the smell of paint that none of the rooms have ever been lived in. Noelle gives me a quick tour, taking in a huge bedroom and lounge, a cosy little kitchenette, and a bathroom with a tub big enough to fit an entire rugby team.

I wander through the rooms in a disorientated daze, feeling more like an impostor at every turn. It seems impossible that I'm actually going to be living here. That all this empty space is mine to fill. It's a million times nicer than the grimy five-person flat-share I was living in during my last job, where nobody seemed to know how to wash their dishes or flush their shits. And it's a million times more private than when I moved back in with my parents…

Mam and Dad tried to act supportive when my sudden lack of income left me knocking at their door. They said not to worry – everybody makes mistakes. I was welcome to stay as long as I needed. But I could tell, deep down, they were disappointed in me. Embarrassed. Maybe even a little resentful. And why shouldn't they be? They'd given me the best of everything. Slaved away for years to put me through school. Sent me out into the world with every opportunity to succeed. And what did I go and do? Fuck it all up at the very first hurdle.

Mam's method of coping was to pretend I was a teenager again. She kept barging into my room to collect my dirty laundry, leaving assorted pieces of fruit behind her, like she was afraid I was developing scurvy. Dad, meanwhile, took it upon himself to help me find a new job. He started emailing me random ads he found online, despite the fact I wasn't remotely qualified for any of them.

'Look Dad,' I'd tell him. 'It says you need a master's degree and three years' experience.'

'But it's an *entry-level position*,' he'd snap. 'And the pay is peanuts. Just send in your CV and see what happens.'

I started applying to everything he sent me, just to shut him up. But most of my CVs were either ignored or met with generic rejection letters, and the handful of interviews I did get invited to all ended abruptly when it came to the question of why I left my previous role.

Dad – desperate to get rid of me – started turning his attention further afield. He found job listings in the UK. In Canada. In Australia.

'There's no recession Down Under,' he told me over dinner one evening. 'They'll take any worker they can get their hands on. Even the ones who've been rejected back home.'

But the thought of moving to a new country terrified me. If I couldn't make it in Ireland, where everything was mild as mayonnaise, how the hell was I supposed to survive in Australia, where the sun would incinerate me within minutes, and a killer spider could be lurking under every toilet seat?

Eventually, I started avoiding Dad. Mam too. And my few friends who were still in Dublin, while I was at it. I started spending more and more time alone in my room, surrounded by a growing mountain of crisp packets and cider cans. Sleeping all afternoon and sending out CVs all night, the blue glow of my laptop screen replacing the natural light of day.

When the job at WellCat finally came along, I accepted it without a second thought. Even though the pay was terrible, and it was a field I had no interest in. Even though I'd have to move to the middle of nowhere and leave behind everything I knew. Because they were the only company who didn't ask for references. The only one who made no effort whatsoever to look into my background. And I knew that if I turned them down, I'd never get another shot at a second chance.

'I think that's everything,' says Noelle, concluding the tour back at the front door.

'Thank you,' I say. 'For all your help today. I really appreciate it.'

'My pleasure,' she grins. 'A new starter at the office is the most exciting thing that's happened in Ashcross all year.' She reaches out and turns the handle, pulling open the door. 'Anyway, I'll leave you to get settled. Unless you had any other questions before I go?'

A sudden jolt of adrenaline shoots up my spine. I'd almost forgotten about Valentina in the thrill of exploring the apartment. But if I don't ask about her now, I might never get another chance. 'Actually, there was one thing...'

'Mmhmm?'

'I was wondering if you could finish telling me about Valentina?'

'Ah,' she sighs. 'That again.'

It's clear she doesn't want to talk about it. But I can't back down now. 'You still haven't explained why exactly she got fired...'

'Look, it's a long story. And *Ninety Day Milkmaid* will be starting any minute.'

'Please! I'm begging you... Just a quick explanation.'

Her eyes narrow, glinting with suspicion. 'Why's this so important to you, anyway? What do you care about some girl you never even met?'

I hesitate, staring down at my scuffed leather shoes. Do I tell her the truth about how I was fired too? Or would that be too dangerous? She seems easy-going enough, in her own sardonic way. But that's no guarantee of understanding. What if she reacts badly? Decides I'm incompetent – too much of a liability – and the company would be better off without me?

No, better not to risk it.

'...I'm just curious, I guess.'

'Well, you know what they say. Curiosity killed the WellCat employee.' She winks half-heartedly, stepping out into the hallway. 'Anyway, I should really get going.'

'No, wait!' I say, beckoning her back inside. I guess I don't have any choice... 'The truth is, I was also fired from my last job. And it's not an experience I'm eager to repeat. So I guess I'm just trying to figure out how I can learn from Valentina's mistakes.

To make sure I don't fall into the same trap she did.'

She raises an eyebrow, like she's weighing up the story. And then her face suddenly softens. 'Alright,' she sighs. 'I didn't know that. But if I tell you, you have to promise to keep it to yourself.'

'Of course. I swear!'

She steps back inside the apartment and closes the door behind her. 'Did Maeve mention anything to you about Future Fish?'

'*Future Fish*? I don't think so.' I'm sure I'd remember something as strange sounding as that.

'That doesn't surprise me. We're not supposed to talk about it. But I bet she did tell you to stay out of the lab, right?'

I nod, remembering our awkward conversation in the meeting room this morning.

'That's because the lab is where Future Fish is being developed.'

'But…what is it?' I ask.

'A new flavour.'

'Of cat food, you mean?'

'Exactly. The Product Innovation Manager comes up with a new flavour every year or two. A few weeks ago, Maeve sent around an email announcing the next one would be called Future Fish. She said it was still in development, but they were hoping to have it on shelves by next spring. All pretty standard stuff.'

I nod again. I'm struggling to see what any of this has to do with Valentina, but I know better than to go interrupting her.

'But then she started going on about how this wasn't just any old flavour. It was the golden ticket to overtaking Miss Meow and solving all our financial woes. She went on a whole big spiel about how we were investing in new technology to develop a cutting-edge product. Like nothing the industry had ever seen before. She didn't go into too much detail, but she did make a big song and dance about keeping it confidential. We were forbidden – and she literally said *forbidden* – from mentioning it to anybody outside the company until further notice.

'Well, poor Valentina – she must not have read the email properly. Or maybe she just didn't understand all the jargon Maeve was spouting. Either way, some hack journalist from *Pet People Ireland* rang up a few days later asking if we had anything to contribute to a story they were running on *the future of pet food*. Usually, those requests would go through to Stevie, the Media Officer, but he was off sick that day, so it came through to Valentina instead. I suppose she thought she was being helpful when she forwarded them Maeve's email about Future Fish.'

'Oh God,' I groan. 'I can see where this is going…'

Noelle smiles sadly. 'They ended up running an entire web feature on Future Fish, chock-full of speculation about what its *secret* could be. Under normal circumstances, we would have killed for that sort of publicity. But Maeve was livid. She fired Valentina on the spot, then called the rest of us in for an emergency meeting. Went on a big rant about how none of us were taking her seriously. How she was going to have to start cracking down on security. That's when she introduced the rule against going into the lab. Before that, you weren't really supposed to go down there unless you had a good reason to, but there was never any of the secrecy we have today.

'She's been paranoid about Future Fish ever since. Flat-out refuses to give away any more details, and goes absolutely mental

Four

The next few days are smooth sailing. I relax slowly into my new routine, no longer worried about repeating Valentina's mistakes. After all, sending out information about something you've explicitly been told not to is a pretty stupid thing to do.

Life in Ashcross is just as dull as I imagined – from the workdays copying and pasting emails to the evenings getting tipsy alone in front of the TV. But despite the long list of downsides, there are a few undeniable perks to being trapped here in purgatory. For one thing, Noelle is a lot more laid-back than my old supervisor, Liam. She seems to do very little actual work, spending most of the day drinking tea and reading tabloids. My commute to the office isn't too bad either – just a ten-minute stroll along a winding, coastal road. The endless grey sea makes for bleak scenery, but it beats being stuck on some crowded Dublin bus – surrounded by smug businessmen and obnoxious schoolkids, with the obligatory junkie couple roaring at each other down the back.

But the best part by far – the one thing that actually makes me glad to be in Ashcross – is getting to see Kevin every day. I've been leaving the apartment earlier and earlier each morning, just so I'll be able to chat to him a little longer on the way in. By the time Thursday rolls around, I'm setting out at a quarter past eight, practically skipping down the road on my way to see my receptionist Romeo.

He sits in his usual place at the front desk, dressed in a shiny blue football jersey. I have no idea what team it's for, but I fully support the way it shows off his biceps. His head is down, eyes fixed on his computer screen, and he doesn't seem to hear me come in. I step closer, about to hit him with a *good morning*, when I suddenly spot the other figure lurking in the room. Maeve stands at one of the filing cabinets behind the front desk, sipping from a tall takeaway coffee as she flicks through a pile of post. I haven't spoken to her again since my first day at WellCat, and the sight of her still makes my palms sweat.

'Good morning, Marcus,' she says, looking up from her envelopes. 'How's your first week in Ashcross been going?'

'Grand, thanks,' I croak.

'I hope your accommodation has been up to scratch?'

'The place is lovely, yeah. I couldn't believe it when I first saw it.'

'Neither could I,' she grins. 'I was sceptical when Noelle first suggested moving you into her building, but the photos weren't half as bad as I was expecting.' She takes a swig of coffee, leaving a bright red lipstick stain on the lid. 'I trust things are going well on the work front too?'

I nod. 'So far so good.'

'You're not having any issues?'

'None that I'm aware of.'

'Wonderful, wonderful. Although there was one little thing I wanted to address...'

My stomach tightens. I haven't done something wrong already, have I? 'Oh really? What's that?'

'Your Personal Progress Reports. You haven't been submitting them.'

'Oh, sorry... I didn't realise I was supposed to.'

'Noelle probably didn't even mention them, did she? It's hard enough getting her to fill out her own reports, let alone asking her to take responsibility for somebody else's.' She closes her eyes, pinching the bridge of her nose. 'You're supposed to submit one every evening. It's pretty straightforward – just a log of how you've spent your time that day, divided up into fifteen-minute increments.'

'It's so they can monitor you more closely,' says Kevin, without looking up from his computer. 'Like a self-service panopticon.'

Maeve glares at him, drumming her fingers along the side of her cup. 'It's not about *monitoring* anybody. It's just a simple tool to help you keep track of your productivity. It's for your own benefit more than anything else, so you're free to spend as much or as little time on it as you like. But submitting it every evening *is* mandatory.'

'I'll make sure to do it today,' I say, hanging my head in penitence. 'Sorry again.'

'It's fine,' she sighs. 'Noelle's the one who should be apologising, not you. Just make sure she walks you through it by close of play today. Anyway' – she picks up the stack of post and tucks it under her arm – 'I'll leave you to it. Have a good Thursday, lads.'

She turns around and sets off down the hallway, leaving Kevin and me alone again.

'Lord give me patience,' he mutters, as soon as she's out of earshot. 'I can't stand that woman.'

I hesitate, surprised to hear him being so negative. He's usually such a ray of sunshine.

'It's her obsession with *productivity*,' he continues. 'Coupled with a total lack of respect for human dignity. It's like we're all machines to her, and she thinks she can just press a button and programme us to do whatever demeaning little task she dreams up next.'

'She can be a little intense,' I agree.

'More than a *little*. You know, sometimes I'm tempted to hand in my notice and escape this hellhole once and for all.'

'Really?' I ask, my heart sinking. 'You'd leave WellCat?'

He considers this for a moment, holding his head up high. And then his shoulders sag down in surrender. 'Probably not,' he sighs. 'I mean, I would if I could. But jobs in Ashcross are hard to come by. You've got to take what you can get. Especially when you're a college dropout like me.'

'*You* dropped out of college?' I ask, in a more judgemental tone than I meant to. 'I mean, it's no big deal, obviously. But I would have thought an avid reader like you would be in their element in academia.'

'It wasn't the amount of reading that was the problem,' he

says. 'It was the content. I originally wanted to study philosophy, but my guidance counsellor convinced me to do business studies instead. *You should choose a degree that will get you a good job*, he said. And like an idiot, I believed him. But I ended up hating every minute of it. I know it's a cliché, but I've never really been motivated by money. And sitting there in all those lectures, where the only thing I was learning was how to turn a profit, I sometimes felt like, what's the point, you know? Why am I wasting my time on this, when I could be doing something that actually helps people? Something that makes the world a better place?'

I nod solemnly. If anybody else talked like this, I'd dismiss them as naïve and idealistic. But Kevin looks so good in that football jersey, it's impossible to disagree with him.

'Of course, somebody like Maeve would never understand that,' he continues. 'She's too consumed by greed to think beyond her own bank balance. You know, I was just talking to Grace about this the other day, and she said that—'

'Hang on,' I say, cutting him off. 'Who's Grace?'

'Oh, just an old friend of mine. You wouldn't know her.'

'I see. And by *old friend*, you don't mean…*girlfriend*, do you?'

'No,' he snorts. 'Grace is most definitely not my girlfriend.'

Phew.

'So…you don't have a girlfriend at the moment?' I ask.

'Nope.'

'And have you had one recently?'

'Not really.'

'Have you had one ever?'

He hesitates, adjusting his glasses. 'Look, Mark, I don't usually talk about this in the office, but to be honest with you, I'm not really interested in girls. My heart is set on a different target.'

A strange squeaking sound escapes my throat, somewhere between a laugh and a squeal. I knew it. I fucking knew it! Kevin doesn't like girls. 'Oh really?' I say, trying to play it cool. 'Funny you should mention that, because I'm not interested in girls either.'

'That doesn't surprise me,' he grins. 'I get the feeling we have a lot in common.'

'I get that feeling too...'

For a few seconds, neither one of us speaks. We just stare dreamily into each other's eyes. I can feel my face turning beetroot red, but I don't even care. This is the most romantic thing that's happened to me in months.

'Anyway,' he says, breaking the spell. 'You should probably head on to your desk. You don't want Maeve to start accusing you of slacking off.'

There's a spring in my step as I set off down the hallway, like the whole office has suddenly burst into colour. I know I shouldn't get my hopes up too high yet. Just because Kevin is into guys doesn't necessarily mean he'll be into *me*. But still, there's clearly something going on between us. An uncommon connection. Two souls cast from the same mould. He said so himself.

I'm still smiling like an idiot as I switch on my computer. Not even the thirty-odd customer emails in my inbox can dampen my spirits. As I scan through the subject lines, most are ones I've encountered before. The same questions coming up again and again. The same comments. The same complaints. *Is your Super*

Silky Salmon sustainably sourced? I cut my finger on a WellCat can and demand compensation! Can I get some free samples for my 'cooking with cat food' channel?

But then, at the bottom of the inbox, I spot a subject line I haven't seen before. Three simple words, screaming out at me from the screen.

FUCK FUTURE FISH!

My immediate instinct is just to delete it. It sounds like spam, after all. The sort of thing that could have some nasty virus attached. But isn't Future Fish the name of the new flavour Noelle was telling me about? The one Valentina got fired for leaking? The one nobody outside the office is even supposed to know about?

Maybe I'd better take a quick peek, in case it's something important…

DEAR WELLCAT EMPLOYEES,

THIS IS YOUR FINAL WARNING. WE DEMAND YOU PUT AN END TO PROJECT FUTURE FISH IMMEDIATELY. FISH ARE SENTIENT BEINGS, CAPABLE OF EXPERIENCING PAIN AND FEAR. YOU HAVE NO RIGHT TO TORTURE THEM IN YOUR SICK FRANKENFISH EXPERIMENTS.

YOU MAY HAVE GOTTEN AWAY WITH YOUR PREVIOUS CRIMES, BUT THIS TIME YOU WON'T BE SO LUCKY.

PUT AN END TO PROJECT FUTURE FISH WITHIN THREE DAYS, OR YOU'LL START

SUFFERING ALONG WITH THE FISH.
WE'LL BE WATCHING,
FRIENDS OF THE FISH

'Eh… I think you'd better have a look at this,' I say, turning towards Noelle. 'There's a really weird email in the inbox.'

'Ooh, I love the weird ones.' She scoots her chair over to my computer, eyes twinkling with anticipation. But her smile quickly fades as she reads what's on the screen.

'It's bad, isn't it?' I ask.

'Not really,' she shrugs. 'Just more of the usual shite.'

'Wait, what? You mean you've had something like this before?'

'Oh yeah,' she grins. 'We get them all the time.'

'*All the time*!?' A little warning would have been nice, in that case. It's not like *responding to threats of violence* was listed in the job description. 'So, what am I supposed to do with it? Send back a reply saying *thank you for your feedback and have a nice day*?'

'Just delete it, I suppose. That's what I usually do.' She turns back to her own computer, like there's nothing more to say. But I can't let it go that easily.

'Don't you think the tone is a little aggressive, though? It sounds like they're talking about hurting somebody.'

'People will say all sorts of shite in an email. You learn not to take it too seriously.'

'What about the part where they mention Future Fish? Shouldn't we take *that* seriously?'

'Shh!' She glances over towards the far side of the room, where Maeve is chatting away to a pair of younger, blonde women. 'Keep your voice down, will you? You don't want herself catching wind of this.'

'Wait, you mean Maeve doesn't know? Surely we should tell her!'

Her eyes widen, cheeks puffing out like an angry frog. 'Look, why don't we go for a little walk? If anybody asks, tell them we're just popping out for a fag.'

'But I don't smoke.'

She stands up, grabbing my wrist and yanking me after her.

'You do now.'

Five

Noelle drags me across the room, past rows of spreadsheets and slumped shoulders, and out into the empty hallway. I try to break free – to retreat towards my desk. Sneaking around having secret conversations isn't something I want to be doing. But Noelle is an unstoppable force, and I'm an easily moveable object.

'Everything alright there?' asks Kevin, as we barrel through the door to reception.

'Grand,' grunts Noelle. 'We're just popping out for a smoke.' She holds up a battered pack of cigarettes as proof.

'*Mark*,' says Kevin, shaking his head. 'I'm disappointed in you. How can you go around sucking on those cancer sticks?'

'Oh, no… I don't smoke!'

'Your body is a temple, you know. I've given up trying to convince Noelle to quit, but I would have expected better from you.'

'But I'm not… I mean, I'm just…' I stutter, struggling to think straight under the weight of his disapproval. What if this is a dealbreaker for him? What if he could never love a smoker?

'It's my fault,' says Noelle. 'I've corrupted Mark. Forced him to take up all sorts of filthy habits. But we're legally entitled to a smoke break, and there's nothing you can do to stop us!'

Next thing I know, she's pulling me out the front door and around the side of the building. I try to shake her off again, to turn back and explain myself to Kevin. But it's no use. Her fingers knead into the doughy flesh of my arm, dragging me down the ramp to the underground car park. The herd of stray cats scatters from our path as we stagger across the concrete. It's only when we're right outside the emergency exit, close enough to smell the rubbish steaming in the bins, that she finally releases me. I rub sullenly at my arm, already feeling a nasty bruise coming on.

'That's better,' she sighs, leaning back against the wall. 'No paranoid bosses to eavesdrop out here.'

She lights up a cigarette, then offers me the pack. But I shake my head. 'I told you, I don't smoke. Even though Kevin now thinks I do.'

'Ah, would you forget about Kevin for one second? I thought you wanted to talk about those emails.'

'I do want to talk about them! But I don't understand why we had to come all the way out here to do it.'

She takes a long, slow drag, exhaling a thick cloud of smoke. The smell is disgusting, but at least it masks whatever's rotting in the bin. 'Look, sorry if I was a bit short with you in there. I know you didn't mean any harm. It's just, I really don't want Maeve sticking her nose into this.'

'Why not though? It seems like the sort of thing she should probably be aware of.'

'In theory, maybe. But you know what she's like. She'd probably drag us into an emergency meeting, make us fill out a fifty-page incident report form, then insist on checking in on the situation every day for the next year. It'd be an absolute nightmare. Enough to rob a person of the will to live.'

'But won't she be angry if she finds out we haven't told her?'

'Of course, she'll be furious! But how's she going to find out if we don't tell her?' She winks, exhaling another cloud of smoke.

'I don't know…' I cough, fanning a hand in front of my face. 'I just don't want to get into trouble over this.'

'Look,' she sighs. 'You're not going to get into trouble. Even if Maeve does catch on, it's me who'll be on the chopping block. You reported the email to your supervisor, just like you were supposed to. I'm the one who failed to escalate it further.'

I pause to consider this, watching one of the stray cats climb up on top of the bin. It's a filthy old thing – all matted fur and milky eyes, looking more like a demon than any sort of domesticated pet. Noelle reaches a hand out to stroke it, but it dodges her fingertips and leaps up into the vent.

'Fine,' I say at last. I still don't like keeping secrets from Maeve, but there is a certain logic to what Noelle is saying. 'I'll keep my mouth shut if that's what you want. But regardless of Maeve, aren't you at all worried about the email?'

'Nah,' she shrugs. 'Why should I be?'

'It sounded a little threatening to me. Saying if we didn't stop Future Fish, they were going to make us suffer…'

'Like I said, you learn not to take that stuff seriously. People like to talk big from behind their keyboards, but ninety-nine percent of them would never have the balls to follow through.'

'What if this person is part of the one percent though? They could do something crazy. Like show up at the office and shoot the place up.'

'Yeah right,' she laughs, going to light up a second cigarette. 'As if anything that dramatic would ever happen in Ashcross.'

'This isn't funny,' I snap, snatching the lighter from her hand.

'Oi! Give that back, you little prick!'

'Not until you start taking this seriously.'

'Alright, alright.' She grabs the lighter and cradles it to her lips. 'I'm taking it very seriously. But I'm not sure what you expect me to do about an anonymous email.'

I sigh. I'm not sure either. But surely we should be doing *something*. 'You don't have any idea who these Friends of the Fish people are?' I ask.

'Nope. We've been getting their crap for years, but it's all totally anonymous.'

'*Years?* But I thought Future Fish was only announced recently.'

'It was,' she says. 'But the hate mail goes back much further. Ever since the incident with the salmon farm.'

'Hang on,' I say. 'What incident with the salmon farm?'

'Oh, it happened years ago. Right after Maeve took over as CEO. One of her big strategic goals was building our own farm up on the Donegal coast, so we wouldn't have to rely on third-party suppliers any more. Not a bad idea in theory, but she was overly optimistic with the budget. Wanted to rush it through as quickly as possible, and refused to listen to any of the warnings. Well surprise, surprise, there were some issues with the permits, and the opening had to be delayed. Everything was in place, including staff and salmon stocks, but legally, we couldn't begin operations. This dragged on for months and months, with the costs getting higher and higher, and the return on our investment getting further and further away. In the end, Maeve decided to cut her losses and close the place down. All the workers were made redundant, and the poor fish had to be euthanised.'

'Jesus Christ,' I say. 'Sounds like a major shitshow.'

'It was,' grins Noelle. 'There was a whole kerfuffle about it in the media. The local mayor was furious, saying the farm was supposed to be a boost for the economy, but we'd gone and pulled the rug out from under them by messing up the permits. There were a few hit pieces about Maeve in the tabloids, but nothing too serious. The storm died down after a couple of weeks, when the next big scandal came along. But then, a month or two later, the hate mail started arriving.'

'You mean these Friends of the Fish people?' I ask.

'Exactly. They flooded our inbox with emails, callings us *animal abusers* and *murderers*. Saying we had the blood of innocent salmon on our hands. I guess they thought we should have released the unused stock into the wild rather than euthanising them. Never mind the fact that that would have been totally illegal, and the fish probably wouldn't have survived anyway. A few of the nutters even threatened to show up at the office and stage a protest. You know, the ones where they take off all their clothes and cover themselves in fake blood. The funny thing is, I'm pretty sure they were all Americans. They wouldn't know Ashcross from the arse end of Antarctica. But I guess they read about the salmon farm online and started sharing it around their groups. Egging each other on and getting all worked up, until they were frothing at the mouth. It took years for the hate mail to die down.'

'And now they're starting up a fresh crusade over Future Fish?'

'Looks like it,' she says. 'Although this is nothing compared to last time. Either they've gone soft, or there are fewer of them involved this time around.'

'Well, whoever they are, where did they get all that stuff about *experiments* and *Frankenfish*? They make us sound like a bunch of mad scientists.'

'Your guess is as good as mine,' she shrugs. 'Maybe they heard *Future Fish* and let their imaginations run wild. Started picturing some B-movie sci-fi shite. Which you couldn't really blame them for doing, to be fair. I always said that was a stupid name.'

I shake my head, tapping my shoe against the cement. This still doesn't make sense to me. 'But how can they get so angry without having any proof? How can they threaten to hurt somebody over something that's not even true?'

'Because people don't care about the truth,' she says. 'The truth is boring. It's depressing. An anchor dragging them down into cold, mundane reality. What people want is some excitement. Something they can fight against or defend. Something to give their lives a bit of meaning, whether it makes any sense or not.'

I sigh, still not understanding, and let my eyes wander over towards the emergency exit. On the far side – separated by just a thin sheet of metal – lies the basement. The laboratory. And whatever Future Fish really is.

'What *does* go on in there?' I ask. 'I mean, if it's not fish torture, what do the researchers get up to all day?'

'Not much, to be honest. There's only one guy working down there, and he's more of an *innovator* than an actual scientist. Spends all his time mixing food colourings and flavour samples, then sends them off to focus groups for cat owners. I can tell you one thing though; there are no live animals on site. It's not that kind of lab.' She stubs her cigarette out against the wall and tosses it into the bin. 'Anyway, we should probably be getting back inside. You don't want Kevin to start thinking you're some sort of chain-smoker.'

I take one last look at the emergency exit, then turn and follow her back up to street level. Whatever's going on with Future Fish, it's got nothing to do with me. Maeve told me to stay out of the lab, and I'm only too happy to comply.

The rest of the day is mercifully quiet. I brew myself a nice strong cup of tea, pop on a *soothing rain sounds* playlist, and do my best to forget about Future Fish and the strange email. Noelle offers me a lift home at half-five, but I politely decline. For the first time since I arrived in Ashcross, there's actually a bit of blue in the sky, and I want to make the most of it by walking. Besides, I'm in no particular rush to be getting back to the apartment. My only plans for the evening are heating up a frozen pizza and eating it in the bathtub.

I polish off one last email after Noelle leaves, then shut down my computer and begin packing up. Somewhere in the back of my mind, I have a nagging feeling I'm forgetting something. Some unfinished task or unresolved issue. But no matter how hard I try, I can't put my finger on it, and in the end, I write it off as lingering anxiety from the Future Fish email.

Kevin is watering the drooping houseplant when I arrive at reception. He gently parts the brown leaves, sprinkling a tiny yellow watering can onto the dusty black soil. I've got a feeling these attentions might be too little, too late. The plant has already departed for chlorophyll heaven.

'Mark!' he says, waving at me. 'Have you got a second to chat?'

'Sure, yeah.' More than a second, Kevin. I've got all the time in the world.

He sits down on the itchy green couch and pats the cushion beside him. I sidle over as nonchalantly as possible, aiming for that perfect close-but-not-*too*-close distance between us.

'So…' he says, fidgeting around with the spout of the watering can. 'I wanted to talk a bit more about our conversation earlier.'

'You mean the smoking thing? Because I swear, I've only had, like, five cigarettes in my entire life! My uncle died of lung cancer, and I—'

'No, no, not that. I mean our conversation this morning. When we talked about…not being interested in girls. Loving differently from everybody else.'

'Oh, right.' That's a lot more romantic than lung cancer.

'I was thinking it might be nice to talk about it a bit more. To properly share our stories with each other. It can be a lonely road, as I'm sure you know, but having somebody to walk it with makes all the difference.'

'Of course,' I say. 'I'd love to.'

Just then, the door to the corridor crashes open, and a balding middle-aged man from the accounting department comes barrelling into the room.

'Yeah, yeah,' he bleats into his phone. 'I'll do it after I drop Saoirse off at karate… Relax, there'll be plenty of time… For God's sake, I said *relax!*'

He shoves the front door open with his shoulder, letting it slam shut behind him.

'Maybe here's not the best place to discuss this,' mumbles Kevin, as soon as the coast is clear. 'Maeve would lose her mind if she heard us discussing personal issues in the workplace. Are you free this Saturday?'

'Sure, yeah. I'm free all weekend.'

'Why don't we meet up for a cup of tea?' he asks. 'There's this lovely little café called the Black Cat on Main Street.'

'A cup of tea? You mean…just the two of us?'

'Yeah,' he grins. 'Just the two of us. If that's something you'd be interested in?'

A choir of angels hallelujahs in my head. Can this really be happening? Did Kevin just ask me out!? 'Yeah, I'd definitely be interested in that.'

'Brilliant,' he beams. 'I'll see you there at noon on Saturday.'

I step outside in a delighted daze. Sunlight streams down through a gap in the clouds, and everything is going my way. A date with Kevin! It feels too good to be true, yet strangely inevitable at the same time. Like dying and finding out there really is a heaven, and it's exactly like you imagined.

I can already picture the two of us sitting there in a cosy little café, soft jazz floating through the air as we play footsie under the table. We'll take things slowly at first, ending the afternoon with nothing more than a chaste kiss. Date number two is where we'll get into the heavy petting, snuggled up together at the back of some dimly lit cinema. And then on date number three – a romantic candlelit dinner – I'll invite him back to my place to seal the deal.

The thought of being in a relationship again is exhilarating. It would almost be enough to make life in Ashcross worth living. But beneath the excitement, a part of me is terrified. This will be my first proper date since breaking up with Neil. And the way things ended there didn't exactly leave me with an over-abundance of confidence...

Neil called it quits after I moved back in with my parents. He didn't even give me the courtesy of an in-person meeting – just phoned up like a cold-caller asking if I was interested in having my heart broken. And the worst part was, this didn't even surprise me. Things had been going sour for a few months already, and I suppose my new status as an unemployed loser was just the last straw in a long series of disappointments for him.

The two of us were in the same year at college, and up until that point, our lives had progressed in tandem. We knew all the same people, went to all the same parties, and spent all the morning-afters nursing our hangovers together. But everything changed after graduation. Neil went straight into a master's degree, while I started the job at the advertising agency. Within just a couple of weeks, it was like we were living in two different worlds. He was still floating happily through student heaven, spending all day at the library, the gym and the campus bar, while I was getting dragged down deeper and deeper into nine-to-half-five hell.

He couldn't understand why I was always so tired. Why I'd lost interest in going out and seeing friends. Why the only thing I wanted to do in the evenings was eat takeaway and watch trash TV. I tried to explain what it was like. That work was a vampire sucking up all my energy, leaving nothing left over for myself. That the office had become the main stage of my life, and evenings and weekends were just a waiting room in-between. But he told me my attitude was making things worse. I was gaining weight and letting myself go. I'd feel so much better if I just *made more of an effort*.

I still remember the disdain in his voice as he delivered the final blow. I was lying on top of the duvet in my childhood bedroom, trying to be as quiet as possible so my parents wouldn't overhear. But Neil wasn't holding anything back.

'I'm sorry Mark, but this just isn't working. I need to be with somebody who knows what they want from life. Somebody who has goals and the ambition to achieve them.'

I wanted to tell him that was easy for him to say. He was still sitting pretty in the ivory tower of academia. He hadn't even begun to face the real world yet. Hadn't realised how it grinds you down and crushes your spirit. How it strips your dreams away one by one, until the only *goal* you're left with is making it to the end of another day.

But I knew he'd never understand. And so, I kept my mouth shut and stared up at the glow-in-the-dark stars on the ceiling as he listed off his reasons. And when he finally hung up the phone, marking the irrevocable end of our two-year relationship, the only thing I felt was exhaustion.

Six

Noelle is at the dentist the next morning, leaving me to hold down the fort alone. Not having her around makes me extremely nervous, and I can't shake the feeling that something terrible is going to happen. Like an angry customer ringing up and threatening to sue the company for millions. Or our email account getting hacked and sending out ads for *lonely housewives in Ashcross.*

The first hour passes without any disasters – just a few spam emails offering discount Viagra. Slowly but surely, I begin to relax. Maybe everything will be okay after all. Maybe I don't need Noelle to babysit me. But then, just before ten, another email arrives to trample my budding confidence.

RE: FUCK FUTURE FISH! reads the subject line.

My heart starts to pound as I open the full email. I knew we'd probably hear from those Friends of the Fish people again sooner or later, but I figured it would take at least a few days. And I assumed Noelle would be here for backup when it happened…

Hey WellCat people,

Sorry about that last email. Although we totally do disapprove of Project Future Fish, we're actually a non-violent organisation. We don't want to inflict suffering on anybody – human or fish.

My comrade was just showing off when he sent that (trying to impress his new girlfriend, no doubt). He didn't really mean it. So please don't report us to the police or anything.

Anyways, have a nice day,

Friends of the Fish

I stare stupidly at the screen, letting the words sink in. And then a shell-shocked chuckle rumbles up from my stomach. That's not quite what I was expecting when I opened the email… Sinister ramblings? Yes. Vicious abuse? Sure. A full-blown bomb scare? Maybe. But not a polite apology. And definitely not a *have a nice day*. I hate to admit it, but maybe Noelle was right. Maybe the Friends of the Fish really are nothing to worry about.

I reread the message a few more times, making sure I haven't missed anything. Just as I'm finishing my third pass, I hear Noelle pull out her chair beside me.

'Welcome back,' I mumble, eyes glued to my screen. 'How was the dentist?'

But she doesn't reply.

'We just got another one of those Future Fish emails,' I continue, without looking up. 'But this one is a lot more… friendly.'

There are a few seconds of silence, and then finally a response. 'And what *Future Fish emails* would these be?'

My spirit nearly leaves my body when I hear the voice. Because it's not Noelle after all. It's Maeve.

'S-sorry,' I stutter, trying not to panic. 'I didn't see you there.'

'I was just coming over to talk about your Personal Progress Reports. You failed to submit one again last night.'

Shit! The report… I knew I was forgetting something last night. 'Sorry about that. It must have slipped my mind. I'll ask Noelle to help me with it as soon as she's back from the dentist.'

'Is *this* the email you were talking about?' She leans over towards my screen, ignoring everything I've just said. A few seconds pass in terrifying silence, and then she straightens back up. 'Where did this come from?' she asks, in a calm but deadly tone.

'Somebody sent it in to the customer service inbox.'

'And when was this?'

'Just a minute ago. Literally.'

'I see. And you said this was *another one*. Meaning you've received something similar before?'

I nod, swallowing down a lump in my throat. 'Yeah. We got one yesterday as well.'

She inhales sharply, springing to her feet. 'I think you'd better come with me.'

I stand up and follow her towards the door, my stomach churning like we've just hit a patch of turbulence. Why, oh why did I let Noelle talk me into keeping the emails secret?

She leads me down the hallway and through a door marked *Large Meeting Room*. Inside is a long table with a laptop and projector at the far end. Like the smaller room where we had our meeting on my first day, the walls are lined with posters of classic WellCat ads. There's one with a sexy fireman rescuing a kitten from a tree, and another with a grumpy cat looking unimpressed by the tin of off-brand tuna before him.

'Sit,' says Maeve, pointing at a chair. She drags the laptop down along the table and shoves it into my face. 'Open up your email.'

I do as she commands, fingers trembling as I input my password.

She pounces on the computer as soon as I'm finished, spinning it around to face her and scanning her eyes across the screen. 'Where's the other one?'

'The other what?'

'The other email. You said you received it yesterday, but I'm not seeing it here.'

'Oh, right… I deleted that one.'

Her eyes widen. 'You *deleted* it?'

'I thought it was spam, so I figured that was the safest thing to do.'

'And what exactly did the spam say?'

'Nothing much. It was just a load of angry rambling.'

She takes a deep breath, pinching the bridge of her nose. 'This is an extremely serious matter, Marcus. You should have forwarded it to me immediately.'

'Sorry. I didn't realise.'

'Did you show it to anybody else?'

'Just Noelle.'

'And she was the one who told you to delete it, was she?'

I tug at the collar of my shirt, feeling a sticky patch of sweat well up. I don't want to get Noelle into trouble, but I don't want to lie to Maeve either. And Noelle *did* say to blame her if Maeve ever found out about the emails...

'You know what?' she says. 'It doesn't even matter. Let's just focus on correcting our course going forward.' She sighs, like the effort of suffering such fools has taken years off her life. 'I suppose Noelle also told you all about Future Fish?'

'Sort of. She just said it's a new flavour coming out soon.'

'It's more than just a *new flavour*. It's the culmination of everything I've been working towards since I took over as CEO. The silver bullet that's finally going to put down Miss Meow. The entire future of the company hinges on its success, which is why we can't afford to be complacent in the face of threats like these. Do you understand what I'm saying to you?'

'Eh...I think so.'

'Good. Now wait here. I need to check something before I decide how to deal with this.'

She stands up and strides out of the room, slamming the door behind her. The projector screen rattles ominously in her wake.

I slouch down in my seat, letting out a long, slow breath. Sweat drips down my spine, pooling like an oasis in the small of my back. I have no idea where Maeve has gone, or what exactly she needs to *check*, but something tells me this isn't going to end well. I stare anxiously at the door, waiting for her to return, and brace myself for the inevitable *go pack up your things*.

When she finally does reappear, she's followed by a man in a long white coat. The sight of him instantly lifts my spirits. Tall and broad, with dark hair and a neatly trimmed beard, he looks like the sexy dad from a family holiday ad. I assume he must work in the building, although I've never seen him around before.

'Marcus, this is Dominic,' says Maeve, closing the door behind them. 'Dominic is our Product Innovation Manager.'

'Nice to meet you,' I say, standing up to shake his hand. His grip is firm and reassuring, and I hold onto it slightly longer than I probably should.

'You too,' he replies, sitting down and reaching straight for the laptop. 'Is this it, then?'

'That's it,' says Maeve, taking a seat beside him. 'What do you think?'

He makes a faint humming sound as he reads, then sits back and scratches his beard. 'Hard to say. There's nothing in there that isn't already public knowledge, so I wouldn't be too worried about an information leak. But at the same time, somebody is clearly trying to mess with us.'

'Those same stupid activists as last time,' adds Maeve.

'Looks like it,' he shrugs. 'But what's the worst they can do? Start a petition and try to drum up some negative publicity? Fine. We play the *hard-working local business* card and wait for the whole thing to blow over.'

'It's not the activists themselves I'm worried about,' says Maeve. 'It's what they might uncover if they start digging around in our business.'

'Right. You mean the—'

She clears her throat, cutting him off, and nods over in my direction.

'Sorry…' he mumbles. 'You mean the *thing*. In the *place*. That we still have to take care of.'

'Precisely.'

'But how would they ever find out about that?' he asks. 'They'd have to break into the office and force down the security door. No way a bunch of puny, protein-deprived vegans could ever pull that off, even if they had the balls to try.'

'Maybe you're right,' says Maeve. 'But we can't afford to take any chances. Not with so much riding on Future Fish. You remember how bad the publicity was after we had to close down the salmon farm, right? And that wasn't even our fault. The media would crucify us if they found out about *this*.'

'So what are you planning to do about it? Take the email to the Guards and see if they can track down the sender?'

'No,' she says. 'We can't risk getting the police involved. Better to beef up our own defences instead. We could expand the CCTV system. Or hire a security guard.'

'And how are we going to afford that?' he asks, with a sceptical look.

'Leave the finances to me,' she snaps. 'I'm sure the bank will be willing to increase our loan again. We'll be able to pay them back tenfold once Future Fish hits the market.'

'Alright,' he says, holding his hands up in surrender. 'I'll take your word for it.'

'Good.'

'If that's all for now,' he says. 'I'd better be getting back downstairs. The results from the latest focus group have just come in, and I need to put together a report for the Board.' He stands up, tucking his chair into the table, then leans over and kisses her on the cheek.

'I told you, not in the office!' she hisses, shoving him away.

'Relax,' he laughs. 'There's nobody here except Marcus. And he doesn't mind. Do you, Marcus?'

'No, no, don't mind me,' I mumble, trying not to blush. Despite feeling like the world's biggest third wheel, I'm strangely flattered by Dominic's confidence.

'Just get out of here, will you?' says Maeve. 'Marcus and I still have some business to attend to.'

'Alright. I'll see you later so.' He squeezes her shoulder, then gives me a wink as he heads for the door. I turn to watch him go, his long white coat billowing behind him as he disappears down the hallway.

And then it's just me and Maeve again. Picking up from the same terrifying point where we left off.

'I'm not sure how much of that you picked up on,' she says. 'But it seems some online trolls might be mobilising against us. It's nothing to worry about. For now, anyway. But best to keep an eye out in case the situation escalates.'

I nod slowly, trying to come off as calm and collected. She's clearly hiding something from me. But right now, I don't care what it is. The only thing that matters in this moment is getting out of the room with my job still intact.

'Now, the reason I'm telling you all this,' she continues, 'is that you have an important role to play in helping us maintain our defences.'

'I do?'

'You're responsible for monitoring our customer service inbox. That means you hear first-hand from people who might be unhappy with us.'

'I suppose so...'

'So, if you see anybody mentioning Future Fish, you can be the first one to raise the alarm. No matter how small or trivial it may seem, it's imperative that you pass the information on to me immediately. Clearly, you didn't understand the significance of that last email. But you won't go making the same mistake again, will you?'

I shake my head.

'Good. I knew I could count on you.' She smiles the least reassuring smile I've ever seen, then begins typing away on the laptop. 'Now, unless you have any other questions, I think it's time for you to be getting back to work.'

I rise shakily to my feet, mumbling a *thank you* as I stumble towards the door. Out in the hallway, I collapse against the wall.

Holy shit.

I can't believe I got off that easily. Maeve could have eviscerated me in there – and been perfectly justified in doing so. But instead, she's sent me on my way with nothing more than a slap on the wrist. I must have caught her in a good mood. Or maybe luck was finally on my side for once. Either way, you can bet your ass I've learned my lesson.

From now on, I'll be telling Maeve everything I hear about Future Fish. Whether it's an email, a phone call, or a letter in the post. Whether it's a whisper in the hallway or a message on the bathroom wall... There's no way I'm keeping anything from her again.

Seven

Saturday morning is wet and miserable. Even by Ashcross standards, things are looking bleak, with thunderclouds rumbling in from the horizon and a vicious wind whipping the ocean into foam. On any other day like this, I'd do anything to avoid leaving the house. Even getting out from under the duvet would require a miracle of willpower. But this morning, I can't wait to get going. Because today is my date with Kevin!

I pore over the contents of my wardrobe, searching for something flattering to wear. But my options are severely limited. I could only bring one suitcase with me on the bus, and that was reserved for work clothes and toiletries, with the rest of my things scheduled for delivery on Sunday. I've always had a terrible sense of fashion, and I figured living out of a suitcase for a few days wouldn't particularly bother me. But that was before I knew I'd be having a date with the potential love of my life.

Now I'm kicking myself for not paying that extra seven fifty for next-day delivery.

In the end, I settle for a pair of black slacks and the least formal shirt I can find. I set out from the apartment at half-eleven, which coincidentally is the exact same time the clouds decide to burst. Despite the best efforts of my flimsy little umbrella, I'm soaked to the bone by the time I reach the café. I pause inside the door, shaking myself off like a wet dog, and scan the sea of tables for Kevin's face. But there's no sign of him.

Even more disappointingly, the place is a far cry from the cosy little hideaway I'd been imagining. Instead of plush leather couches and a roaring fire, there are cheap plastic tables and harsh fluorescent lighting. Instead of a few other couples scattered intimately around the room, the only other customers are a trio of decrepit nuns, huddled together like a penguin colony on the verge of extinction.

I trudge over to the counter, shoes squelching with every step, and order a pot of tea from the tired-looking waitress. She smiles half-heartedly, revealing a row of lipstick-stained teeth, and tells me she'll bring it over to the table. I seat myself by the back window – as far as possible from the nuns. I don't think any of them are the same one who assaulted me with holy water on my first day in Ashcross, but I'm not taking any chances. I'm already wet enough.

The windows are covered with condensation, and I entertain myself by drawing tiny little love hearts while I wait for Kevin. He arrives a few minutes later, waving over at me as he pulls down the hood of his bright yellow raincoat. I wave back with one hand, hastily wiping away the love hearts with the other. But then, with a mortified shudder, I realise it's not me he's greeting. It's the nuns.

'How are you, Mr O'Mahoney?' calls the oldest of the trio. She's got an authoritarian air about her, like she used to just love beating children with rulers back in the day.

'Grand thanks, Sister Grace.' He nods politely at each nun in turn. 'Sister Helen. Sister Rose.'

'Nasty old weather we're having,' says the smallest one, who I think is Sister Helen. She seems friendlier than Sister Grace, judging by her serene smile. Although on closer inspection, she might just be senile.

'It is indeed,' says Kevin. 'But please God it passes soon.'

'Will you join us for a cup of tea?' asks Sister Rose, giving the chair beside her a seductive pat.

'I wish I could, Sister, but my friend is waiting for me. We'll have to catch up some other time.'

'Your friend would be welcome to join us too,' she croons. 'A bit of company would do our old souls a world of good.'

He hesitates, and for one awful moment, I'm afraid he's going to give in. But then he smiles politely and shakes his head. 'Sorry Sister, but I think my friend and I would prefer a bit of privacy.'

She tries to convince him for a few more seconds, until finally he manages to slip away.

'Sorry to keep you waiting,' he whispers, joining me at the table. 'The Sisters mean well, but they'll talk your ear off if you're not careful.'

'No worries,' I reply, feeling strangely flattered. It's not every day you beat three Brides of Christ in the battle for a man's attention. 'How do you even know that many nuns?'

'Ah, you know, it's a small town. Everybody knows everybody.' He shrugs. 'Anyway, how are you? You look absolutely drenched!'

'Sorry, yeah. The umbrella I brought with me from Dublin couldn't handle the Ashcross weather. I've never seen this much rain in my life! But I suppose I shouldn't complain, since I'm here with you now...'

I smile suggestively, but he doesn't seem to notice.

'You definitely *can* complain about the weather,' he laughs. 'It's all anybody around here ever does. You should hear Sister Rose going on about the pain in her hip whenever it snows.'

I grit my teeth, wishing we could stop talking about the stupid nuns already. But before either of us can say anything else, a shadow falls across the table. I look up to see the haggard waitress standing there with a tray.

'Here you go, love,' she says, placing a mug of milky-white tea in front of me. 'And what can I get you this morning, Kevin?'

'Just a tea please, Sandra. Black.'

'Coming right up.'

She turns and drags her feet back over to the counter, leaving the two of us alone again.

'So...' he says, running a finger along the edge of the sugar bowl. 'Thanks for agreeing to meet me here today. I know the invitation was a little out of the blue, and I hope it didn't make you uncomfortable.'

'Not at all! I was hoping you'd ask.'

'That's good,' he grins. 'It's just, I've been accused of being a little too forward about these things in the past.'

'A little forwardness is a good thing, if you ask me. You never know what could happen until you take that chance.'

'Exactly! But sometimes I feel like I have to repress a part of myself at the office. People will say it's *unprofessional* or *inappropriate* to express my true identity. Of course, they only say that when it's people like us doing the expressing. For all the so-called *normal* people, it's totally fine.'

'I know what you mean,' I sigh. The minefield of being out and proud at work. 'But you can't let other people's opinions hold you back. Just be yourself, and if they don't like it, screw them!'

'You're right,' he says, beaming over at me from across the table. He leans forward, sliding his hand towards mine. 'It's so great being able to talk to you like this. There's never really been anybody like me in the office before. Never anybody who was a fellow...you know...'

I nod, sipping coyly at my tea. Of course I know what he means. *A fellow homosexual.*

'...a fellow servant of Christ.'

I choke, tea spouting from my mouth like a filthy fountain. 'Sorry, what!?'

'I said, there's never been anybody else in the office who was serious about serving the Lord. We've had plenty of fair-weather Catholics, of course. The sort who go to mass on Christmas morning but wouldn't know their Virgin Birth from their Immaculate Conception.'

'Oh...'

His eyes narrow behind his glasses. 'Hang on. You *are* a Catholic, right? Not some sort of Protestant or something?'

'Eh...' Technically I am a Catholic, in the sense that I was forced to make my confirmation in primary school, and I've never formally been excommunicated. But for all intents and purposes, I'm just another godless homosexual.

'What am I saying?' he laughs. 'Of course you are. Why else would you be such a big fan of Catholic theology?'

'*Catholic theology?*'

He nods. 'Lewis N. Lewison. Remember, we were talking about him on your first day?'

'Oh, right.' *That's* what that stupid book was about?

I stare down at my tea, stirring in lump after lump of sugar. Am I losing my mind, or does none of this make sense? How can Kevin be a hardcore Catholic *and* openly gay? I thought they didn't allow that…

'So, the other day,' I say, trying to keep my voice steady, 'when you said you weren't interested in girls, what you meant was…?'

'I've been thinking about entering the seminary. But Father Marsh says I'm not ready yet. That just because things went badly for me at college, I shouldn't turn my back on the entire secular world.'

'You're thinking about becoming a priest, you mean? Going totally celibate?'

'Those are the rules,' he shrugs. 'Not that it's ever seemed like a particularly heavy burden to me.'

Somewhere in the back of my mind, this thought offers small comfort. At least if I can't have him, nobody else can either.

'And you?' he says. 'You meant the same thing too, right?'

'What same thing?'

'That you were also thinking about entering the seminary. When you said you weren't interested in girls either.'

'Oh, right…'

His eyes bore into me, pinning me down like a butterfly on a board. I know I should tell him the truth. Set the record straight before things get even more confusing. But I have no idea where to even begin. No idea how far back to rewind the tape before things start making sense. And before I can figure it out, Sandra the waitress reappears at the table.

'Here's your tea, love.'

'Cheers,' says Kevin, blowing on the cup as she trudges back towards the counter. 'By the way, I saw you and Maeve heading into the meeting room yesterday. I hope she didn't give you any trouble.'

'No, no,' I mumble. 'No trouble at all. We were just talking about Future Fish.'

'Future Fish?' His whole body stiffens. 'No good ever comes from those two words.'

'It was fine,' I say. 'Maeve was annoyed at me for not telling her about an email, but she let me off with just a warning.'

'I see,' he says, clearly intrigued. '…And what email was this?'

Next thing I know, I'm launching off into the entire story, from Maeve catching me reading the email, to Dominic appearing in the meeting room, to the two of them making cryptic comments about something they didn't want discovered. I know I probably shouldn't be telling him all this, but I can't stop myself once I've started. I just don't want to give him the opportunity to ask me about becoming a priest again.

'Lord have mercy,' he says, as I finish the story. 'Those Friends of the Fish characters are a bunch of loons, but in this case, there might be some truth to what they're saying.'

'What, you mean there really are fish being experimented on in the basement?'

'No, no. Nothing as outlandish as that. But there's clearly something suspicious going on with Future Fish. Maybe even something dangerous. Why else would Maeve be so desperate to keep it secret?'

I squirm around in my seat, not liking where this is headed. 'What do you mean *something dangerous*? It's just a new cat-food flavour, right? How dangerous could it be?'

'It's not the cat food itself that I'm worried about. It's the lengths Maeve will go to to make it a success. She's obsessed with beating Miss Meow. With claiming the top spot in the industry. What if her greed is corrupting her, leading her down the path to sin? What if she's lying, or stealing, or exploiting other people?'

I stare down at my empty teacup, not saying anything. Suddenly I don't want to be here any more. I want to run screaming from the café and get far away from Kevin. But the rain is still bucketing down outside, and I can't think of an excuse to just get up and leave.

'What we need to do now,' he says, 'is carry out a proper investigation. Go down to the basement and figure out what's really going on. It should be easy enough, as long as we choose the right moment. I know the code for the laboratory, and I've got a spare set of keys. We just need to make sure nobody else is around.'

'I don't know,' I say. 'This sounds like a bad idea.'

'I know it's scary, but you need to be strong. Weren't we just talking about becoming spiritual leaders? About shepherding our community closer towards God? How can we hope to protect our flock if we're afraid to investigate injustice?'

'Actually,' I mumble. 'About that whole becoming a priest thing…'

'*Come on,*' he hisses, cutting me off. Lightning flashes outside the window, illuminating his eyes like two red-hot brands. 'I'm asking you to help me, as a fellow servant of Christ. And I won't take no for an answer.'

Eight

Noelle is in hysterics when I tell her the story.

'I'm sorry,' she wheezes, clutching the kitchen table for support. 'I know I shouldn't laugh. But I can just imagine the look on your face. You must have been mortified!'

We're standing in the middle of my apartment, surrounded by a mountain of soggy cardboard boxes. Outside the window, rain is pouring down, and for all I know, Kevin is still sitting there in the café with Sister Grace and co.

I got the call from the delivery driver right after the conversation turned to breaking into the lab. He was clearly in a bad mood, telling me I had fifteen minutes to appear at the apartment before he dumped all my boxes out into the rain. Even though he was the one in the wrong – the delivery was scheduled for tomorrow, not today – I didn't talk back or complain. I was just happy to have an excuse to get out of that café. I tossed a couple euro onto the table, mumbled an apology to Kevin, then sprinted back to the apartment as fast as my unfit legs would carry me.

The delivery van was sitting in the car park when I arrived, but there was no sign of the driver. After checking around the back of the building, bracing myself for an earful, I eventually found him sipping tea with Noelle in the foyer. She introduced him as Johnny, saying she'd spotted him out in the rain and invited him inside to dry off. She acted like she was only being a good Samaritan, but I'm pretty sure there was some flirting going on. And I can't say I blame her. He did have a certain rugged charm about him, in that burly red-faced construction worker sort of way. I felt like an awful cockblocker as I signed for the boxes and sent him off in his van. But Noelle didn't seem to mind. She even offered to come up to the apartment and help me unpack.

'I think I was more shocked than embarrassed,' I say, trying to preserve some shred of dignity. 'How was I supposed to know Kevin was such a hardcore Catholic?'

She bites her lip, shoulders shaking with repressed laughter. 'How could you *not* know? It's all he ever talks about! Father Marsh's latest sermon, his yearly pilgrimage to Lourdes, that time he saw the Pope live in the Phoenix Park and the Holy Spirit appeared to him as a pigeon…'

'Hang on,' I say, pointing a boxcutter in accusation. 'You mean you knew all along? You knew he was obsessed with Jesus, and you didn't think to mention it? You must have realised I fancied him!'

'Sorry… I thought you'd figure it out for yourself before you had a chance to develop any serious feelings. But it looks like things escalated faster than I was anticipating.'

'It's fine,' I grumble. 'Whatever. I didn't develop any *serious feelings.*'

I'm still annoyed at her, but admitting that will only make me look even stupider. Instead, I focus my attention on slicing open a box. Inside is a jumble of mismatched socks and suspiciously stained underwear. I haul it into the bedroom, not wanting Noelle to see my unmentionables, and begin sorting the socks into pairs.

'What did you say to him, anyway?' she calls from the kitchen. 'When he asked you to go down to the lab?'

'I didn't say anything. Your boyfriend Johnny rang up at just the right moment, and I seized the opportunity to get the hell out of there.'

'Hang on a second,' she cackles, sticking her head through the bedroom doorway. 'You mean you didn't say no? He still thinks you're going to help him investigate Future Fish?'

'I never said I'd help him.'

'But you never said you wouldn't, either!' She doubles over in a fresh fit of laughter, and I hurl a pair of balled-up boxers at her head.

But then, as the pants splat against the wall and flop sadly down to the ground, I start laughing too. Because how could you not, in a situation this absurd? You've got to laugh to keep yourself from crying.

Besides, in a way it's actually a relief that Kevin has turned out to be totally unobtainable. If there was still a chance of something happening between us, I might have been tempted to help him. To go behind Maeve's back and sneak into the lab. To risk it all for romance. At least this way, I can keep a clear head on my shoulders.

'You won't tell Maeve about this, will you?' I ask, as Noelle returns from the kitchen with a boxful of bedsheets.

'Of course not. You know I tell her as little as possible. And besides, I wouldn't dream of ratting out Saint Kevin.'

'Thank you,' I say, looking back down at my socks.

The only question that leaves is whether *I'm* going to tell Maeve. I know I probably should. She made it crystal-clear at our last meeting that I was expected to pass on any Future Fish-related information I came across. And an employee planning to snoop around the lab sounds like exactly the sort of thing she'd want to know about. But could I really throw Kevin under the bus like that? Despite everything that's happened, he's still my friend. And I can't imagine him selling me out if the roles were reversed.

I turn this dilemma over and over as I stuff the socks into a drawer. But no matter which way I look at it, it's a lose-lose situation. Damned if I betray Kevin, and damned if I don't tell Maeve. In the end, the only resolution I can come to is to keep my head down and hope the whole thing blows over. After all, it's nothing but talk at this stage. Maybe Kevin will abandon the plan. Come to his senses and realise it's not worth risking his job.

'I'm not sure what I'd even tell her,' says Noelle, folding up a wrinkled duvet cover. 'Did Kevin say what exactly he was expecting to find down in the lab?'

'Nope. He just said it could be something dangerous.'

'God only knows what goes on in that head of his. But if it

annoys Maeve, then I fully support it.' She finishes folding the sheets and sets them in a neat stack on top of the dresser. 'Now then, what's next?'

'Thanks for your help,' I say. 'But feel free to head on whenever you need to. I don't want to keep you here all day.'

'Don't worry about it,' she replies. 'It's not like I've got anything better to be doing.'

'Are you sure? I feel bad taking up your entire afternoon.'

'Yeah, yeah. It's grand. I used to spend all my weekends looking after Mam. Taking her to the hospital for tests, cooking her dinner, helping her in and out of the shower. Now that she's gone, I haven't quite figured out what to do with myself.'

'Sorry… That must be weird for you.'

She shrugs, breaking down one of the empty boxes. 'There are worse problems to have than too much time on your hands. I suppose I just need to get out more.'

'Maybe you should join a sports club. My aunty Geraldine took up MMA after her husband died, and she says beating the shit out of people is very therapeutic.'

'Hmmm. Sports has never really been my cup of tea, but I *was* thinking about giving online dating a try. Maybe I could find myself a nice man. Preferably a rich one, with no snotty little children running around.'

I shudder, memories of WildAtlanticGay coming back to haunt me. 'I'm not sure I'd recommend that, to be honest. My experience of dating apps in Ashcross has been pretty bleak so far.'

'Maybe I need to get out of Ashcross then.'

'Go on holiday, you mean?'

'Maybe,' she shrugs. 'Or else pack my bags and get out for good. I never planned on staying here permanently when I moved back from Cork.'

'Oh.' I stare down at the bubble-wrapped succulents I've just been unpacking onto the bed. The thought of Noelle leaving Ashcross has me strangely distraught. 'Where would you go? Back to Cork?'

'That's the thing...' she sighs, sitting down on top of the duvet. A dozen tiny cactuses roll over behind her. 'The doctors were only giving Mam six months when I decided to come back. I figured it would be painful, but quick, and then I could get back to my own life. But those six months ended up turning into three years. Which was great, of course. But a lot changed in that time. The company I was working for went bust with the recession, and all my friends moved on to different cities. Even if I did go back now, there wouldn't be much of a life waiting for me.'

'Couldn't you go somewhere else then? Somewhere entirely new?'

'I suppose so. Mam's insurance covered all her medical expenses, and I've spent practically nothing the last few years. Even that silly car barely put a dent in my savings. The problem is, I'd have no idea where to go. And no idea how to even begin deciding. The world is my oyster, but I can't get the slimy fecker open.'

'You could pick somewhere at random?' I suggest. 'Spin a globe around and see where your finger lands?'

'And end up in the middle of Siberia? Or some remote tribal island where they'd throw me in a volcano? No thanks. I know running away and starting a new life sounds exciting when you're young. But the older you get, the harder it is to start over. You just don't have the energy any more. You think about all the time and effort it would take, and you wonder if you wouldn't be better off just staying home and watching TV.'

'But you said yourself that you wanted to get out. So surely the effort would be worth it?'

'Fair point,' she says, with a self-conscious smile. 'Maybe I'm just a coward. Or maybe I need somebody to come along and give me a push. Set me going in the right direction, like a little paper sailboat, so all I have to do is keep moving forward.'

I nod slowly, trying to think of something inspiring to say. But nothing comes to me. I'm not exactly an expert on living your best life.

'Anyway,' she says, standing back up. 'Enough of that nonsense. Somebody with real problems would roll their eyes into the back of their skull if they heard me… Now, let's get started on another box.'

By the time she leaves, three hours later, everything has been unpacked and put in its proper place. Books have been shelved in alphabetical order, shirts have been hung in a colour-coded rainbow, and toiletries have been lined up from smallest to tallest along the edge of the tub. I collapse in a sweaty heap on the bed, exhausted from the exertion. All that bending and lifting is probably the most exercise I've done since secondary school PE class.

As I lie there on top of the duvet, surrounded by the silent apartment, a strange sense of loneliness begins creeping over me.

You'd think having all my own things around me would make me feel more at home. But somehow, it does the exact opposite. The place felt like a hotel before – cold and impersonal, but only temporary. Now it feels permanent. Like I'm going to be stuck in this town for the rest of my life. Like my days are going to slip by one after the other, draining away in a dull, grey blur. And the one bright spot – the one star in the sky I thought I could follow – has just been snuffed out.

Kevin doesn't love me. And he never will.

In a moment of desperation, I reach out for my phone. I haven't logged into Grindr again since my first day in Ashcross, when the sight of that lonely screen – only one creepy old guy in range – was depressing enough to last me a lifetime. But maybe it's worth another shot. Maybe somebody new has come online…

The first thing I see is a notification. *Seven new messages from WildAtlanticGay.*

Hi.

Hi.

Dick pic.

Hi.

Dick pic.

Ass pic.

Hi.

I ignore this depressing porn, flicking straight through to the list of nearby guys. But once again, there's nobody else in sight. It's just me, WildAtlanticGay, and the great black void. With a sigh of resignation, I toss my phone down the side of the bed and head to the kitchen for a glass of wine.

One glass quickly turns into two, then two into three. And at that stage, you might as well just finish the entire bottle. Tipsy, but still not satisfied, I rummage through the cupboards in search of more. I'm all out of wine, but there is a shoulder of tequila I picked up with some vague notion of having a housewarming. I glance over at the kitchen clock. It's only half-five – still a little early for shots. But if you mix it with orange juice, that's technically a cocktail. And everybody knows you can drink cocktails at any time of day.

After three glasses of this sickly-sweet mixture, I start having second thoughts about WildAtlanticGay. Maybe I was too quick to judge before. Maybe I should at least give him a chance. Sure, he's three times my age, and there's a significant possibility he wants to kill me and wear my skin. But nobody's perfect. And if my only other option is dying alone, what have I really got to lose?

I fish my phone out from the side of the bed, already composing a compliment about the subtle lighting of his ass pic. But when I open up the app, I find a fresh message waiting for me. And this time, it's not from WildAtlanticGay.

Hey man, how's it going? :)

The username is an American flag, followed by a right-pointing arrow, an Irish flag, and then a little yellow face in a party hat. I squint at these hieroglyphics, struggling to decipher their meaning through the fog of tequila. But then I spot something far more interesting. The profile picture. It shows a tall guy in baggy shorts and a flannel shirt standing in the shade on a palm-lined beach. His face is half-hidden under the brim of a baseball cap, but you can tell from the jawline alone that he's at least a nine out of ten.

From LA, reads his bio. *Just arrived in Ashcross. Looking for a cool guy to show me around.*

My heart starts to pound as I put together a reply. I'm a cool guy. I can show him around!

It's going well, I type, relying heavily on autocorrect. *Just having a little pre-dinner cocktail. How about you?*

He responds immediately, which I take to be a good sign.

I'm great. Just a little jetlagged. I only got here yesterday.

Welcome to Ashcross – the asshole of Ireland. What brings you to town?

Just visiting family. My mom grew up here, before she moved to the States, and one of my aunts still lives in the old family house.

And how long are you in town for?

Just a couple of weeks, then I'm heading back to LA. How about you? Are you a local?

Damn. I was hoping he might have been moving here permanently. But still, a hot guy in town for two weeks is nothing to sniff at. A lot can happen in that time…

I'm from Dublin originally, but I just moved here for work.

Awesome! How do you like it so far?

I let out a tequila-scented belch, resisting the urge to go off on a rant. Experience has taught me that guys don't respond well to negativity on dating apps. You've got to act like your life is perfect. Like you've got everything under control. Describe yourself as *an ambitious young professional with a healthy lifestyle*, even though *a mediocre underachiever with a mild alcohol problem* would probably be more accurate.

It's great, I lie. *Although I'm still pretty new in town. I haven't got to know anywhere other than my office.*

What sort of place do you work at?

A cat-food company. The second biggest independent pet-food producer in Ireland, apparently.

Cool. I love cats! What do you do there?

I hesitate, trying to think of a way to spin *Customer Service Assistant* into something more impressive. But I'm too tipsy to come up with anything clever.

Nothing very interesting. Just answering emails from customers all day.

Sounds interesting to me. You must read some crazy stuff!

Crazy doesn't even begin to cover it. You have no idea the stories I could tell…

Well, why don't you tell me a few of them over a drink one evening? :)

A drink? Damn. That was fast! From saying hello to scheduling a date in less than five minutes. And to think, I was seriously considering hooking up with WildAtlanticGay…

Yeah, I'd love to go for a drink!

Great. Let's say Thursday. Know any cool bars in town?

Shit. I still haven't been to any pubs in Ashcross. But even if I had, I seriously doubt any of them could be described as *cool*. I close the app and open a search engine. Feeling optimistic, I start out with *gay bars in Ashcross*. But shockingly enough, nothing comes up. I remove the *gay* and try again, and this time there's a grand total of three results. The one with the highest rating is called *The Black Veil*. According to one review, it's *a cosy little hole in the wall with a shabby-chic interior, located right in the heart of vibrant Ashcross.*

I close down the search engine and return to Grindr.

There's this one pub called the Black Veil which is pretty cool. I could meet you there at 6?

Perfect. I'm Sean, by the way :)

Mark :)

I lie back on the bed and stretch my arms out in delight. I guess it's true what they say about one door opening when another one closes. What happened with Kevin is already old news. Now I've got somebody else to focus on. Somebody bigger and better. Somebody who seems just as nice as Kevin, and is possibly even hotter to boot...

I just hope things with him will go a little more smoothly.

Nine

I avoid Kevin the next week, pretending to be on my phone or running late for a meeting whenever I pass through reception. He sends me a few texts, asking when we can *continue our conversation from the café*, but I pretend I haven't seen them. I know I should just bite the bullet and tell him the truth. That I'm not really a Catholic or an aspiring priest, and when we met up in the café, I thought it was a hot date. But I can't do it. It's just too awkward. And so I carry on ghosting him and hope he'll give up eventually.

I make it all the way to Wednesday without getting roped into a conversation. But on Thursday morning, my luck finally runs out. I barge through the front door, planning to charge past Kevin's desk as quickly as possible.

'Mark!' he calls, trying to wave me over.

'Sorry,' I call back. 'Can't talk right now. Have to get to the toilet ASAP. Got a nasty case of diarrhoea coming on!'

It's only when I hear the sniggering behind me that I realise Kevin isn't the only person in the room. I freeze, halfway through the door to the hallway, and slowly turn around.

Dominic is standing in the corner of the room, next to the sad potted plant. Two bleach-blonde women sit tittering on the itchy green couch beside him.

'Morning, Marcus,' he says, with a sympathetic grimace.

'Morning, Dominic…'

'Have you met Shelley and Fi yet?' he asks, gesturing down at the women on the couch.

I've seen the two of them hanging around Maeve before, whispering away in their matching South Dublin accents. They're both in their early thirties, with the same unnaturally smooth foreheads and suspiciously orange tan. But where Shelley is short and round, Fi is tall and full of angles.

'Eh…hi there,' I mumble, trying not to blush.

'Marcus here is the newest member of the under-forties club at WellCat,' says Dominic. 'That makes five of us now.'

Shelley gives me a caustic smile, like she was perfectly happy with the club's membership the way it was before. Fi's wave, meanwhile, feels slightly more sincere.

'So tell me, Marcus,' says Dominic. 'Did you get up to much on your first weekend in Ashcross?'

'Not really…' I begin. But something cuts me off before I can finish.

It's Kevin. Staring out at me from behind the front desk. His eyes are wide, his lips pinched tight, as he beckons me over with a frantic wave. I shake my head, nodding at Dominic, and pray Kevin will have the cop-on to keep quiet around him.

'Is Marcus alright?' asks Fi.

'I think he's having a stroke,' says Shelley.

'Sorry,' I splutter, turning back towards Dominic. 'I mean, I didn't do much over the weekend. Just got a little drunk on Saturday and then was hungover on Sunday.'

'Nice one,' he grins. 'Where did you go on Saturday?'

'What? Nowhere. I just had a few drinks at home.'

'Ah,' he says, raising an eyebrow. 'Did you have somebody over?'

'No, no. It was just me.'

'Oh...' He clears his throat. 'So you got drunk alone in your apartment? That must have been...fun.'

Shelley and Fi exchange a look, then both of them burst out laughing.

I feel my face blowing up like a red balloon and retreat towards the hallway. Kevin starts waving me over again, but I pretend I can't see him. I mumble a *see you later* to Dominic, then turn around and throw myself through the doorway.

I hurry down the corridor, not slowing down until I'm safely at my desk. My cheeks are on fire, my stomach twisted up into a pretzel of shame. That entire exchange was a disaster. Like a meteor hitting the Earth and wiping out all my dignity. Shelley and Fi are going to tell everybody I'm a weirdo, and Dominic will probably never talk to me again...

And then, just when I think my morning can't get any worse, a message from Kevin arrives on my phone.

Good idea playing it cool in front of Dominic and his floozies.

The coast is clear now, if you want to come back and finish our conversation from Saturday?

Sorry, I reply. *I'd love to chat, but things are manic this morning. A million emails have come in overnight.*

How about lunchtime, then?

I'm all booked up, I lie. *Noelle and I are heading to the chipper.*

This evening?

I'm meeting somebody for drinks. Sorry.

This one is technically true, although I've left out a few key details about my date with Sean.

Come on, Mark. This is serious. We all enjoy a nice drink or two, but is that really more important than doing the Lord's work?

I roll my eyes at that one, setting the phone aside and focusing on my inbox. Despite what I may have told Kevin, hardly any emails have come in overnight. I scan through the short list of subject lines, keeping an eye out for any mentions of Future Fish. But there's nothing. Just the same old questions about ingredients and nutrition, as well as one woman offering up her cat's modelling services for our next ad campaign.

I work through the list at a leisurely pace, knowing there's no need to hurry on such a quiet day. But despite this slowdown, I still manage to polish off the last email just after lunchtime.

'I've cleared the inbox for today,' I say, turning towards Noelle.

'Nice one,' she replies, with a half-hearted thumbs up. Her eyes are locked onto her own computer screen, where the homepage of a particularly trashy tabloid is open.

'Anything else you need help with?'

'Hmmm. Have you checked the junk folder?'

'Yep. Nothing but mail-order brides and Nigerian princes.'

'Nothing else that needs doing until tomorrow then.' She lets out a little snort, clicking on a headline reading *Fitness Influencer's Gory Accident at Spin Class.*

'Are you sure?' I ask, glancing up at the clock. 'It's only half-one. There's still four hours to go...'

'Well, you can always keep an eye on the inbox in case anything shows up this afternoon. But try not to reply to them *too* quickly. We don't want those whack jobs thinking they've got us at their beck and call.'

'And if nothing else comes in?'

She shrugs. 'Just sit back and relax so.'

I turn towards my computer, fully intending to comply with these instructions. But the thought of lounging around doing nothing makes me nervous. 'There definitely isn't *anything* else I could be working on?'

'Look,' she sighs, starting to lose patience. 'I'd let you go home early if it was up to me. But Maeve would lose her rag if I did that.'

'But won't she also be angry if she sees me sitting here twiddling my thumbs?'

'Of course she will! There's nothing she hates more than people slacking off on her time. The trick is to make sure you *look* busy, even if you aren't really. Just keep your head down and don't be afraid to get creative with your personal progress report.'

I pause to consider this. But I'm still not convinced. 'Surely she'll notice if I'm not being productive?'

'You'd think so, but no. She has this idea in her head that everybody's working at maximum capacity at all times. I'm not sure where she gets it from, but it seems to make her happy. Like a queen bee watching her minions slave away. I tried telling her I could get by without a replacement for Valentina, but she wasn't having any of it. She said people would think the business was struggling if we started cutting down on staff.'

The comment about not needing to replace Valentina stings a little, but I try not to dwell on it. 'So, you're saying I definitely won't get into trouble, as long as I just *pretend* to be working?'

'Exactly. So long as you maintain the illusion, Maeve will be none the wiser.'

'Alright. Fine...'

I slump back in my chair and begin brainstorming ways to pass the time. Catching up on current affairs seems like the most respectable option, so I decide to start there. But the news gets old quickly. It's just the same old doom and gloom, over and over. Politicians lying. Celebrities dying. The earth frying. I switch to Facebook, hoping for something a bit more light-hearted. But that's just more of the same, with a few photos of people doing stupid poses on beaches. In a moment of desperation, I even look up the weather forecast. But that's the bleakest of all. Rain, rain, rain and more rain.

Just as I'm zooming in on a map of today's pollen count, despite never having suffered from hay fever in my life, Noelle stands up and pulls on her coat.

'I'm just popping out for a smoke,' she announces. 'Do you want to come?'

'No thanks.'

'Are you sure now? You don't want to go make lovey eyes at Saint Kevin?'

'Get lost,' I grumble, shooing her away.

'Alright, alright,' she laughs. 'But you'll be bored out of your mind without me.'

I turn back to my map as soon as she's gone, trying to muster up some enthusiasm for the fact that there are apparently three different types of pollen allergies. But her little joke about Kevin has thrown me off kilter. Filled my head back up with thoughts of Future Fish and the lab.

And then an idea occurs to me. Something else I could be looking up to pass the time. Something far more interesting than tree, grass, and ragweed...

I know I probably shouldn't. Only fools tempt fate when they could be leaving well enough alone. But a quick peek couldn't hurt. Especially with Noelle out smoking, and nobody else sitting close enough to see what's going on on my screen.

Fingers trembling, I type *WellCat Future Fish* into the search bar.

I'm not sure what exactly I'm expecting to find. Some more information on Friends of the Fish, maybe – a website or manifesto explaining who they really are. Maybe even some clue as to what Kevin thinks could be lurking in the basement. But the first result that comes up is a video. It was uploaded to YouTube just twelve hours ago, by a user called WatcherInTheWest. My heart starts to pound as I read the title.

Is this cat food company secretly conducting extra-terrestrial research?

A voice in my head screams at me to turn back now. To close down the window and pretend I never saw a thing. But it's too late for that. I'm already fishing a pair of tangled earphones from my pocket and plugging them into the computer. I glance around the room, making sure nobody is watching, then click *play*.

The video opens on a black screen. Haunting synth music echoes in the background, like a knock-off of some nineties sci-fi theme. A picture of the WellCat office gradually fades into view. It was taken on an unusually sunny afternoon, with clear blue skies and sunlight streaming down onto the footpath outside. I recognise it as the same one from the *About Us* page on our website.

'This is the office of Irish pet-food company WellCat,' announces a voice over the music. It sounds unnaturally deep and distorted, like that vocal effect used by serial killers in films. 'Just a few metres below, in the basement of the building, is the laboratory where secret experiments are alleged to be taking place.'

Cut to an image of a fuzzy white spot floating against the night sky. Based on the context, I can only assume it's supposed to be a UFO.

'The story of the Ashcross Alien begins on June eighteenth, just one month prior to time of recording. That night, between eleven pm and three am, there were nine independent reports of strange lights hovering in the sky off the coast of Galway. The image you see on screen was captured by Fearghus O'Maoileoin, a local farmer whose name will be familiar to many viewers in connection with a previous incident of cattle mutilation.'

The UFO is replaced by an unflattering close-up of a toothless man in a flat cap. I can't tell whether it's a mugshot or just a very unfortunate selfie.

'Two of the reports about the nocturnal lights were radioed in from pilots to air traffic control at Shannon Airport, prompting the Irish Aviation Authority to carry out a full investigation. The official verdict was a shower of meteors burning up on entry to the Earth's atmosphere. But viewers in the know will recognise all the hallmarks of an extra-terrestrial visitation. Several witnesses additionally described seeing the lights descend rapidly down towards the Atlantic before disappearing completely, leading some to speculate that the vessel may have crashed or been forced to carry out an emergency landing.'

Cut to moonlight reflecting on dark water. I squint at the grainy image, half expecting to see an alien clinging to a life ring. But it looks just like any old stock photo of the ocean.

'The story could easily have ended there, going down in history as yet another suspicious incident swept under the rug by the authorities. But a seemingly unrelated occurrence a few weeks later has raised the eyebrows of many observers. On July second, the following article appeared on a popular pet-food website...'

A screenshot of *Pet People Ireland* pops up on screen. At the top of the page is a headline reading: *The Secret Science Behind WellCat's Future Fish*. Underneath is a wall of text too small to read, along with an illustration of what looks like a strand of DNA.

It must be the article Noelle told me about. The one that got Valentina fired.

'The article was quickly deleted,' continues the voiceover, 'but not before it had been screenshot and shared on several animal rights forums. Much of the initial commentary speculated that the *secret science* was referring to some sort of genetic modification experiment. But the story soon came to the attention of the extra-terrestrial investigation community, who were quick to put together the close proximity of Ashcross to Galway, as well as the suspicious timing of the post – just two weeks after the UFO sighting.'

Cut to a CGI rendering of an alien on an operating table. It's classic B-movie stuff – giant round head on a tiny grey body, bulging black eyes reflecting the light.

'Could the rumours be true? Has an extra-terrestrial specimen, living or dead, been recovered from the crash site and taken to Ashcross? Is this so-called cat-food company a front for a secret EU research facility? And is *Future Fish* the codename for an as-yet-unidentified alien lifeform, accidentally leaked to the pet-food press and then hastily covered up? The evidence is compelling, but not yet conclusive. That's why I, WatcherInTheWest, have taken it upon myself to launch my own personal investigation. I've already arrived in Ashcross and begun reconnaissance work in the local area. Stay tuned for more updates in the coming days, and don't forget to like and subscribe in the meantime.'

The video ends there. I remove my headphones in a daze, not sure whether I should be laughing or crying. First animal experiments, and now…aliens? And just when I thought this town couldn't get any stranger. I rest my head against the wall, too bewildered to continue fake-working, and wait for Noelle to get back from her smoke break.

'What's the goss?' she asks, reappearing a few minutes later. 'You look like a fortune teller has just shown you the Death card.'

'It's hard to explain,' I mumble, pasting the video link into an email. 'Just check your inbox. And make sure you've got your headphones in first.'

'More animal rights shite?' she yawns.

'No. Something even stranger.'

I watch out of the corner of my eye as she opens up the video. Her expression – bored and disillusioned to begin with – quickly brightens into mild curiosity, before freefalling into full-on chaotic delight.

'Jesus Christ!' she laughs, yanking her earphones out at the end. 'You weren't lying. That was brilliant!'

'I'm not sure *brilliant* is the word I'd use.'

'You know what I mean. It was a wild ride!'

'Hang on,' I say, eyeing her with suspicion. 'You don't actually believe in any of that alien shite, do you?'

'Of course not. If there was any intelligent life out there, they would've nuked the Earth a long time ago. But it's still fun to think about.'

'Well, fun or not, we should probably show this to Maeve. We don't want her finding out about it the same way she did with the Friends of the Fish emails...'

'I suppose you're right,' she sighs. 'You can pop the link into an email, like you did for me.'

'No,' I say, rising to my feet. 'Better to do it in person. It could be hours before she sees an email, and something tells me she'd want to know about this as soon as possible.'

'Alright,' shrugs Noelle. 'It's your funeral.'

Ten

Maeve's reaction to the alien video is just as terrifying as I imagined. Her jaw clenches tighter and tighter as she watches, until I can practically hear her teeth cracking.

'This can't be for real,' she mutters. 'Somebody must be messing with us...'

She spends the rest of the afternoon hovering over my desk, grilling me with a series of follow-up questions. Where did I find the video? Have I ever heard of this WatcherInTheWest person before? Can I subscribe to his channel so I'll get a notification if he posts any more content? Noelle is absolutely no help, picking up her phone and pretending to be in the middle of a call every time Maeve comes near. The only thing that gets me through it is thinking about my date with Sean later this evening.

I head straight from the office to the Black Veil pub, managing to avoid Kevin on the way out by hiding myself amongst a group of after-work joggers. The pub is located right next to the seafront, on a corner with a particularly off-putting smell of fish. A rusty metal sign hangs above the doorway, showing an old-timey wench in a massive skirt pulling back a dark curtain. I can tell from the exterior alone that that review I read was full of shit – there's nothing remotely *cosy* or *chic* about this place. But it's too late to change venues now. All I can do is push open the door and step inside.

The interior glows like a phosphorescent cave – the single, green-shaded lamp reflected dozens of times over in the sticky stains splattered across the floor. An eerie silence hangs in the air, with no music or radio station playing in the background. The only sound at all is the hushed conversation of three balding middle-aged men at the bar. I linger in the doorway, getting the impression this probably isn't the sort of place that welcomes non-regulars. But neither the bartender nor the three drinkers seem to notice my arrival, so I go ahead and seat myself at a booth in the corner.

My phone starts to vibrate as soon as I sit down. I pick it up, praying it's not a last-minute cancellation from Sean. But it turns out it's only a message from Kevin.

Mark, we need to talk ASAP. The situation just got a lot more complicated.

I groan, in no mood for this latest bit of nonsense. But before I can decide how to reply, the door of the pub creaks open. A tall, dark stranger comes strutting in. Even through the gloomy half-light, I can tell it's Sean straightaway. He looks almost identical to his photo – the same flannel shirt rolled up to the elbows, the same sparkling white teeth and stubble-covered jawline.

He spots me right away, approaching the table with a self-assured smile. 'You must be Mark,' he says, extending a hand. A sleeve of tattoos covers his forearm – an incongruous mixture of cartoon characters and occult symbols.

'And you must be Sean,' I reply, awkwardly accepting his hand-clasp-back-pat. 'Nice to meet you.'

He slides down into the seat opposite, gazing around the room with a tourist's delight. 'This place is amazing. I love a good dive bar!'

'Sorry it's such a kip. They must be renovating or something.'

'No, no. This is exactly what I was expecting. I could tell from your profile you weren't one of those fancy-schmancy type of guys.'

'Eh…thanks,' I reply, not sure if I should be offended. 'Can I get you something to drink?'

'I'll take a Guinness, thanks.'

I extract myself from the booth as elegantly as possible and head towards the bar. The three middle-aged men pause their conversation as I approach. They don't say anything, or even look directly at me, but I can feel the judgment radiating from the corners of their eyes.

'Two pints of Guinness,' I say to the barman. He's slightly younger than his customers, with thinning red hair and a filthy dishtowel thrown over one shoulder.

'That all?' he grunts.

I nod, handing over a twenty and waiting for my change. As I head back to the table, I hear one of the men whisper something behind me. The other two erupt in howls of laughter.

'So,' says Sean, once the drinks are set down and the *cheers*-ing out of the way. 'How was your day?'

'Oh, you know, just an ordinary workday. Nothing too exciting.' Besides the alleged alien in the basement. But that seems a bit intense to bring up on a first date. 'How about you?'

'My day was great! I've just been exploring around town, checking out some of the local hiking trails.'

'I didn't know there were any hiking trails in Ashcross...' And if I did, I would have avoided them at all costs. 'Did you walk anywhere nice?'

'I followed this one route up to the remains of an old Neolithic tomb. A sort of stone door leading down to an underground chamber. It was incredible! You'd never see anything like that in LA.'

'*Neolithic?* That's like...thousands of years old, right?'

'Exactly,' he grins, taking a sip of his pint. 'I love old shit like that.'

'Right, yeah. Me too...'

'Back in high school, I was totally obsessed with Ancient Egypt. I used to read all these books about the culture and religion and stuff. Did you know modern engineers still don't understand how they built the Pyramids?'

'Eh, no...I didn't know that. And I didn't know there were any old tombs in Ashcross either. How did you even find out about that one?'

'My aunt told me. The one I'm staying with.'

'And what's she? Some sort of archaeologist?'

'Not exactly,' he laughs. 'She's a nurse at the hospital up in the city. She's just really into history, I guess.'

The conversation flows freely from here, Sean telling me all about his family and his impressions of Ashcross so far. He buzzes with a giddy enthusiasm for the town, which I find endearing, even if I can't relate. Things are going well, as far as I can tell. But a dark cloud still hovers at the back of my mind.

'Too bad you're only in town temporarily,' I sigh. 'You said you're leaving in a couple weeks, right?'

He nods, his smile dimming. 'I'm supposed to be flying back next Saturday. Although I've actually been thinking about staying on a bit longer...'

'Oh yeah?' I sit up a little straighter in the booth. 'How much longer?'

'Until next fall, maybe. I was thinking about working abroad for a year or two anyways. Maybe heading to Korea to teach English or something. But now that I'm here, I feel like this might be the right place for me.'

'You'd really stay in Ashcross for an entire year?'

'Why not?' he shrugs, downing the last of his beer. 'The only real issue would be finding a job. I don't have many savings to my name, so I can't afford to slack off for too long.'

'Finding a job in Ashcross could be tricky,' I concede. 'It's not exactly an employment hotspot.'

'I take it that means you don't know anybody who's hiring?'

I think back over all the businesses I've visited in the last week, scanning my memory for a *help wanted* sign. But nothing comes to mind. 'I don't think so. Sorry.'

'Too bad,' he sighs, looking down at his empty glass. He opens his mouth, like he's about to say something else, then shakes his head and jumps to his feet. 'My round!'

I check my phone again as he heads towards the bar. Another

message has come in from Kevin.

Listen, Maeve is going mental over some video about an alien. She's asked me to start ringing up security companies to get quotes for expanding the CCTV system. We need to make our move ASAP!

I roll my eyes, switching the phone to silent, and shove it down deep in my pocket. Some people just don't know when to quit, do they?

Sean returns a minute later, clutching another pint of Guinness in each hand. But this time, instead of resuming his seat on the opposite side of the booth, he squeezes in next to me.

'So,' he says, his thigh pressing up against mine. 'Enough about me. I want to hear more about *you* now.'

'Oh, well, I'm not sure how much there is to tell...'

'Come on. Everybody has a story.'

'But mine's not very interesting.' Unless you have a fetish for failures. A kink for people getting fired from their jobs and having to move back in with their parents… But I can't go telling him my whole sad history. He'll think I'm a loser.

'I'm sure that's not true,' he says, sliding his hand on top of mine. 'You seem pretty interesting to me.'

I mumble a self-conscious 'thank you', eyes dropping down to our interlocked fingers. His are long and tanned, like a Classical bronze statue. Mine are fat and pasty, like a Neanderthal cave painting.

His face begins drifting closer towards mine, the distance between our lips getting smaller and smaller. But before the kiss can connect, something snatches my attention away. It's the men at the bar. All three of them are staring over at us, the one in the middle muttering darkly to the others. I can't make out what he's saying, but it doesn't take a psychic to intuit that it's not something friendly.

'Everything okay?' asks Sean, pulling back. 'I hope that wasn't too forward of me.'

'No, no, not at all. It's just…those guys at the bar have been staring at us.'

He turns around to take a look, fingers tightening over mine. 'Assholes,' he mutters. 'What's their problem?'

'Who knows… Probably best to ignore them though.'

'No way. You can't let bullies like that intimidate you. Trust me, there's only one way to deal with this.' He stands up from the table, letting my hand fall down onto the empty booth.

'Come on, just forget about it,' I plead. But he doesn't seem to hear me.

'Hey man,' he calls across the room. 'You got a problem?'

None of the men respond.

'I said, *you got a problem?*' repeats Sean, advancing across the sticky floor. I look around for the bartender, hoping he might be able to defuse the situation. But there's no sign of him.

It's only when Sean is within striking distance that the man in the middle finally speaks up. 'No problem here,' he grunts. 'Or at least there wasn't, until you lads showed up.'

'What's that supposed to mean?' hisses Sean, grabbing him by the collar.

'It means, we don't want your type coming around here. This is a quiet, family establishment.'

'So what, we can't sit here and enjoy a drink, just because we're gay?'

'*Gay?*' says the man, frowning in confusion. 'Nobody cares

which way you swing. Sure, Johnny here is bisexual.' He gestures over at the moustachioed man on his right, who winks suggestively at Sean.

'Oh,' says Sean, letting go of the man's collar. He slouches sideways, unsure how to take this. 'Well, if you're not a bunch of bigots, then what's the problem?'

'The problem,' says the pot-bellied guy on the left, 'is that we don't want a load of Yanks coming over and turning Ashcross into another tourist trap. We work hard to keep this place off the radar, so the locals can still afford to live here. So why don't you take yourself back to Temple Bar and your twenty-euro pints, and leave us alone in peace?'

Sean stares at him for a second, like he's struggling to process this. And then his face hardens with a fresh wave of indignation. 'Well guess what, old man? I'm here, I'm…um, American, and I'm not going anywhere. And if you've got a problem with that, we can take it outside.'

'Relax,' says the man in the middle, rolling his eyes. 'Nobody's looking for a fight.'

'Well too bad,' says Sean, shoving him back against the bar. 'Because you've just found one.'

I open my mouth, about to try and intervene – to tell Sean to calm down and not do anything stupid. But the voice of the bartender beats me to it.

'Oi!' he shouts, emerging from a door in the corner. 'What the hell is going on here?'

'Nothing…' says Sean, taking a step back.

'It didn't look like *nothing* to me.'

'Listen man, he started it.'

'And I suppose you were going to finish it, were you?'

Sean shrugs. 'Maybe I was.'

'Well, the only thing you'll be finishing now is that pint. And then you'll be taking yourself outside immediately after.'

'That's not fair! You can't just—'

'It's my pub; I can do what I want. Now finish your drink and fuck off.'

Sean storms back to the table, muttering under his breath. He picks up his pint and downs it in one go. 'Come on,' he grunts, holding out his palm. 'Let's get out of here.'

I leave my Guinness unfinished and take his hand. We march across the dingy room, past the bartender and the three leering men, and out into the blinding light of day. It's only when the door is safely shut behind us that I realise I'm shaking.

'Holy shit,' I mumble. 'That was insane! I can't believe you almost got into a fight.'

'Sorry,' he sighs. 'I didn't mean to ruin our evening.'

He leans back against the side of the pub, kicking one leg up behind him, and hits me with a pair of puppy-dog eyes. I know I should be angry with him – he could have gotten us into serious trouble back there. But now that the immediate danger has passed, the whole incident seems kind of exciting.

'It's fine,' I say. 'Let's just get out of here.'

'Sounds good to me,' he says. 'Know any other good bars in town?'

'Eh…' It's clear neither one of us wants the date to end here. But wandering into another unknown pub feels like a bad idea. And we're not quite at the going-home-together stage yet either. 'Why don't we go for a walk along the beach?' I suggest. 'It's not a bad evening, and the off-licence will still be open. We can grab some wine and watch the sunset.'

'Why, Mark…' he grins, throwing an arm over my shoulder. 'If I didn't know any better, I'd think you were trying to seduce me!'

Fifteen minutes later, we're strolling along the sand, two bottles of wine and a naggin of whiskey in hand. The sun is just beginning to slip below the horizon, sending streaks of orange and pink bleeding out into the sky. For just a brief moment, if you keep your eyes on the ocean, you could almost forget what a shithole Ashcross is.

We chat away about all sorts of nonsense, from favourite films to childhood pets. The shoreline carries us further and further away from town, until soon there isn't a single other soul in sight. It's only when the sky has faded to black that we finally turn back towards the distant lights of Ashcross. Sean turns out to have an impressive knowledge of astronomy, pointing out various stars and constellations sparkling in the sky. Scorpius. Ursa Major. Cassiopeia. I'm far too tipsy to actually focus on any of them, but it feels incredibly romantic all the same.

'Here's where I get off,' I announce, as we reach a roundabout at the edge of town. Sean is carrying on north towards his aunt's house, while I'm switching back onto the main road.

'Alright,' he says, taking my hands in his. 'Thanks for an amazing evening. I hope we can do it again sometime.'

'I hope so too. Before you have to go back to the States…'

He smiles sadly, moving his hands down to my waist. 'Hey, don't say that. There's still a chance I could find a job and stay.'

'I wish there was something I could do to help you,' I sigh. 'It would be too depressing if you disappeared now.'

'Well, there is *one* thing you could do…' His fingers wander around into the small of my back, setting my spine all atingle. 'You could ask around to see if any of your colleagues know of any jobs going. If it's not too much trouble, that is…'

'Of course. I can do that. My supervisor is a local, so she'd know better than anyone what's going on in town.'

'Amazing,' he grins, going in for another kiss. There's nobody around to ruin the moment this time, so I just close my eyes and let it happen. The touch is softer than I was expecting. Tender, almost. With hints of red wine and sea salt, and something bittersweet I can't quite put my finger on. 'Hey,' he says, pulling away. 'Speaking of your supervisor…this might sound crazy, but do you think I could maybe get a job at your company?'

'A job at WellCat?' Even through the alcohol haze, I can tell that might be a bad idea. I don't want to recommend somebody who's such a loose cannon. But that kiss felt so good, there's no way I can refuse him. 'I'm not sure. But I can ask around tomorrow and let you know.'

'You're my hero,' he says, with another quick peck. 'Anyways, I'd better run. My aunt is already going to kill me for staying out so late.'

I pull my phone from my pocket once we've gone our separate ways. It's been on silent ever since the pub, and it turns out I've missed several calls and messages from Kevin.

Time is running out, Mark. Are you free to meet up this evening?

Hi Mark, I've just called by your apartment, but you weren't home. What's going on?

PLEASE MARK. FROM ONE SERVANT OF CHRIST

TO ANOTHER, I NEED YOUR HELP!

I stagger back and forth from the effort of reading and walking at the same time. All this Kevin shit is really starting to get old. It's one thing talking about it at the office, but blowing up my phone all evening is a whole other level of annoying. And the worst part is, it's never going to end. Not as long as Kevin is under the illusion that I'm some sort of aspiring priest…

So maybe it's time to set the record straight. Put a stop to this nonsense once and for all.

Hi Kevin, I type, the letters dancing in front of my eyes. *Sorry I missed your calls. I was on a hot date with a guy called Sean. I hate to break it to you, but I don't want to be a priest. I don't even believe in God. So you're just going to have to find somebody else to help you investigate Future Fish. Maybe one of those skanky nuns…*

I read back over the message, making sure I've captured the right tone. And then, with a satisfied grunt, I slam my thumb down and click *send*.

Eleven

The hangover hits me hard and heavy the next morning. I lie awake in bed, eyes screwed tight against the daylight, and take stock of the damage to my system. Moderate headache (should be manageable after a couple of painkillers). Mild nausea (not bad enough to keep me from holding down breakfast). A vague sense of existential dread (not entirely attributable to the hangover). All in all, it feels like I've gotten off lightly. Especially considering that bottle of whiskey we cracked open on the beach. For such a magical evening, it's a price I'd gladly pay again.

I sit up, ignoring the sudden rush of vertigo, and reach out blearily for my phone. And that's when it all comes hurtling back to me. The text! Oh God, the text... Heart pounding, I open up the conversation with Kevin and begin reading back over my message. But I only get halfway through before I have to stop. It's so cringy, so crazy-sounding, I feel like I'm about to vomit all over the duvet. He hasn't responded yet, but I can tell from the little blue ticks that he's read it. He must be furious with me. And who could blame him? I swear to God, I'm never drinking again…

Hey Kevin, I type, holding down a fresh wave of nausea. *Sorry about last night. I was off my face when I sent that. Please just ignore it.*

I wait a few minutes, anxious for his reply. But the phone remains silent, the little ticks still grey. He hasn't even read it. With a sigh, I set the phone aside and drag myself towards the shower. I'll just have to apologise properly when I get into the office.

I move at half my usual pace as I get dressed and force down a bowl of sugary cereal. My limbs feel like they've doubled in length, every action requiring a miracle of coordination. By the time I finally crawl out the front door, it's already five past nine. I'm running seriously late.

I power-walk down the road as quickly as possible, ignoring the sandpaper scraping against my skull. Although I'm sure Noelle won't care if I'm a few minutes late, I don't want Maeve to think I'm some sort of slacker. But as soon as I turn the corner onto Atlantic Lane, I realise there's no need to worry. Nobody's going to notice I was a few minutes late. In fact, nobody's going to be paying me any attention at all this morning.

The first thing that hits me is the lights. Flashing blue and white, they stab like needles into my hungover eyes. I blink the pain away, squinting through the multicoloured glare, and realise the lights are coming from an ambulance. It's parked just outside the office, beside the ramp to the car park. A few dozen onlookers are gathered outside, but I can't see anybody in need of urgent medical attention.

I make my way to the edge of the crowd, trying to see in through the door to the office. But a portly police officer is blocking the way.

'What's going on?' I ask, to nobody in particular.

'We don't know yet,' replies a woman, holding her phone up at the ready in case something worth filming comes along. She taps her heel on the pavement, like she can hardly bear the anticipation. I'm pretty sure she's not a WellCat employee. Just some random rubbernecker off the street, hoping for a bit of blood and gore to spice up her morning. 'The paramedics went in twenty minutes ago, but nobody's come out since. And your man's not letting anybody else inside...' She makes a sour face at the Guard in front of the door. He stares off stoically into the distance, ignoring the impatient mob before him.

I linger at the edge of the crowd, not sure what I should be doing. There's no sign of Noelle or Kevin. And no Maeve either.

After several anxious minutes, the sea of people begins to part. A pair of paramedics in high-vis emerge from the building. They push something along between them, but I can't get a look in over the shoulders of the people in front of me. It's only when I stand right up on my tippy toes, leaning against a lamp post for support, that I finally see what it is.

A stretcher. Covered in one of those emergency tinfoil blankets. With a motionless body laying stiff underneath. The head is so bloody, I can barely make out its features. But there's no way I'd ever mistake that face...

'Kevin!'

Next thing I know, I'm shoving my way through the crowd. Elbowing man, woman, and child aside without remorse. Pure instinct drives me forward, and I have no idea what I'm going to do when I reach my target. I just know that I have to get to Kevin. I have to make sure he's alright.

I break through the final row of onlookers and grab hold of the edge of the stretcher. The paramedics are still pushing it towards the ambulance, and I stumble along helplessly beside them.

'Kevin! Can you hear me?'

His eyes are closed, his breathing strained and painful-sounding. A dark slick of blood spreads out from his temple. It looks serious. Potentially life-altering. Maybe even…

'Is he going to be alright?' I demand, turning to the paramedic at the back of the stretcher. Tears well up in my eyes, choking my voice into a hysteric sob. 'Why isn't he answering me!?'

'We're doing everything we can,' replies the paramedic, with all the empathy of a self-service checkout. 'Please stand back.'

'Kevin! Kevin! Are you alright? Answer me!'

His eyelids flutter open, like scraps of paper floating on the wind. 'Mark…is that you?'

'It's me, Kevin. It's me!'

'I thought you weren't coming…' He stares up at the sky, like he can't see me walking along beside him.

'What happened to you, Kevin? Did you have some sort of accident?'

'No… No accident.'

'What, then? What happened to your head?'

The stretcher comes to a halt at the back of the ambulance,

a ramp slowly descending towards the footpath. We don't have much time.

'I was a… I was a…attacked.'

'*Attacked?* You mean somebody else did this? Somebody hurt you?'

He nods, wincing at the effort.

'Who was it? Who did this to you!?'

'It was…it was…'

They're pushing him up the ramp now, my hands slipping off the side of the stretcher. 'It was *who*, Kevin? Tell me!'

He draws in a long, gurgling breath, struggling to work up the strength to answer.

But it's too late.

The door slams shut. The ambulance speeds off down the street. I chase after it for a few seconds, screaming at the driver to stop. But it's no good. He's already gone.

I collapse onto my knees in the middle of the road. My head is spinning, my heart beating so fast I'm afraid it might burst. This can't be happening. It doesn't make sense. Why would anybody want to hurt Kevin? The thought of him lying alone in that ambulance, tubes and needles snaking through his body, is just too awful to bear…

I kneel there in a heap on the concrete, totally oblivious to my surroundings, until the *honk* of an oncoming car brings me back to my senses. I rise shakily to my feet and stagger over towards the door to the office. The bulk of the crowd has already dispersed, all the gawkers and gossips moving on with their mornings. Only a dozen or so WellCat employees remain. They mill around outside the door, waiting for some sign of normality to return. Noelle emerges from the car park just as I'm heading over to join them.

'What's going on?' she asks, waving me over. 'There was an ambulance blocking the car park, and I couldn't get in.'

'It's Kevin,' I whimper. 'He's hurt. They've taken him away to hospital.'

'Jesus Christ. What happened to him?'

'I'm not sure. He had a cut on his head, and there was blood everywhere. I think somebody attacked him.'

'*Attacked him?* Who in their right mind would lay a hand on Kevin?'

'I don't know. He didn't say...'

She stares over at the office wall, like she's searching the concrete for a hidden clue. 'Maybe it was a burglary,' she says. 'We do get them around here from time to time.'

'Maybe... But I don't think so. It looked awfully violent for just a random break-in.'

She raises an eyebrow, studying my expression. 'What are you suggesting?'

'I'm not sure exactly...but what if this has something to do with that alien video? The guy doing the voiceover was talking about coming to Ashcross. Carrying out some sort of *reconnaissance*. Maybe he tried to break into the office to investigate Future Fish. Maybe Kevin caught him, and things got violent.'

She bites her lip, chewing this over. 'I don't know... Making stupid videos is a far cry from actually hurting somebody.'

'Well, somebody clearly hurt him!' I snap, tears stinging my eyes. 'You didn't see him coming out on that stretcher. You don't know what it was like!'

'I'm sorry,' she says, giving my shoulder a squeeze. 'You're right. I have no idea what happened. I'm just saying we should wait for more information before jumping to conclusions. Kevin will be able to explain everything once he's out of hospital.'

I close my eyes, forcing down a deep breath. She's right about needing more information. But I'm not just going to sit around waiting for it. 'Do you know which hospital they'll be taking him to?'

'Probably St Edna's, up in Galway. It's the closest one. About a forty-minute drive.'

'Can you take me there?'

'Of course. We'll head over straight after work.'

'No, we need to go *now*. I have to talk to Kevin.'

'I know you want to see him, but we can't just run off in the middle of the morning. Not unless you want Maeve to—'

'PLEASE!'

She freezes, taken aback by this sudden outburst.

'I'm sorry,' I mumble. 'It's just…Kevin and I had a bit of an argument last night. I sent him a stupid text, and now he's pissed off at me. If something happens to him… I mean, if he doesn't make it through this, and that's the last thing I ever said to him…'

'Here now,' she says, getting a little teary-eyed herself. 'You can't start thinking like that. Kevin's going to be just fine. And after everything that's happened, I'm sure he won't even remember your silly little squabble. But you have to be patient. Maeve will start asking questions if we disappear now. And I don't think either one of us wants to deal with that. Besides, they'll probably be running tests on him for the next few hours. Better to go this evening, when he's had a chance to rest.'

'Alright,' I sigh. As much as I hate to admit it, her plan does make sense. I'll just have to sit tight for a few more hours.

Just as our conversation is reaching its conclusion, an excited murmur begins rippling through the crowd. Maeve appears at the front door, flanked by two more Guards. She whispers something to the one out front, then turns to address her waiting audience.

'Alright folks, show's over. Please make your way inside and try to start catching up on your work.'

We file into the office one by one. Maeve stands just outside the door, giving each person a curt smile as they pass. I'm not sure if it's supposed to be comforting, or if she's just carrying out a headcount to make sure nobody's run off to the pub. I watch her make the same face over and over to all the people ahead of me. But then, just as my turn is approaching, her expression suddenly changes. The smile disappears, replaced by a stony-eyed stare.

'*Good morning, Marcus,*' she hisses, enough ice in her voice to sink the *Titanic*.

'Eh…good morning.'

I glance back over my shoulder, nearly tripping over the doorstep. But the smile has already returned to her face. Like that little flash of hostility was meant for me and me alone. But why? What could I possibly have done to provoke such a reaction? Other than showing up a few minutes late for work…

The mood is tense for the rest of the morning. Everybody is clearly shaken up by what's happened, but nobody seems to want to talk about it. I try to focus on my work, hoping the distraction will make the time between now and seeing Kevin pass faster.

But it's impossible. There's no way I can concentrate while he's lying wounded in a hospital bed. I try texting him again, just to make sure he's conscious. But there's still no response.

Noelle invites me out for lunch, but I politely decline. Every time I think about eating, Kevin's blood-soaked face flashes through my mind, sending a spurt of bile rushing up my throat. She heads on without me, leaving me to spend the lunchbreak alone at my desk. I end up scrolling through the website of the local newspaper, hoping there might be an article about this morning's incident. If it really was a burglary, that seems like the sort of thing they should probably be reporting. But there's nothing. Just a load of angry letters to the editor about the council's plans to build a cycle lane along Main Street. It's the most tedious content I've ever encountered, but I still read every single line.

Just as lunch is coming to an end, my phone starts to vibrate on the table beside me. I snatch it up with a furious swoop. This could be it! Finally, some news on how Kevin's doing. Proof he's still alive. Maybe even an explanation for who attacked him…

But it turns out it's not Kevin. It's Sean.

Hey man. Hope the head's not too sore today :) Did you have a chance to ask your supervisor if there were any jobs going?

I flip the phone over, simmering with frustration. Is he for real right now? How am I supposed to ask about vacancies when I have no idea if Kevin is even breathing?

But after taking a few seconds, I realise how unreasonable I'm being. Of course Sean doesn't know what a bad time this is. How could he? He has no idea what happened to Kevin. No idea what's going on in my head. To him, it's just a normal morning-after, and all he's doing is following up on something we discussed last night.

With a sigh, I pick my phone back up and begin typing a reply.

Sorry, not yet. Things are a little crazy at the moment. One of my co-workers had an accident this morning and he had to be rushed to hospital.

Shit man, he replies. *Sorry to hear that. I hope you're okay.*

I'm fine. It's my co-worker I'm worried about. He looked like he was in pretty bad shape, and I have no idea how long they're going to keep him in for.

My guilt intensifies as I read back over his reply. It was totally out of order getting annoyed at him before. Just look how sweet he's being now that I've explained the situation…

But then, a few seconds later, another message arrives. One that makes me slam the phone down so hard the battery falls out.

So…does that mean his job is up for grabs?

Twelve

Noelle and I head for the hospital at exactly half-five. While others take their time shutting down computers and pulling on coats, we charge up the hallway like two out-of-shape greyhounds. Neither one of us speaks as we pass through reception. The sight of Kevin's empty chair – so small and fragile against the blank white wall – is too depressing for words. Even the cats in the car park are surprisingly quiet, some lingering domestic instinct telling them this is no time for begging.

We cruise down Main Street and up into the hills, leaving the grey walls of Ashcross far behind us. As we twist and turn through a maze of green hedgerows, it occurs to me that this is the first time I have left town since I arrived there. I would have thought I'd be happy to get out – heading back home for a long weekend, or popping down to Shannon airport to catch a flight to Spain. But the only thing I feel right now is a knot of dread tightening in my chest.

Noelle focuses on the road, making no attempt at conversation, and I flick through my phone to pass the time. I still haven't replied to Sean's last text – the one where he asked if Kevin's job was *up for grabs*. I keep telling myself I should just get over it. Who cares if he was a little rude? Am I really going to throw away my chances with a hot guy over one stupid text?

But his lack of manners isn't the only thing that's nagging at me. Somewhere in the back of my mind, a new suspicion is brewing. I try to force it down, to pretend I don't see it, but it keeps bubbling back up to the surface. Sean arriving in town… the alien video appearing…Kevin getting attacked in the office. What if they're all connected? What if Sean is the guy from the video? And what if he's the one who hurt Kevin?

I shake my head, telling myself to stop being so paranoid. There's no way Sean's some sort of alien freak. No way he spends all day on dodgy internet forums trading photos of UFOs. The timing of his arrival is suspicious, sure, but he's too good-looking to be such a loser.

St Edna's is a small, one-storey hospital on the outskirts of Galway. The surroundings are grim – a concrete dual-carriageway, a few rows of cookie-cutter houses, and a waterlogged park with a single, lonely goalpost. But after two weeks in Ashcross, it feels like a glorious return to civilisation. If I wasn't so worried about Kevin right now, I might even get excited.

'Let me do the talking when we get inside,' says Noelle, as we climb out of the car. 'We're a little early for visiting hours, but there shouldn't be a problem.'

We hurry across the car park and into a high-ceilinged reception, where the stench of disinfectant hangs heavy in the air. To the right is a row of sterile plastic chairs. To the left, a gift shop selling *Get Well Soon* balloons. A friendly-looking woman in a fake-looking wig sits at the front desk.

'Ah, there's Jackie!' calls Noelle. 'Long time, no see.'

'Jesus, is that Noelle?' says the woman, holding her glasses out in front of her. 'I wouldn't even have recognised you! How long's it been now since poor Helen passed?'

'It'll be five months next Saturday.'

'God rest her,' says Jackie, bowing her head. 'And what brings you in today?'

'A young lad from work was in an accident this morning. Kevin O'Mahoney. We just wanted to make sure he was alright.'

'Let's see, Kevin O'Mahoney...' She types away at her computer, false nails clacking noisily on the keys. 'There we are. He's in room six, just down the corridor and on your right.'

'Thanks a million,' says Noelle, putting her hand on my shoulder and spinning me away from the desk. 'Listen,' she whispers, 'I'm going to stay here and catch up with Jackie. You go ahead and have your chat with Kevin. I'll come find you later.'

'Alright, thanks,' I mumble.

The door to room six is closed when I arrive. I pause outside, bracing myself for the worst, then knock once, twice, three times.

No answer.

'Hello?' I call out, turning the handle and sticking my head into the gap.

But there's still no response. The room is silent as a grave, the blinds shut tight and all the lights switched off. Through the gloom, I can just make out the shapes of two curtained-off beds. I approach the one nearest the door and peer down at the head on the pillow.

'Kevin?'

But it's not him. Just a withered old man in an oxygen mask lying perfectly still. For a second, I'm afraid he might be dead, and I wonder if I should go find a doctor. But then he lets out a low, mournful moan, and I realise he's only sleeping. With a shudder, I close the curtains and hurry over to the bed nearest the window.

This time I find what I'm looking for.

'Kevin? Are you awake?'

His eyes are closed, but I can see his chest moving up and down under the starched blue bedsheet. The blood from earlier has been washed away, replaced by a spotless white gauze. It's the first time I've ever seen him without his glasses on. He looks exposed. Vulnerable, somehow. Like a wounded angel fallen from heaven.

'Who's there?' he groans, eyelids flickering open.

'It's me, Mark.'

'Oh.' He glances over in my direction, then stares pointedly up at the ceiling. '…Great.'

'Are you alright? Can you see me?' I reach across the bed and pull open the blinds. A stream of watery sunlight floods into the room.

'I'm fine,' he groans, covering his eyes.

'Thank God,' I sigh, collapsing onto the bedside chair. 'I was so worried about you.'

He snorts. 'Were you now?'

'Of course I was!'

'Hmm…' He rolls over towards the wall, hiding his face from view.

I stare at the back of his blonde head, waiting for him to say something else. But he remains silent. 'Is something wrong, Kevin? Is this about the text?'

'What text?'

'The one I sent you last night. When I…cleared up our little misunderstanding.'

'Oh. *That* text.'

'Because like I said, I'm sorry. I was off my face when I sent it, and I didn't mean for the tone to be so blunt.'

'Who cares about the tone?' he snaps, rolling back over to face me. 'Do you think I've never received a drunken text before? The issue isn't that you were talking shite. It's that you've been lying to me this entire time.'

'I'm sorry,' I mumble. 'But technically, I never actually lied to you. You just assumed I was a hardcore Catholic, and I never managed to correct you…'

'Don't try to argue semantics! You let me believe you were going to help me. We were going to investigate Future Fish together. It's a two-person job you know, sneaking into the laboratory. One person to search the room while the other keeps a lookout on the stairs. Well, thanks to you and your duplicity, I ended up with nobody looking out for me. I never even heard the footsteps coming.'

'Wait, you mean you already went down there?'

He rolls his eyes. 'Yes, I *already went down there*. Why did you think I was so desperate to get in touch with you last night? With Maeve eyeing up security improvements, I couldn't risk waiting a single day longer.'

'And that's where you got hurt? That's where…somebody attacked you?'

'Exactly. Because you weren't there to help me.'

'Jesus, Kevin. I'm sorry…' Somewhere in the back of my mind, I'm aware it's not entirely fair of him to blame this on me. But there are more important things to be worrying about right now. 'What did he look like, the guy who attacked you? Did he mention anything about an alien?'

He huffs, like the patience of a saint is required to deal with such a simpleton. 'What are you talking about, Mark? It wasn't a *he*, it was a *she*. And you already know what Maeve looks like.'

'Maeve? You mean *Maeve* is the one who attacked you!?'

He nods. 'Who else would come skulking around the office in the early hours of the morning?'

'But *why*?' I ask, struggling to process this. 'I mean, what happened down there? Did you actually find Future Fish?'

'No,' he sighs. 'Maeve walked in on me before I had a chance. I thought I'd left myself enough time to be in and out of the laboratory before anybody else arrived, but for some reason, she decided to come in earlier than usual. I was just carrying out an initial survey of the room when I heard the door clicking open behind me. She started screaming and roaring before I could even turn around to face her. Threatening to fire me, to call the police, to have me locked up in an insane asylum. I tried to calm her down, saying I was doing this for her own good, but that just made her angrier.

'Eventually, it got to the point where I was afraid things might get physical. I'm not sure why exactly, but something compelled me to pull out my Bible and start reciting the Lord's Prayer. *Our Father, who art in heaven, hallowed be thy name...* Maeve went berserk when she heard it. Her whole face turned bright red, and she started barking at me like a rabid dog. She snatched the Good Book from my hands and ripped the whole thing clean in two. And then she started stamping on the pieces, crushing them under her heel like she was trying to put out a fire. That's when I realised how dangerous the situation really was. Because it turns out Maeve isn't just consumed by greed. She's possessed by it.'

'Hang on,' I say, with a nervous twitch. 'When you say *possessed*, you don't mean, like...by a demon, do you?'

He nods solemnly. 'I'm afraid so. Some infernal entity must have tempted her with promises of wealth and tricked her into giving up control of her body.'

'But...we're not talking about a literal *demon*, are we? As in, pointy horns and a pitchfork?'

'Don't be ridiculous,' he snaps. 'There are no horns or pitchforks. Demons are incorporeal.'

I stand up, head spinning, and stagger over to the watercooler in the corner. The tiny paper cone only holds a single mouthful, and I knock it back in one go. 'You can't be serious, Kevin.'

'I've never been more serious about anything in my life.'

The fire in his eyes tells me this is no exaggeration. Once again, I'm reminded of an angel. But not the friendly, halo-wearing kind. This is some Old Testament sword-grinding shit.

'Is your head okay, Kevin? Did the doctor mention anything about a concussion?'

'My head is fine!'

'But there's no such thing as demons...'

He pulls himself up into a seated position. The hospital gown drifts down over his shoulder, revealing an inky black bruise on his collarbone. 'Just because *you* don't believe in something doesn't mean it's not true. There have been countless cases of demonic possession documented over the centuries, by believers and non-believers alike.'

'Alright, fine...' There's clearly no point arguing with him on this. 'But even if demons are real, what makes you so sure Maeve is possessed by one?'

'As if her frenzied desecration of the Word of God wasn't proof enough, there was also the superhuman strength when she pushed me.'

'*Pushed you?* Is that when you hurt your head?'

He nods self-consciously. 'Once I realised what I was dealing with, I knew I had to get out of the laboratory. These things are beyond the power of a layperson. Maeve was still blocking the doorway, so my only option was to try and slip past her. But she caught hold of my jumper and shoved me back into the room. She was far stronger than any woman her size should be, as though the demon was lending her its power. How else could she have knocked a man like me off my feet and sent me flying through the air?

'I must have hit the edge of a table on my way down, because the last thing I remember before everything went black is a terrible pain in my head. When I came to, I was already outside on the stretcher. And that's when you finally decided to show up...'

'Jesus, Kevin. I'm sorry that happened to you.' He tells the story with such conviction, I have to take a second to remind myself it's all nonsense. The demon part, anyway. I can believe Maeve lost her temper and ripped up his Bible. I can even see her pushing him back when he tried to run past her. She probably didn't mean to hurt him – it was just a freak accident that he fell and hit his head. But all the same, that's still assault. 'Have you spoken to the Guards yet?' I ask him.

'They already came in to interview me. Apparently, Maeve told them I tripped over my own shoelace and fell down the stairs. She made it sound like I was some clumsy buffoon who was always bumping my head on things.'

'But you told them the truth, right? That it was all her fault?'

'What's the point?' he grunts. 'I switched the CCTV off before going down, so it would just be my word against hers. And she's the rich, respectable business leader. Besides, even if they did believe me, there's nothing the Guards could do. What this situation requires is an exorcist.'

'You're not seriously thinking about *exorcising* her, are you?'

'Of course I am. For her own safety, and the safety of those around her. We can't allow the demon to pursue its diabolical agenda unchecked.'

'Oh.' I turn back to the watercooler, hands trembling. This time I down three cones, one after the other. Water sloshes over my chin, soaking down onto my chest, like a contestant in the world's most disappointing wet t-shirt competition. 'And what exactly is this *diabolical agenda?*'

'The same as any other demon's. Leading its victims away from God. Damning their souls for all eternity. I suspect this particular one is using Future Fish as a way to spread its blasphemy. Infusing every tin with spiritual poison and shipping them out across the country.'

'So what are you planning to do about it?' I ask him. 'Tie Maeve to a bed and pour holy water all over her?'

'Of course not. Father Marsh will be the one applying the holy water. But there are several steps we need to go through first. As soon as the doctor releases me, I'm heading straight to church to explain the situation to Father. He'll need to write to the bishop for permission to carry out an exorcism. There'll also have to be a full medical examination to rule out plain old mental illness.'

'Are you sure this is a good idea?' I ask, sinking back down into the bedside chair. 'Maeve's not just going to sit back and let you accuse her of being a demon. You could lose your job over this…'

He shrugs. 'I'm pretty sure that ship has already sailed.'

'You mean she's given you the sack?'

'Not yet, but it's only a matter of time. She's probably just waiting until I'm released from hospital. It would be bad optics to fire somebody before the doctor's signed them off.'

'Well, maybe it's not too late! If you apologise – come up with some excuse for why you were in the lab – she might let you stay!'

He huffs, holding his head up high. 'I have no intention of apologising to that creature.'

'But you can't just throw your job away! Getting fired is a nightmare; take it from me.'

'For God's sake Mark, it's just a job. There are bigger things at stake here. Although I suppose you wouldn't understand that, since you're just a...' He trails off, pinching his lips.

'I'm just a what, Kevin?'

'Never mind. Just forget it.'

'No. Tell me. What am I?'

'Fine,' he sighs. 'If you must know... You're a slave to your lust. Another modern-day materialist who doesn't believe in anything bigger than himself.'

I flinch, more hurt by this than I would have expected. 'That's not fair. I may not be religious like you, but I still believe in lots of things.'

'Oh yeah? Name one.'

'Eh...'

He raises an eyebrow.

'...World peace?'

'Come on, Mark. Get serious.'

'Hang on,' I say. 'Just give me a second to think about it.'

But before I can come up with anything better, there's a knock at the door. Noelle's shaggy head pokes into the room.

'Everything alright in here?' she asks.

'Grand,' I reply. 'We're just having a chat.'

'Are you almost done, or do you need some more time?'

'Just a few more minutes,' I say.

'Alright,' she nods, beginning to back out.

But Kevin stops her with a conspicuous yawn. 'No,' he says. 'I think we're done here. I appreciate you coming to visit, Mark, but I need to get some rest.'

Thirteen

Somebody is sitting at Kevin's desk on Monday morning. I catch sight of him through the front door and instantly get a bad feeling. Like a black cat crossing my path. Or a charity worker making eye contact on the street. Tall, wiry, and dressed in a dark grey suit, he lounges back with his boots on the table and some trashy lads' magazine open on his lap. But who the hell is he? And what's he doing in Kevin's chair?

My heart starts to pound as I go to push open the door. But it won't budge. I try pulling, then pushing again. But still nothing. The sound of the lock rattling around in its socket attracts the man's attention. He looks up from his boobs and sports cars, raising an irritated eyebrow in my direction. I gesture at the lock, miming an apology, and watch as he unfolds himself like a spider from the chair. He moves slowly towards the door, stretching his arms out and yawning, like he wants to make sure I know just how unhurried he is.

'What do you want?' he grunts into the intercom. He's got the gravelly voice of a chain-smoker, with a set of hideous yellow teeth to match.

'Eh…I work here.'

'Do you now?' He looks me slowly up and down through the glass, eyes shadowed with suspicion. 'Name?'

'Mark.'

'Mark *what?*'

'McGuire.'

He produces a stack of plastic cards from his pocket and begins flicking through them. 'McGuire… McGuire… There's the little bastard.' With a magician's sleight of hand, he extracts a card from the deck and sends it spinning out through the letterbox.

I bend over to pick it up from the chewing-gum-splotched pavement. Other than a small sticker with my surname along the bottom, it's totally blank. 'What's this for?' I ask, looking back up.

'For swiping into the building, you dope. You'll need it every time you come in from now on, so don't go forgetting it. It's twenty quid for a replacement if you do.' With a rotten brown smile, he turns around and saunters back over to his chair.

I look around for somewhere to put the card and spot a shiny new swipe machine to the right of the door. After scanning the plastic across it, a little red light turns green, and the lock releases with a mechanical *click*. I try the door again, and this time it swings open to let me inside.

'So, eh…who exactly are you?' I ask, taking a tentative step towards the desk. 'Some sort of temporary receptionist?'

'Do I look like a fucking *receptionist*?' he growls, pointing to a badge on his chest. All it says is *JD*.

'Well, you are sitting at reception…'

'Don't get smart with me, you little weasel. I'm sitting here because I'm the new Head of Security. So you'd do well to show me a bit of respect.'

'*Head of Security*?' Jesus Christ… I guess Kevin was right about Maeve wanting to beef up the office's defences. And after seeing that alien video, I can't say I blame her. But did she really have to choose this asshole? Could she not have found somebody who was at least *slightly* less of a scumbag?

'That's right,' he says. 'And I've got my eye on you, Mark McGuire. So you'd better watch yourself.'

I glare at him, trying to think of a clever comeback. But something about the look in his eyes tells me not to push him. I swallow my pride, stare down at the floor, and set off along the corridor without another word.

Noelle is already sitting at her desk when I arrive in the main room. She stares at her computer screen, scrolling through some celebrity gossip column, and nearly jumps out of her skin when I grunt a *good morning*.

'Morning,' she replies. 'Is everything alright?'

'Everything's fine,' I grumble, kicking my bag under the table. 'Or at least it was, until I met that new Dick-Head of Security.'

'JD, you mean? Did the two of yous not get along?'

'*Not get along* would be the understatement of the century. I don't think I've ever gone from not knowing somebody to hating their guts in such a short space of time.'

'That's a shame,' she grins. 'I thought he was quite charming.'

'*Charming?* Jesus Christ. Please don't tell me you fancy that guy.'

'He has a certain appeal, is all I'm saying.'

'He looks like he's made out of leather!'

'All the better. I've always had a thing for a man with a tan…'

'Stop,' I groan, turning away. 'I don't want to hear any more about your disturbing fetishes. The sooner I can forget that asshole, the better.'

I open up my inbox and go to start the day's work, hoping the familiar flow of emails will help me forget about JD. But the first subject line on the list is one I've never seen before. A notification from YouTube, reading *WatcherInTheWest has uploaded a new video*. For a second I'm confused, wondering what it's all about, until I remember WatcherInTheWest is the person who posted the alien video. Maeve made me subscribe to his channel in case he uploaded any more. With a sigh, I stick my headphones in and click the link in the email.

Update on the Ashcross Alien reads the title of the video. I'm expecting more grainy footage and distorted voices, but this one is different. It opens with a teenaged girl sitting at a desk. A harsh yellow light shines down onto her face, casting a shadowy silhouette on the wall behind her. At first glance, you might assume it was just another low-budget makeup tutorial. But this girl is clearly no beauty guru. Her greasy brown hair is tied back in a limp ponytail, and the only product she's applied is inch-thick black eyeliner.

'Hello all you truth-seekers,' she begins, in a high-pitched, nasal tone. 'Thanks for tuning in. Now, I know what you're probably thinking. *Who is this random girl? And what's she doing on WatcherInTheWest's channel?* Well, surprise… It's me! WatcherInTheWest herself. I'm sure you've got a million and one questions, but don't worry. All will be revealed over the course of this video.'

Despite her dishevelled appearance, she addresses the camera with a commanding air of confidence, and I find myself sitting up a little straighter as I listen.

'Before I get into the investigation, I thought I'd begin by giving you all a proper introduction. My real name is Sally Hayes. I'm nineteen years old and currently studying journalism in Galway, Ireland. I know some of you have been watching my videos for years, and I just wanted to let you know how grateful I am for your support. Seriously, thank you so much. There was also a big spike in subscribers after my exposé on the Ashcross Alien. So, welcome to all you newcomers too.'

I glance down at the bottom of the screen, where the number of subscribers to her channel is listed. Nearly thirteen thousand. Not bad for such a niche-interest weirdo.

'So, you're probably wondering, why have I kept this all secret up until now? Why didn't I just show you my face from the get-go? Well, the simple answer is that I was afraid of being persecuted for speaking the truth. I work as a carer at the weekends, so I have to be careful about what I put online. The agency who gives me my hours will fire anybody who posts something they don't like, no matter how much evidence they have to back it up. Take my friend Chloe, for example, who got axed for raising awareness about the dangers of vaccines. I was afraid the same thing would happen to me if I spoke up about extra-terrestrials.

'But after seeing the support for my last video, there was no way I could stay silent any longer. Truth is sacred, and we all have a duty to share it. To counter the lies of the mainstream media and our useless education system. I decided to quit my job and drop out of college, so I could investigate the Ashcross Alien full-time. To put everything on the line in my quest for truth. Because if this story really is as big as I think it is, it could change the entire course of history.'

She pauses, reaching out to grab something off-screen.

'But I can't do it alone. Without a job, or any savings to my name, I've only got enough money to last a few weeks. That's why I've decided to start selling these...'

She lifts a baggy black t-shirt up to camera. Across the front is a cartoon UFO, hovering above a crudely drawn map of Ireland. Underneath, a row of bold white letters proudly proclaims, *I BELIEVE IN THE ASHCROSS ALIEN.*

'You can find a link to my shop in the description below. I'm also accepting donations, if you'd like to contribute directly to the investigation. If you can't afford to give any money, just clicking *like* and *subscribe* would go a long way.'

She sets the t-shirt down, then leans forward and waves at the camera.

'Anyway, that's all for now. Stay tuned for more updates in the coming days.'

And that's it. The video ends there.

I sit back in my chair, letting it all sink in, and nearly jump out of my skin when I notice Noelle's face beside me.

'What was that?' she asks, eyes wide with curiosity.

'The latest alien video,' I tell her. 'In case the last one wasn't weird enough.'

'But what was *she* doing in it? I mean, where was the guy from before?'

'Apparently she *is* the guy from before, minus the creepy voice distortion.'

'Jesus Christ. Are you serious?' She squints at the screen, forehead creasing. 'I assumed the person behind the computer was some beardy old weirdo, not a little girl who wouldn't even get served a cider without her ID.'

'I know what you mean,' I nod. 'Although I'm not sure if that makes it more or less disturbing.'

'More, if you ask me...'

'Well, either way, I guess I'd better send it on to Maeve.'

'No,' she says. 'You've already done enough. Just send me the link and let me handle this one.'

'Alright,' I shrug. 'If you insist.'

I copy the URL into an email and forward it on to her, hoping that will be the end of this morning's madness. But as I click through to my inbox, I find a message waiting from Maeve. *Update re Kevin O'Mahoney*, reads the subject line.

Dear all,

Please note that as of this morning, Kevin O'Mahoney is no longer an employee at WellCat.

Until a replacement has been appointed, please come to me with any administrative queries you previously would have addressed to Kevin. Please contact our new

Head of Security, JD Macintyre, regarding any building or maintenance issues.

Best,

M

My heart sinks as I read, plunging down through my chest and coming to rest in the murky depths of my stomach. I had a feeling this was going to happen. But that doesn't make it any less depressing now that it's arrived. I know things have been weird between Kevin and me recently, but I figured we'd get back to normal sooner or later. The whole Catholic-homosexual mix-up would be forgiven and forgotten, and we could start over as friends. Him with the knowledge I had no interest in theology, and me accepting the fact that the only man he'd ever fancy was Jesus...

But there'll be none of that now. Kevin is gone forever, his desk usurped by a human dumpster fire.

Before I've even begun coming to terms with this first piece of news, a second email pops up at the top of my inbox. And this time, it's addressed to me personally.

Marcus,

See me in the large meeting room immediately.

M

I stand up automatically, pulse accelerating in my chest. Why the hell would Maeve want to see me? And why now, right after announcing that Kevin has been fired? Something tells me it isn't just for a cup of tea and a chat about my feelings.

Fourteen

Stepping into the meeting room is like descending into a shark tank. Maeve paces up and down beside the long, empty table, eyes glinting hungrily under the fluorescent lights. A cold-blooded smile spreads across her face as she turns to take in my arrival. Like the meal she's been waiting for has finally been served. Like she can already taste the blood in the water.

'Sit,' she says, pointing at the table.

I comply in silence, hands shaking as I pull out a chair. Maeve remains standing.

'Let's cut to the chase,' she begins, in a voice devoid of all emotion. 'I suppose you already know why you're here?'

'Eh…not exactly.'

'Well, why don't you take a guess?'

I stare down at my hands, too terrified to make eye contact. 'I really don't know. Sorry.'

'Here's a hint – think back to Friday morning.'

'Friday morning?' When Kevin was taken away in the ambulance... When everybody was standing around outside... When Maeve gave me that mysterious glare as we filed back into the office. I still don't understand what that was all about. She looked so angry, so filled with resentment. Like I'd committed some heinous crime that demanded swift justice. But I hadn't done anything wrong, had I? Other than showing up a few minutes late... 'You mean when Kevin got hurt?'

'Exactly,' she says, gripping the edge of the table. 'I couldn't help noticing you were the last one to speak to him. Whispering in his ear as he was loaded onto the ambulance. Getting in the way of the paramedics.'

'Right, yeah. I just wanted to make sure he was alright.'

She nods, pursing her lips in a parody of sympathy. 'Of course you did. The two of you were awfully close, weren't you? Always huddled together having secret conversations.'

'Sure, I guess so...' Usually, the thought of Kevin and I getting *close* would be enough to give me a semi. But the current situation is distinctly unarousing.

'And that's why you looked so upset when you saw him on that stretcher?'

'Exactly. It was horrible seeing him like that.'

She frowns, closing her eyes, like she's struggling to understand some convoluted concept. 'But his injuries weren't *that* serious, were they? Just a little cut on the forehead. Hardly anything life-threatening.'

'I suppose so. But it was hard to tell at the time. There was so much blood.'

'Does blood make you squeamish, Marcus? Do you get light-headed at the slightest hint of red?'

'Not really...'

'Then there must have been something else bothering you, if it wasn't the blood.'

'Something else bothering me?'

'Something to account for your hysterical reaction.'

I swallow down a lump in my throat, not liking where this is headed. 'Like what?'

'Oh, I don't know...' She pauses, looking pensive, then slams her fists down onto the table. 'Maybe the fact that your plot to sabotage Future Fish had failed!?'

'My plot to...what?' Suddenly I really do feel light-headed, like somebody's unplugged the blood supply from my brain. 'I have no idea what you're talking about.'

'Oh please,' she snorts, squeezing the table edge until her knuckles turn white. 'I caught Kevin red-handed in the laboratory. He didn't even try to deny what he was doing – just started spewing some Bible-bashing nonsense.'

'But that has nothing to do with me. I wasn't in the lab. I've never been anywhere near it!'

'You may not have been down there when I arrived, but you were on your way, weren't you?'

'What? No, of course not! I had no idea what Kevin was doing. I was running late that morning, and I didn't arrive at the office until the ambulance was already outside.'

She shakes her head, like this is all a colossal waste of time. 'If you had no idea what he was doing, then how come you were texting each other in the midst of the crime?'

'*Texting each other?*'

She smirks, seizing the advantage. 'Poor old Kevin dropped his phone when he fell over. And do you know what I happened to see when I bent down to pick it up for him? *One new message from Mark WellCat.*'

Shit. The apology I sent him for my drunken message the night before. I'd forgotten all about it. 'Oh, that? I can explain...'

'I'd certainly hope so. Because last time I checked, there was only one *Mark* on my payroll.'

For a second, I consider whipping my phone out and showing her the message. Proving I refused to help Kevin with the break-in. But that would only get me into even deeper trouble. She'd see I knew what he was planning, yet I failed to report it.

'That was a personal message,' I say. 'It had nothing to do with him breaking in.'

'Oh please. How thick do you think I am?'

'I'm telling you the truth! I wasn't involved in any of this. I swear to God, I'd never do something like that!'

She glares down at me, petrifying my every muscle like a snake-haired Medusa. 'I wish I could believe you,' she says. 'You've been a good worker so far. But it's putting too much trust in people that got me into this mess in the first place. I knew Kevin was odd, but I assumed he was harmless. Never did I dream he'd betray me like this. Three years he's been working here. *Three years*. And then, out of nowhere, this knife in my back... We had our differences, sure, but that doesn't explain it. Somebody must have put him up to this.'

'Somebody like who?' I mumble, unsure where she's going.

'Oh, I don't know…' She eyes me up, her expression blank, like a poker player reading the table. 'One of our rivals maybe. Like, say, Miss Meow?'

'I don't know anything about Miss Meow,' I tell her.

'Are you sure about that?'

'I'd never even heard of them until I started working here!'

She begins pacing up and down the room, pivoting on her heels at the end of each length. 'Maybe you're telling the truth, and maybe you're lying. It's impossible to say for certain. But between Kevin's betrayal and that ridiculous alien video, I can't afford to take any more chances.'

'So, that's it…' I whimper. 'You're firing me too?'

Her pace quickens, up and down the room in an endless loop. Like a zoo lion driven mad by its confinement. And then, suddenly, she stops.

'No,' she sighs. 'I'm not firing you. Not yet, anyway. There's no proof you were involved, so I'd have no grounds for terminating your contract. But I'll be keeping a very close eye on you going forward. If you place so much as a single toe out of line, you can rest assured it will be the last thing you ever do in this office.'

'Thank you,' I stutter, too relieved to think. 'Jesus Christ. Thank you…'

'Don't thank me. This isn't a favour. Now, unless there are any other crimes you'd like to deny, I think it's time for you to be getting back to work.'

I stammer another *thank you* as I stagger towards the door. Every nerve in my body is fried, every braincell struggling to process the fact that I've made it out alive.

Out in the hallway, I head straight for the bathroom. I'm in no state to be getting back to my desk right now. What I need is a few minutes of peace and quiet. A moment alone to try and catch my breath. And the only place I can think to do that is locked in a cubicle.

But as soon as I step through the door to the men's room, the stench of stale piss and anti-perspirant assaults my nostrils. Not exactly the calming oasis I was hoping for. I head back out into the hallway and slip into the disabled bathroom instead. Here, the scent of urine is slightly less pronounced, masked by the floral spray of an air freshener. I undo my belt, pull down my trousers, and collapse onto the toilet seat like I've just run a marathon.

The shock from my showdown with Maeve slowly begins to recede, leaving a black hole of anxiety in its wake. I may have survived my brush with death in the meeting room, but I'm not out of the danger zone yet. My head is still on the chopping block. And Maeve is still standing above me, dressed in a designer suit with matching executioner's hood. All she needs is one good reason to bring the axe crashing down. And knowing her, it won't be long until she finds it.

I slouch down on the toilet seat, sinking deeper and deeper into despair. Just as I'm settling in at rock bottom, a buzzing in my pocket drags me back up to the surface. I reach down for my phone and find a message from Sean.

Hey man, how's it going?

I still haven't replied to his last message – the one when he asked if he could take over Kevin's role. But the outrage I felt back then seems a million miles away now. Kevin is already dead and gone, and he's never coming back. Plus, the person behind the alien video turned out to be some creepy little girl – nothing to do with Sean after all.

Not great, I text back. *Pretty terrible in fact.*

Shit man, do you want to talk about it?

Not really.

Come on. You'll feel better once you've let it all out.

I sigh, sitting back on the toilet seat. Maybe he's right. A problem shared is a problem halved and all that. Especially when the sharing involves vast quantities of alcohol.

Alright, fine. How about a drink this evening?

Sounds great, he replies. *Although I'm also free right now, if you wanted to have a quick call?*

Next thing I know, I'm pouring my heart out over the phoneline. I end up telling him the entire story, from my conversation with Kevin at the café, through to JD and his swipe cards, and the disastrous meeting with Maeve this morning. Letting it all out feels good, and I don't hold back on any of the more emotional moments. I even open up about my whole sad history, explaining why I can't afford to lose another job.

'Damn,' he says, as I conclude the story. 'You really have been going through it.'

'Tell me about it,' I sigh. 'And something tells me it's only going to get worse from here.'

'Well, maybe the whole thing will blow over. Your boss will find something else to get all hot and bothered about, and she'll forget all about you.'

'Maybe. But I wouldn't hold my breath. Maeve doesn't strike me as the type to let go of a grudge. Even if a bus ran her over on the way to work, she'd probably come back as a ghost to haunt me.'

'Oh shit,' he laughs. 'She sounds like a nasty piece of work.'

'She really is… I'm not sure what I did to deserve her.'

'You didn't do anything, man. All bosses are assholes.'

'Really?' I ask, with a bitter little laugh. '*All* of them?'

'One hundred per cent,' he replies, sounding entirely serious.

'And where did you get that statistic?'

'From my own personal experience. I must have worked a dozen different jobs since graduating high school, and not a single one of my managers has been a decent human being.'

I laugh again, this time with less bitterness.

'But don't take my word for it,' he continues. 'There have been entire studies showing CEOs are disproportionately likely to be psychopaths. It's *science*.'

'I suppose that makes sense,' I concede. 'You've got to be ruthless to claw your way to the top.'

'They probably look for that quality when they're hiring a new boss. You walk into the interview, and they ask you to list your experience tormenting lowly underlings.'

'And then to give an example of a time you crushed the spirit of an idealistic young graduate,' I add.

'And if you let slip even one single shred of empathy, they throw you out on your ass!'

There's another round of laughter, and then an awkward silence sets in. Like neither one of us is sure if we're still joking. I trace my finger along the gaps in the wall tiles, thinking over what Sean's just said. 'If all bosses are really that bad,' I reason, 'maybe I should just throw in the towel now. Accept the life of an unemployed loser, rather than climbing up a ladder I'm always going to fall down.'

There's another pause. Somewhere on the other end of the line, I hear a woman talking. It must be his aunt. Or maybe the TV. 'You're not seriously thinking about quitting, are you?' he asks. 'About walking away from WellCat?'

I close my eyes, imagining what it would feel like to hand in my resignation. The thrill of satisfaction at the shock on Maeve's face. The sudden rush of freedom as I left the office forever. But then I start thinking about what would happen afterwards. When I ran out of money, and I couldn't afford to pay rent anymore. When I was forced to crawl back to Dublin, my tail between my legs. To face all the people who doubted me before. Like Dad. My ex, Neil. And my old manager, Liam. And what would they say, when they saw me then? When all their doubts about me turned out to be true? *We knew it, we knew it. We could have told you all along. He was always a loser. A fuck-up. A ruiner. Nobody ever wanted him around.*

Suddenly I'm furious, white-hot rage coursing through my veins.

'No,' I grunt into the phone. 'I can't give up now. I can't let those fuckers win.'

'That's the spirit!' claps Sean.

I stand up from the toilet, hitching up my trousers, and begin pacing back and forth along the length of the bathroom. 'I should have just ratted Kevin out when I had the chance,' I say. 'I thought I was doing him a favour by keeping his secret, but what difference did it really make? He still ended up getting fired. Our friendship still fell apart. At least if I'd told Maeve what he was planning, I might have been able to save myself.'

'You're right,' says Sean. 'But maybe it's not too late to tell her now?'

I shake my head. 'That would only make things worse. But I can at least make sure I don't repeat the same mistakes. I can stop being such a stupid coward and start standing up for myself for once. Maeve may be an asshole, and there's no way I can change that. But you know what they say… If you can't beat them, join them.'

I pause in front of the bathroom mirror, inspecting my reflection. The face staring back at me looks the same as always. The same pasty skin and pudgy cheeks. The same wavering hairline threatening to recede at any moment. But the expression behind the eyes looks different from before. It's harder. Sharper, somehow. Like a photo that's suddenly come into focus.

'Thank you,' I tell Sean. 'For the advice. And for listening to me rant… Sorry if things got a little heavy there.'

'No problem. That's what I'm here for.' His voice softens, taking on the seductive tone of a lounge singer. 'And for the record, I know we haven't been seeing each other very long, but I'd never break up with you over some stupid job. Your last boyfriend was an idiot.'

A warm feeling spreads over me, like snuggling under a duvet on a cold winter night. How could I ever have been angry at Sean? How could I have suspected him of being an alien freak? In the last half hour alone, he's already shown me more support than Neil did over the entire course of our two-year relationship.

'By the way,' I say, 'sorry I couldn't help you with the whole getting-a-job-at-WellCat thing. If it was up to me, I'd hire you on the spot. But considering all the bad blood between Maeve and me, I think my putting in a good word for you would only hurt your case.'

'No stress,' he laughs. 'I understand. It's not your fault.'

'I hope you can find something else though. It would be awful if you had to go back to LA after all this.'

'Don't worry about that. I'm not going anywhere. If a job at WellCat is off the table, I'll just have to figure something else out.'

Fifteen

The call with Sean leaves me more motivated than ever. I march straight back to my desk and dive headfirst into the waiting pile of work. After wasting all day Friday catastrophising about Kevin, I now have dozens of emails to catch up on. Getting through them all seemed like an impossible task this morning. A Herculean labour for the information age. But now I realise it's just a test. Of my resolve and my will to succeed. And there's no way I'm going to fail.

My foot begins to twitch as I set to work, like some long-defunct engine that's suddenly sparked back to life. After powering through the afternoon and on into the evening – working well past the official home time of half-five – I finally manage to catch up on where I'm supposed to be. I stagger home to the apartment, exhausted but satisfied, and sleep more soundly than I have in months.

This same foot-twitching momentum carries me through the next day, and the one after that. Things are going smoothly, as far as I can tell, with no more threatening emails or run-ins with Maeve. JD is still an asshole, harassing me every time I pass through reception, but I'm getting better at ignoring him. Slowly but surely, despite all the odds, I feel my confidence beginning to return.

And then Monday morning arrives, and I hit the first bump in my new road.

It starts as I'm approaching the office. A strange sound echoes across town, bouncing off the decaying buildings and rising above the usual din of car engines and seagulls. At times, it sounds like somebody shouting. But the tone is distorted, crackling with static. Like it's being broadcast through some ancient radio. There are words in there somewhere, but I can't wrap my head around them.

I peer up and down Main Street, searching for the source of the sound. But all I can see is empty grey pavement. It's only when I'm turning the corner onto the office that I finally spot it. A figure on the footpath, fifty metres up ahead, roaring into a shiny plastic megaphone. They're facing towards the office, with only the back of their head visible from where I'm standing. But I'd recognise that blond hair anywhere.

Kevin.

My first instinct is to sprint down the road. To scream out his name and start waving like a maniac. But I stop – catch myself – take a long, slow breath. I'm supposed to be prioritising my own interests now. Not getting caught up in the silly little dramas of estranged friends.

But still, a quick hello couldn't hurt…

I make my way down the footpath, strolling at a nonchalant pace. The words he's shouting into the megaphone become clearer and clearer the closer I get.

'…NO MAN CAN SERVE TWO MASTERS! FOR EITHER HE WILL HATE THE ONE AND LOVE THE OTHER OR ELSE HE WILL HOLD TO THE ONE AND DESPISE THE OTHER! YOU CANNOT SERVE BOTH GOD AND…MARK!'

'Oh, hi Kevin. I didn't see you there.'

He lowers the megaphone, giving me a sheepish smile.

'It's nice to see you back on your feet,' I say. 'You're looking much better.'

And it's true, he is. The bruise on his temple is beginning to heal, the angry purples and blacks replaced by gentler shades of grey and brown. The colour has come back to his cheeks too, the dark patches under his eyes receding like shadows. He's even got the bristly beginnings of a beard coming in. But despite these improvements, a certain frailness remains. Like a single gust of wind would be enough to blow him out to sea.

'Thanks. The doctor let me out yesterday. He said I just need a couple days' rest, and then I should be good as new.'

'So, eh…what are you doing here?'

'I'm preaching the Word of the Lord.'

'Sure, yeah. I got that. But shouldn't you be in bed or something? This doesn't look like *resting*.'

He frowns, pushing his glasses up his nose. 'How could I just lie around doing nothing at a time like this? Now that I know

Maeve is possessed, I can't rest until the exorcism is complete.'

'Of course not,' I sigh. 'How could you?' I was hoping the stay in hospital might have cooled his zeal. Made him realise how insane this whole demon theory is. But it looks like he's still as fanatical as ever. 'Just try to take it easy, will you? You don't want to get yourself all worked up while you're still recovering.'

He rolls his eyes. 'That's what Father Marsh said too. That I was getting myself *all worked up* over nothing.'

'You mean even the priest thinks this is a bad idea?'

He shrugs, staring sullenly down the road. 'He says I don't know what I'm talking about. That I'm not qualified to diagnose demonic possession.'

'Well, I never thought I'd find myself agreeing with a priest, but maybe he's got a point?'

'That's only because he hasn't seen what I've seen! I *know* Maeve is evil. I *know* what she's capable of. And if Father Marsh won't come to her, I'm just going to have to bring her to him. That's why I'm standing out here reciting these Bible verses. I'm hoping I can still get through to the human part of her. The part that hasn't been entirely consumed by greed. Maybe I can inspire her to resist the demon. To seek the help she so clearly needs.'

I take a deep breath, reminding myself this isn't my problem anymore. I'm done trying to talk Kevin out of his crazy schemes. If he wants to stand on the street corner screaming like a lunatic, that's his business. Nothing to do with me. 'Sure, Kevin. Whatever you say... Although I doubt anybody can actually hear you from inside the building.'

'That's what I was afraid of,' he sighs. 'But the new guy at the front desk won't let me inside, so standing here with the megaphone is the best I can do.'

'Hang on…' I say, a fresh suspicion taking form. 'You're not planning on breaking in again, are you? Trying to sneak past JD and force your way into the lab?'

'Now why would I go and do that?' he scowls.

'I don't know. Maybe you want to pick up where you left off last time. Get back to investigating Future Fish, and the eh… demon.'

'There's no reason for me to make another descent into that den of sin. I've already got all the proof I need about Maeve. Besides, even if I did want to get back in, I wouldn't go through the front door. I wouldn't go through any doors at all.'

'Alright,' I shrug. 'If you say so… I'd better get going anyway. It's almost nine, and I can't be late for work.'

I turn around and set off down the pavement. But before I've taken two steps, I feel him grabbing my elbow and pulling me back. 'Wait,' he says. 'Before you go… I've been meaning to apologise for the way I spoke to you at the hospital. I know you were just trying to help. And you and Noelle are the only people from the office who even came to visit.'

'Thanks Kevin. But you don't need to apologise.'

'No, I do. Especially for the part when I called you a…a slave to your lust. I'm sorry.'

'No worries,' I grin. 'To be fair, that's not an inaccurate way to describe me.'

'You may be a sinner, but you're hardly the worst person in there…' He gestures down the road, towards the concrete block of the WellCat office. 'At least what you're doing is only hurting yourself. But people like Maeve are hurting the entire world.

Hoarding wealth while others starve. Destroying the planet for their own short-term profit. *They're* the ones Jesus condemned in the Gospels. *They're* the ones we should be speaking out against today.'

He's worked himself up into a bit of a frenzy, which I find oddly touching. I couldn't care less what the Bible has to say about me – or about anything else, for that matter – but it's nice to feel like Kevin is back on my side. If only in his own strange way.

'Thanks Kevin. I appreciate that. But I should really get going. It was nice seeing you.'

'You too,' he replies, waving goodbye with one hand and raising the megaphone back up with the other.

'AND AGAIN I SAY UNTO YOU IT IS EASIER FOR A CAMEL TO GO THROUGH THE EYE OF A NEEDLE THAN FOR A RICH MAN TO ENTER INTO THE KINGDOM OF GOD!'

JD is lounging back in his chair when I step through the door to reception.

'Well, well, well,' he heckles. 'It's nine-o-three. You're late.'

'Sorry,' I mumble. 'I'll stay an extra ten minutes this evening to make up for it.'

I make a beeline towards the hallway, hoping to get away from him as quickly as possible. But he springs to his feet and blocks my path.

'Not so fast,' he growls. 'You've got some explaining to do first. Who was that mentaller you were chatting to outside?'

'I don't know what you're on about,' I reply, trying to slip between him and the wall. But he cuts me off with an iron-grey sleeve.

'Oh yes you do. That pretty boy preacher on the corner. Looks like somebody's been giving him a well-deserved beating.'

I open my mouth, ready to jump to Kevin's defence. But I catch myself just in time. This is clearly some sort of trap. JD already knows who he is, and he's just trying to goad me into saying something incriminating. But I'm not going to fall for it. That sort of cheap ploy might have worked on the old Mark, but the new and improved version is totally impervious. Let him insult Kevin all he wants. I don't care.

'Oh, him? Just some psycho who used to work here. He started trying to sell me a Virgin Mary medal, but I told him to fuck off.'

'Did you now?' An extra wrinkle creases his forehead. 'That wasn't very nice of you.'

'Yeah, well, what was I supposed to do? You can't argue with crazy.'

'Hmmm.' He still doesn't look entirely convinced, but he lowers his arm and lets me pass.

A thrill of adrenaline courses through me as I make my way down the hallway. I can't believe that actually worked! A little badmouthing of Kevin, and JD climbed right down off my back. Maybe being an asshole is easier than I thought. Or maybe I'm just a natural.

'Somebody's in a good mood,' says Noelle, as I sit down at my desk.

'Oh yeah?' I grin. 'And why shouldn't I be?'

'Oh, I don't know. Maybe because it's Monday morning, and we've still got five entire days of this shite until the weekend rolls back around.'

'Mondays aren't so bad. You've just got to make the most of them.'

She recoils, wrinkling her nose. 'Are you on drugs or something?'

'Just high on life,' I wink.

'Jesus Christ. Enough. I'm going out for a smoke.'

I laugh, watching her pull a pack of cigarettes from her desk and storm out of the room. Once she's gone, I turn my attention towards my waiting inbox. Top of my to-do list is responding to a query from a customer asking where in Longford she can get tins of Tuna Tsunami, since her local supermarket keeps selling out. That's an easy one to answer. *I'm afraid I can't help you, as Tuna Tsunami isn't a WellCat product. It's made by Miss Meow.*

Just as I'm about to click *send*, a sudden ringing sound pulls me away from the screen. It's somebody's mobile, coming from close by.

La cu-ca-RA-cha! La cu-ca-RA-cha! goes the ringtone.

I look around, trying to pinpoint the source. But the only phones in sight are the office landlines. *La cu-ca-RA-cha! La cu-ca-RA-cha!* it continues, getting more and more annoying with each repetition. Just as my blood pressure is beginning to spike, I finally figure out where it's coming from. Noelle's mobile, wedged between the seat and the arm of her chair. It must have fallen out of her pocket when she was getting up for her smoke break.

I pick it up and set it safely on her desk, next to the framed photo of her mother and the nurse. *Private number calling* flashes across the screen, the ringtone repeating its enraging melody. People begin to glance over from across the room, shooting daggers in my direction. I smile an apology, gesturing at Noelle's desk to indicate it's not my fault. But that doesn't stop the angry looks. Just as their disapproval is starting to make me sweat, the ringing suddenly cuts out. Silence descends on the room. I breathe a sigh of relief and turn back to my computer.

But then it starts up again. *La cu-ca-RA-cha! La cu-ca-RA-cha!* The people at the neighbouring desks begin swearing and shaking their heads. If this carries on much longer, they're probably going to murder me. I consider turning the volume down or rejecting the stupid call altogether. But messing with somebody else's phone feels like a faux pas. A violation of some sacred technological autonomy. The only other thing I can think to do is go find Noelle and tell her to come deal with it herself. But before I can get up, the phone goes quiet. I stare at the screen for several seconds, not wanting to be fooled twice. But this time, it stays silent.

And then the landline on Noelle's desk starts ringing. I clamp a hand over my mouth, holding down a howl. But then I remember I can actually answer this one. It's a work phone – exempt from the privileges of personal mobiles.

I pick up the receiver and go to say hello. But my flustered mind draws a total blank. How are you supposed to introduce yourself on somebody else's phone again? *Noelle's phone, this is Mark speaking* sounds right for an internal office call. But what if it's a customer? Or some other third party? Should I stick to the classic *WellCat customer service, how may I help you today?*

'Hello?' comes a high-pitched woman's voice. 'Sorry to ring you at work, but you weren't picking up your mobile. And this is an emergency. It looks like we've got competition in town, and they're not messing around. We need to move the plan forward to this afternoon. Did you get the code?'

'Eh… WellCat customer service, how may I help you today?'

Silence on the other end.

'…Noelle's phone, this is Mark speaking.'

'Noelle?' says the woman. 'Who's Noelle? I'm looking for Genevieve. This must be the wrong number.'

A quick beep, then the line goes dead.

I set the receiver down in a daze. I'm not sure what just happened, but something about that exchange definitely felt off. Like we were speaking the same language, but neither one of us could understand the other. I don't think I did anything wrong, other than fumble my introduction. Which means it must have been the woman who was acting strangely…

There *was* something familiar about her voice. Like I'd heard it somewhere before. Like it wasn't really a wrong number. But she wasn't a staff member, and the tone was too familiar for a customer. So who the hell was she?

I scoot my chair back over to my own computer, figuring I'll work it out eventually. After finishing off the email about Miss Meow's Tuna Tsunami, I move on to another one asking about child labour in our supply line. Just as I'm starting in on a third, it suddenly comes back to me. Quick and brutal, like a piano falling from the sky.

That voice. I remember where I heard it before.

It's the girl from the alien video.

Sixteen

Once again, I find myself seeking sanctuary in the disabled toilet. The austere three-by-three metre square is quickly becoming my own personal panic room. The one safe space in the office I can retreat to in times of crisis. If this keeps up much longer, I'll probably start developing some weird Pavlovian response mechanism, and the next time I pop in for an innocent poo, I'll end up having a full-blown panic attack on the toilet seat.

Luckily, things haven't progressed quite that far yet, and for now I'm just trembling slightly as I try to process what I heard on that phone call.

The voice definitely belonged to the alien girl. There's no way that sniffling, nasal tone could have been anybody else. And I don't buy for one second that it was really a wrong number. Not when she admitted herself that she'd been trying to get through to Noelle's mobile beforehand. But how did she get her number in the first place? And why would she be trying to contact her?

I rack my brain, desperate for a rational explanation. Like, maybe the two of them are old acquaintances. The girl could be Noelle's niece. Or an estranged cousin twice removed on her mother's side. It would be a coincidence, sure, but doesn't everybody know everybody down the country? Or maybe she's scamming Noelle. Calling up and pretending to be a regular customer to try and trick her into revealing information about Future Fish.

But neither one of these scenarios seems particularly plausible. I'm sure Noelle would have mentioned if she was related to the alien girl. And it would take a seriously talented scam artist to con somebody as cynical as her. Deep down, I know there's only one explanation that makes sense. Only one way to account for the girl's ominous words. *We need to move the plan forward to this afternoon. Did you get the code?*

Noelle is in cahoots with the alien girl.

It sounds crazy, I know. The very notion is enough to make me question my grip on reality. But madness is par for the course at this stage, and Noelle being in league with a teenage conspiracy theorist would hardly be the weirdest thing to happen in Ashcross.

The only problem is, that still doesn't explain the *why*. Why would Noelle be helping the alien girl? What possible reason could she have for such an unlikely alliance? Kevin's motivation for getting caught up in all this may be insane, but at least it makes sense. He has a demon to slay. A world to save. But Noelle doesn't actually believe in any of that alien shite. She said so herself.

I gaze helplessly around the bathroom, hoping to divine an answer in the dripping of the tap or the hum of the extractor fan. But nothing comes to me. After fifteen minutes of fruitless wondering, I decide it's probably best to head back to my desk. Sitting here going round in circles is only going to drive me crazy. And who knows, maybe things will start to make sense once I've talked to Noelle.

She's back from her smoke break when I return to the main room. Her mobile has disappeared from the spot where I left it, meaning she must already have seen the missed calls. But does she know I talked to the alien girl? And does she have any idea I've realised who she was? I pull my chair out as nonchalantly as possible, trying not to let on that anything is wrong. But of course, this fails spectacularly. One of the wheels gets caught up in the wires under my desk, yanking the extension cord clean out of the wall. Both our computer screens instantly go black.

'Shit!' I mumble, scrambling to plug the cord back in. 'Sorry about that.'

'No worries,' she laughs. 'It's not like I was doing anything important anyway.'

I pull myself back up and clamber into the chair. 'So…' I begin, brushing dust off my trousers. 'How was your smoke break?'

'Grand, yeah.'

'Nothing exciting?'

'Not really,' she shrugs. 'One of the cats looked like she might have been pregnant, but I couldn't get close enough to tell for certain.'

'Oh wow,' I say, trying not to retch at the thought of some

mangy cat giving birth. 'You should have taken a photo… Oh wait, you left your phone in here.'

'Right, yeah. Maybe next time.'

'Speaking of phones, I think somebody was trying to ring you.'

'Thanks. I saw the missed calls.'

'I hope it was nothing important…'

'Probably just one of those robots asking if I'd been in any car accidents recently.' She tries to smile, but the expression's not quite right. Like it's all mouth and no eyes.

'You missed a call on your landline, too.'

'Those bleeding robots. There's no getting away from them!'

'This one wasn't a robot though.'

'Oh.' She stiffens, giving me another wooden grin. 'Who was it then?'

'I'm not sure. They didn't leave a name.'

'Did they leave any message at all?'

'They just said they were looking for *Genevieve*, and they must have gotten the wrong number. But the voice sounded awfully familiar.'

'Hmmm. I'm sure it wasn't anything important, or they'd already have rung back.'

'I don't know. It sounded pretty important to me…'

'Alright. Thanks.' She turns away, going to log back into her computer. 'Anyway, I'd better get back to work. I've got an important meeting this afternoon, and there are a few things I need to finish up beforehand.'

I nod, turning back towards my own computer. Probably best not to push her any further for now, unless I want to risk an open confrontation.

The next few hours pass by without incident. I'm too busy peeking over at Noelle's screen to actually get any work done, but at least there are no more signs of suspicious activity. I even follow her out to the chipper at lunch time, in case she tries to sneak off, but all she does is buy a large battered cod. Slowly but surely, I begin to relax. Maybe I was overreacting before. Maybe this is all just a big misunderstanding, and nothing sinister is really going on.

But then, just before three, she suddenly stands up.

'I'm just popping out for a smoke,' she announces. 'See you in a few minutes.'

'Oh, eh…mind if I join you actually?' I ask. I can't risk letting her out of my sight.

She hesitates, giving me a curious look. 'I thought you didn't smoke?'

'I don't usually, but I've got a craving. And Kevin's not here to judge me any more…'

'Fair enough,' she shrugs. 'Although I've just remembered I'm all out of fags. Why don't you wait here while I pop to the shop, then the two of us can head round back together?'

'Alright,' I mumble, unable to think of any plausible objections. 'See you in a sec.'

She bends over to pick up her handbag and drops her phone inside. And then, with a casual flick of her hair, she slips the framed photo of her mother off the desk and slides that into the bag as well. The whole thing happens so quickly, so effortlessly, I never would have noticed if I wasn't watching her already.

A fresh tendril of dread creeps up my spine. But I try to shake it off. Maybe she's just tidying up her workspace. Respecting that *clear-desk policy* Maeve is always sending passive-aggressive emails about. But why do it now, on her way to the shop? The frame will only weigh her down or get damaged in her bag. It doesn't make any sense...

Unless, of course, she isn't really going shopping.

My eyes narrow as I watch her cross the room. As soon as she's safely out in the hallway, I turn towards her desk and begin rifling through the clutter. There must be a clue to her true intentions somewhere. Some secret diary or hand-drawn map that will reveal what she's really up to. But the pile of printouts propped against her keyboard is just a load of old spreadsheets, and the collection of teacups stacked in the corner contains only mouldy dregs. Her computer is locked, her phone stowed in her purse, leaving my little investigation dead in the water.

I sigh, sitting back in my chair. And then suddenly it hits me. The cigarettes! She always keeps a pack in the drawer of her desk. If she really is going out to buy more, then the drawer must be empty...

I reach out and grab hold of the handle, my fingers trembling over the cold metal. I have no idea which outcome I'm hoping for – an empty drawer to corroborate her story, or a full one to prove she was lying. Either way, I just want an answer. Some semblance of certainty in this storm of confusion.

The drawer slides open, and my heart sinks. Not one, not two, but *three* packs of cigarettes lie fanned out before me. The first one is only half empty, and the second and third are still sealed in plastic. Pictures of black lungs and oozing tumours loom up from the government-issued warnings. *Smoking kills. Smoking clogs the arteries. Smoking turns you into a big fat liar.*

Next thing I know, I'm standing up and following Noelle out of the room. I have no idea what I'm going to do when I find her. I just know that I have to do *something*. I can't just sit back and wait for fortune to roll me through another pile of horseshit.

I pause in the hallway and listen out for any suspicious sounds. But all I can hear is a low hum of voices coming from the meeting room. I tiptoe over to peek through the glass pane in the door and find Dominic presenting a graph to Maeve, Shelley, and a few others. At the bottom is a jagged line reading *WellCat purchase intent Q1-2*. And above it, curving upwards, is *Miss Meow*.

There's something sexy about the way Dominic brandishes his pointer, and my mind instantly begins conjuring a boardroom fantasy... Sales are down. President Dominic is unhappy. If I still want to get my hands on that end-of-year bonus, I'm going to have to find some other way to make it up to him... But I stop myself. Cut the scene. File the script away for another day. Now's not the time for idle daydreams. Especially not when Dominic being here means the lab must be empty...

I step back from the door and turn towards the far end of the corridor. The end where the stairwell descends into shadow, like a passage to the underworld. Could Noelle already have made her way down those dark, narrow stairs? And could I really be about to follow? Just a few hours ago, the idea would have been inconceivable. Disobeying Maeve's orders would have meant certain death. But now, after everything that's happened, it feels like it might be the only way to save my job. Because if Noelle really is doing what I think she's doing, then Maeve is sure to suspect I was involved. Just like she did with Kevin. And that would be more than enough reason for her to finally chop my head off.

I take a few tentative steps forward. The darkness of the stairwell is all-consuming, and I have to squint to make out the handrail. I glance back over my shoulder, making sure the coast is clear. It sounds like Dominic's presentation is still in full swing, which means he and Maeve should be occupied for at least a few more minutes. As long as I move quickly, I should have plenty of time to sneak down, take a look around, and get back up before anybody notices.

With a deep breath and a silent prayer, I begin my descent. The air around me gets colder with every step, and I wrap my arms around myself to keep from shivering. Halfway down is a narrow landing where the stairs double back on themselves. Just as I'm coming into this turn, a sudden creaking sound cuts through the silence. I freeze, one foot in the air, and listen out for any signs of danger. If somebody catches me here, it's game over. No excuse or apology would ever get me off this hook.

But when the noise echoes out again a few seconds later, I breathe a sigh of relief. Because it's not somebody coming to catch me red-handed after all. It's just the vent. The huge metallic tunnel runs the length of the ceiling, faintly reflecting the light from upstairs. The sound must have just been a fan coming on. Or a pregnant cat crawling inside to give birth.

I clear the remaining stairs and come out on another long corridor. It's almost identical to the one above, only with bare concrete walls and just a single naked lightbulb. On the left is a door with a glowing *emergency exit* sign – the one leading out onto the car park, I presume. On the right is another door, spelling out a brass-plated warning – *no unauthorised access.* A shiver runs down my spine as I realise what I'm looking at. The forbidden WellCat laboratory. The cradle of Future Fish.

No light shines out from underneath the door, and the only sound is a faint beeping every two or three seconds. I try turning the handle, but it's locked in place. To the left is a small silver keypad, its buttons numbered from zero to nine. You must need to input a passcode to get inside. Another shiver creeps over me as I remember the alien girl's words on the phone. *We need to move the plan forward to this afternoon. Did you get the code?*

I stand there in the half-light of the hallway, wondering what to do next. The evidence against Noelle is mounting, but it's still just circumstantial. Not nearly enough to rule out a simple misunderstanding. What I need now is something concrete. Something that proves beyond the shadow of a doubt that she's guilty. Only when I have that – when I know exactly what I'm dealing with – will I be able to figure out my next move.

With no time for subtlety, I ball up my fist and give the door three quick knocks. It's heavier than I was expecting, made of solid metal, and my hand barely makes a sound. I try again, more forcefully this time, and manage to elicit a satisfying *boom.* At first there's no response, and the only thing I'm aware of is the stinging pain in my knuckles. But then I hear it. A faint rustling sound, barely audible. Like a mouse in the wall.

I wait a few more seconds, sweat breaking out on my forehead despite the freezing basement air. But there's no more movement. No sign of anybody coming to open the door. I consider calling out Noelle's name, letting her know it's me. But I don't want to give up my position just yet. Instead, I reach into my pocket and pull out my phone. The reception down here is patchy, with just a single bar of signal. But that should be all I need. Heart pounding, I open up my contacts and scroll down to *Noelle WellCat*. There's a few seconds of silence as the call connects, and then a ringing starts up on the far side of the door.

La cu-ca-RA-cha! La cu-ca-RA-cha!

Some frantic shuffling sounds, and then the ringing stops. The call disconnects.

And there it is. The proof I was looking for... Noelle is definitely in the lab.

I know right away what I have to do. There can't be any hesitation this time. No handwringing over ruined friendships or guilting myself into wannabe heroics. I didn't ask to be put in this position, but here I am. And if I want to keep my job – to save myself the humiliation of being fired a second time – then there's only one way out of this. I need to march up those stairs and into that meeting room.

I need to tell Maeve everything I know.

Seventeen

I imagined Maeve reacting to the news in a million different ways. Would she turn bright red, forehead twitching with tension, and explode in an apoplexy of rage? Or harden into ice, cold and lifeless, her words freezing the very blood in my veins? Would she retreat to the safety of smooth corporate speak – *thank you for bringing this to my attention, I'll look into it as a matter of urgency* – or dispense with words altogether, slapping me full-force across the face? I imagined every possible combination of shock and frustration. Every howl of rage and jaw-clench of hatred. But the one thing I never expected to see on her face was fear.

'Go find JD,' she says, eyes wide and glassy like a spooked horse. 'Tell him to meet me in the laboratory. And tell him it's an emergency.'

We're standing in the middle of the hallway, just outside the meeting room. The people inside crane their necks around the doorframe to gawk out at us.

'Sorry everybody,' says Maeve, turning around to face them. 'I just need to pop out for a few minutes. Go ahead and finish up without me.'

She storms off down the corridor before anyone can respond. I watch her disappear into the darkness of the stairwell, then turn uncertainly towards the meeting room. Dominic has finished his presentation, and now Shelley is standing in front of the projector. She glares out at me, like I've just ruined her birthday party, then strides over to the door and slams it in my face.

I stand there shellshocked for a few seconds, then begin trudging towards reception. Talking to JD is the last thing I want to be doing right now. Even Shelley the door-slammer would make for a more appealing conversation partner. But Maeve gave me a direct order, and only a fool would dare disobey her.

JD is reclining in his classic pose, boots up on the desk and hands folded behind his head. On the screen of his computer, some football match is entering its eighty-sixth minute.

'What do you want?' he growls, without looking up. 'Can't you see I'm busy?'

'Maeve sent me to find you. But I can tell her the football was more important if you'd like?'

'Sent you to find me, eh?' He jerks forward, taking his feet off the desk, and leans in closer to the screen. 'Come on… come on… FUCK! YOU USELESS BASTARD!'

On-screen, a player in a red jersey holds his head in dismay. A sea of blue fans erupts in cheers behind him.

'She wants you to meet her in the basement,' I say. 'And she says it's *an emergency.*'

He finally looks away from the football, eyeing me up with a suspicious scowl. 'Really now? And why would she go saying a thing like that?'

'Because she needs your help.'

'No shit, Sherlock. What does she need my help *with?*'

I draw the moment out as long as possible, enjoying the uncertainty in his eyes. '...With helping her catch an intruder in the lab.'

The frown drops off his face, replaced by a look of lip-licking exhilaration. He spins the chair around and leaps to his feet, sending an empty can of energy drink flying onto the floor. 'Good lad,' he says, slapping me on the shoulder as he sprints off down the hallway.

I watch the door swing back and forth in his wake, gradually returning to a state of stillness. It occurs to me then that I have no idea what to do next. Maeve's only instructions were to find JD and send him down to the lab. Now that I've done that, am I supposed to just head back to my desk? The basement is still off-limits, as far as I know. And Maeve must be angry enough at me already for going down there earlier.

Before I can decide what to do, I hear a sound coming out from the direction of the stairwell. A man's voice – shouting. Like he's in the middle of a furious argument. The sound is muffled, bouncing off the walls. But I'm pretty sure it's JD. There are a few seconds of silence, and then another voice shouts back. Louder, this time. And higher-pitched.

It's Noelle. And it sounds like she's in pain.

Next thing I know, I'm racing up the hallway and down the stairs. Panic spurs me forward – no time for health and safety – and I end up tripping over and barrelling shoulder-first into the wall of the landing. The vent groans out a warning as I pause to steady myself. *Slow down, you idiot. You're going to break your neck.* But I can't stop now. I clear the remaining steps two at a time and stumble headfirst into the gloom of the basement.

The door to the lab is still shut tight, but now a tiny sliver of light shines out from underneath. The voices are clearer now, coming from just inside, and I manage to make out the majority of what they're saying:

JD: 'Easy, love. You're only making this harder on yourself.'

Noelle: 'GET YOUR HANDS OFF ME, YOU POXY BASTARD!'

Bang. Bang. CRASH!

Maeve: 'Careful! That computer is worth three times your monthly salary.'

I try pushing the door open, but the handle is still locked in place. 'Hello?' I call out. 'What's going on in there?'

But there's no answer.

'HELLO?' I call again, pounding at the door. 'IS EVERYTHING ALRIGHT!?'

Still no response. But the voices are getting closer now. Noelle keeps screaming at them to get off her, while JD tells her over and over to calm down. Even through the door, I can tell he doesn't really mean it. He's only going through the motions of de-escalating the situation, while deep down, he's getting off on all the violence.

Just as I'm about to resume my knocking, the door suddenly

swings open. JD's sweaty shirt-back appears before me. Both his arms are wrapped around Noelle's waist, dragging her slowly but surely towards the doorway. She puts up a good fight, thrashing about like a shark in a net, but it's clear she's no match for him on strength. Maeve holds the door open, watching on impassively as the pair of them stumble back and forth.

'Stop!' I shout. 'You're hurting her!'

The three of them turn to face me in unison. JD and Noelle freeze mid-struggle, while Maeve just throws her eyes up to heaven. It's only in this sudden stillness that I realise I'm actually looking inside the lab. The secret cave of wonders that's caused all this trouble. I can't make out much over JD's shoulder – just a couple of sterile metal desks and a shelf lined with glass jars. Inside these containers is an assortment of brightly coloured liquids. Banana yellow. Barbicide blue. Blood-bank red. Three or four lie shattered at JD's feet, their contents spreading in a sticky rainbow across the floor.

'Marcus,' says Maeve, tapping her finger against the door. 'You shouldn't be here.'

'Sorry. It's just that I heard shouting, and I wanted to make sure everything was alright…'

'Everything is fine. JD and I have got the situation under control.' Her tone is calm and collected, but I can see the impatience pulling at her eyes. 'You've already done your part by raising the alarm. So why don't you just return to your desk, and we'll discuss the consequences of this later?'

'Eh…alright. Sure.'

I begin backing out the doorway, about to turn and walk away. But the look on Noelle's face freezes me in my tracks. Her mouth hangs open – a capital *O* – as though all the wind has just been knocked out of her. Her eyes swirl around with confusion, before resolving like kaleidoscopes into sudden clarity. Her whole body goes limp, JD staggering to one side to keep her upright.

My eyes drop to the floor as I complete my retreat. I hurry up the stairs, trying to outrun my own guilt, and do my best to block out the conversation below. But a few words still manage to reach me.

JD: 'How the hell are we going to get her up these stairs?'

Maeve: 'We're not. The last thing I need right now is a lawsuit. Just take her out this way.'

A harsh scraping sound, like metal on concrete. The emergency exit opening out onto the car park.

JD: 'Nice one. The bin is right where this trash bag belongs.'

Noelle: 'Fuck off, you slimy scumbag!'

Maeve: 'Hold on, don't let her go yet. We still haven't discussed the matter of that phone she was recording on.'

Noelle: 'That's private property, you blood-sucking leech!'

The rest of the afternoon passes by in a blur. Everybody around me carries on as usual – chatting, drinking tea, typing away at their keyboards – totally oblivious to what's just transpired beneath their feet. I watch their carefree movements with a growing sense of resentment. It must be nice, being innocent. Having nothing more to worry about than how many minutes are left until home time. Meanwhile, my mind is eating itself alive.

I manage to keep the guilt at bay, telling myself Noelle only has herself to blame for what's happened. But that just clears a path for my anxiety. Maeve's words echo over and over in the back of my mind. *We'll discuss the consequences of this later…* Is she still angry at me for going down to the basement, even though I was trying to stop Noelle? Should I have gone to her straight away, rather than waiting to find proof? What if I made the wrong decision, and I end up screwing over both myself and Noelle?

It's over an hour later by the time Maeve finally reappears at her desk. I study her expression, searching for a clue as to what's going on in her head. But she remains impassive as ever. Like this is just an ordinary afternoon, and nothing cruel or unusual could possibly be occurring.

Within minutes of sitting down, she's already sent around an email announcing that Noelle has been fired. The words barely register as I read them. It feels inevitable, a mere formality at this stage. Like a doctor declaring the bloated corpse in the canal is *officially* dead. The only thing that surprises me is how similar it is to the one she sent for Kevin. Besides the name and date, the wording is identical. Like she has a special template saved on her computer. A handy time-saver for whenever she needs to get rid of somebody.

And just like the email about Kevin, this one is also followed up with a personalised message just for me.

Marcus,

Please see me in the large meeting room as soon as possible.

Regards,

M

My legs feel like bags of water as I stand up from the desk. Like you could fill them with goldfish and give them out at the fair. I keep my head down as I cross the room, ignoring the chorus of whispers rising up around me.

The door to the meeting room is closed when I arrive. I pause for a deep breath – which does absolutely nothing to calm me – then knock three times.

'Come in.'

Maeve is already sitting down, arms folded neatly on the table in front of her. I take a seat in the chair opposite.

'So,' she begins, in a matter-of-fact tone. 'How's everything going?'

'Eh…fine, thanks.'

'And how are you finding your workload?'

'My workload?' What's she playing at here? Surely this is no time for small talk. 'It's fine, I guess.'

'You're managing to stay on top of everything?'

'I think so.'

'Not feeling overwhelmed, or stretched too thinly?'

'No, everything's fine work-wise. Although it has been a little hard to concentrate this afternoon. After, you know…'

She nods solemnly. 'That unfortunate incident in the laboratory. That's actually part of the reason I called you in here.'

'I'm sorry for going down there without permission!' I blurt out. 'I know it's against the rules.'

'Don't worry about that now.'

'I would have come to you sooner. It's just, I needed proof of what Noelle was doing.'

'I understand.' Her voice takes on an unnaturally gentle

quality, like a teacher encouraging a particularly slow child. 'You were only doing what you thought was right.'

'So…I'm not in trouble?'

'Of course not. I called you in here because I wanted to thank you.'

'Thank me?'

'And apologise. I never should have doubted you before. Or questioned your loyalty to the company. I'm sure you can understand where I was coming from, after what happened with Kevin. But I see now that I was wrong. I know you and Noelle were close, and it can't have been easy coming to me the way you did. But you made the right decision.'

Relief swells inside me, filling my head up like a balloon. All I can do is blink stupidly as she continues talking.

'I'm sure I don't need to remind you how important Future Fish is. How the entire future of the company hinges on its success. Noelle could have ruined everything if she hadn't been stopped. She's not just some deranged lunatic like Kevin. She's shrewd, and highly manipulative. Did you know she was recording on her phone when I walked in on her?'

I shake my head.

'Trying to gather information on Future Fish, no doubt. Luckily, she didn't manage to find anything important. I'm sure Miss Meow would have paid her a pretty penny for the footage if she did. Maybe even offered her a senior management position for her trouble. Did she ever say anything to suggest she was working for them? That they knew about Future Fish, and they wanted her to rustle up some evidence?'

'Eh…nothing I can think of.'

'Hmmm.' She stares straight in front of her, clicking her tongue. 'I suppose she would have known better than to go around blabbing about it. Especially after the recent levelling-up of our security systems. In any case, she's not coming back. Which means we need to start planning how we move forward without her.'

She sits back in her chair, settling into her natural CEO element. I smile nervously, still totally out of mine.

'Obviously, the ideal scenario would be to find a qualified replacement as soon as possible. But after Kevin and Noelle's betrayals, we can't risk bringing anybody else on board. At least not until after the launch of Future Fish. What that means is that I may have to lean on you for some additional support in the interim. It will likely involve an increase in your workload, but I'm sure you'll find it an invaluable learning experience.' She pauses, raising one perfectly plucked eyebrow. 'How does that sound to you?'

'It sounds great!' Or at least, I think it does... I'm still not entirely sure what she's getting at.

'Brilliant. I'll have our IT provider set up a redirect on Noelle's inbox, so all her emails will be forwarded on to you. You may find it a little overwhelming at first, but I'm sure you'll get into the swing of things soon enough.' She stands up from the table, straightening her blazer. 'I think that's all for now. Probably best for you to be getting back to your desk. You're about to become a very busy man.'

I sit there in stunned silence after she leaves. If I'm understanding correctly, it sounds like she's asking me to cover for Noelle. To step into her shoes while we wait for a replacement.

Which means not only am I not being fired, but I'm being given *extra* work instead. Trusted with more responsibility. Rewarded for my loyalty.

A slow smile spreads across my face. This meeting has gone better than I ever could have imagined. And best of all, there's no more need for second-guessing what happened with Noelle.

I definitely made the right decision.

Eighteen

Kevin is back outside the office the next morning. Only this time, he's not alone. A motley crew of supporters stands assembled behind him, like a makeshift army preparing to charge the front door. There's a jowly middle-aged general in suit and tie, red-faced and panting despite standing perfectly still. Next to him, two conservatively dressed women wield battering-ram buggies, the tiny infants inside blinking about in mute bewilderment. And at the end of the line, reciting a mumbled war cry of *Hail Mary, full of grace*, stand the three elderly nuns Kevin was chatting to at the café. The rest of the troops are armed with homemade signs – black marker on cardboard – which they thrust proudly above their heads.

MATTHEW 6:25.

WELLCAT = HELLCAT.

GOD HATES FUTURE FISH.

'HEAR ME NOW YE PEOPLE OF ASHCROSS,' roars Kevin into the megaphone. His beard has grown out surprisingly quickly, swallowing up his jawline in a mass of blonde bristles. 'I TELL YOU GREED IS NOT JUST ANY OLD SIN. IT IS A CAPITAL ONE. FOR IT LEADS THOSE WHO SURRENDER TO ITS TEMPTATIONS TO COMMIT FURTHER ACTS OF DEGENERACY. A VICIOUS CIRCLE OF SIN UPON SIN. AND WHAT, I ASK YOU, IS THE WAGES OF SIN?'

'DEATH!' chants the line of followers behind him.

Despite the creepy cult vibes, there's something kind of sexy about this new and improved Kevin. Like he's gone from lone wolf to leader of the pack. Alpha male in the Legion of Mary. His voice has taken on a rugged air of charisma, making you want to believe every word he's saying. If his cause was any less insane, I might even be tempted to join the congregation.

But despite this allure, I cross the road to avoid him. I can't risk getting drawn into another conversation right now. Not when JD is probably peeking out from behind the blinds, just waiting for an excuse to start up a fresh round of interrogation.

I make it past the protest without attracting any unwanted attention, breathing a sigh of relief as I step through the front door. But the feeling is short-lived. JD emerges from the shadows in the corner, peering out over my shoulder at the scene on the street. I grit my teeth, bracing myself for the usual tongue-lashing. But all he gives me is a friendly wink.

'Morning boss. Those loonies weren't giving you any trouble, were they?'

'Eh… no. No trouble here.'

'Are you sure, now? You can tell me if they were.'

'Well they weren't. I wasn't even talking to them!'

'Alright. Let me know if they do start bothering you though, yeah?'

My eyes narrow. What sort of twisted web is he spinning here? 'Why, what are you going to do about it? Use it as an excuse to throw me in the gulag?'

'Relax, would you?' he laughs. 'Don't you know we're on the same side now?'

'…We are? Since when?'

'Since yesterday, you dope. Maeve has got you back in her good books after what happened in the basement. Which means it's my job to look out for you. To make sure nobody's giving you a hard time. And to be honest, I wouldn't mind having an excuse to go out there and teach that rabble a lesson.'

'OK…well, thanks, I guess. I'll let you know if there are any issues in future.'

'Nice one,' he says, with another wink. 'You know where to find me.'

I set off uncertainly down the corridor, baffled by this sudden change in character. Are we really *on the same side now*? Or is this just his latest method of messing with me? Would I be naïve to trust him, or stupid to turn down a ceasefire?

But all thoughts of JD disappear from my mind as I open up my inbox. It turns out Maeve wasn't joking when she said I was about to become a very busy man. Along with the usual customer inquiries, there are dozens of messages forwarded from Noelle's address. Apparently, she was busier than she looked, with a mountain of reports needing to be filled out every day. They must have been easy for her – mere muscle memory after so many years – but they're all total gibberish to me.

It's the sort of situation that could easily overwhelm a person. Tossed into the deep end, with neither life ring nor rescue party in sight. No option but to sink or swim. But despite the mounting pressure, I'm feeling oddly confident. I just need to keep calm and resist the urge to panic. Take a deep breath and work my way through it. And what better way to do that than with a lovely cup of tea?

I trundle towards the kitchen, wondering if there'll be any bourbon creams left in the drawer. A weekly supply of biscuits is supposed to be one of the perks of working here, but whichever stingy HR assistant orders them only ever gets enough to last until Monday afternoon. Inside the kitchen, Maeve, Dominic, Shelley, and Fi sit assembled around the small wooden table, gossiping away about 'that bunch of freaks outside'. I mumble an awkward 'good morning' as I pass them and head straight for the biscuit drawer. But all I find is a heap of empty wrappers.

'Alright there, Marcus?' asks Dominic, sipping from an intimidatingly small coffee cup. 'You look like somebody's just died.'

'Sorry. I was just looking for a biscuit…'

'There are none left,' says Fi.

'*Somebody* ate them all yesterday,' adds Shelley, shooting an accusing glare in my direction.

I open my mouth, about to deny all responsibility. But then I decide it's probably best just to back out of the kitchen. 'Right, well, I'll leave you to it. Sorry for interrupting.'

'Don't be silly,' says Maeve. 'This is the kitchen, not a private meeting room. You're welcome to join us.'

'Are you sure? I don't want to intrude...'

'Of course,' she says, with an insistent smile. 'Take a seat.'

I squeeze into the empty chair between Dominic and Shelley, taking extreme care not to touch either one of them.

'How about a coffee?' asks Dominic, springing to his feet. 'We've just been trying out this new blend Shelley brought back from her cousin's café in Dún Laoghaire.'

'Eh...sounds great,' I say, with as much enthusiasm as I can muster. In reality, I can't stand coffee. But refusing him would only make the situation even more awkward.

'One espresso, coming right up.'

I watch on, mystified, as he fiddles around with the fancy coffee machine. A blue light flashes on top, setting a motor whirring into life, and then the whole kitchen counter starts to vibrate. There's a sudden puff of steam, followed by a pleasant tinkling sound as the coffee trickles out.

'Here you go,' he says, handing me one of the tiny cups.

I down the whole thing in one go, just to get it over with. The taste is unholy, like sucking acid out of a battery, but I force myself to smile afterwards. 'Mmm-mmm-mmm. Delicious... What's the name of the café in Dún Laoghaire? I'll have to check it out next time I'm back in Dublin.'

'It's called Moby Dick's,' says Shelley, with a grudging smile. 'My cousin Fiachra is the manager. Tell him you work with me, and he'll give you a discount. Or you can just wait until the end of the day, when they give out free drinks to the homeless.'

'Speaking of the homeless,' says Dominic. 'We were just

talking about Kevin O'Mahoney and the little circus he's set up outside.'

Fi groans, slumping down in her chair. 'I still don't get what they're even angry about.'

'Nobody does,' says Shelley. 'Their signs are just a load of Bible references, as if anybody knows what they mean.'

'He was saying something about greedy people going to hell when I walked past,' says Dominic. 'Although I'm not sure if that was aimed at us specifically.'

'Why would it be aimed at us?' frowns Fi.

'Don't worry about it,' cuts in Maeve. 'It's just Kevin up to his usual tricks – trying to force his beliefs onto other people. Apparently, he has a problem with companies trying to turn a profit. As if creating value for our shareholders were some sort of crime. You know, I could almost see where he was coming from if he was targeting the tax-dodging multinationals in Dublin. But going after an honest business like ours is madness.'

'*Madness*,' echoes Dominic. 'I still can't believe the Guards just left him to get on with it. Surely making that sort of racket should be illegal?'

Fi nods. 'I get that people have the right to free speech or whatever, but can't they at least do it quietly?'

'Exactly,' says Shelley. 'We're not *all* unemployed losers with nothing better to do than stand around shouting. Some of us actually have jobs to do.'

'Whatever happened to those silent protests?' says Dominic. 'You know, the ones where people would duct-tape their mouths shut? Maybe somebody could convince Kevin to switch to that tactic for a while.'

'Oh my god,' snorts Shelley. 'How freaky would it be if they just stood there staring at you? Kevin is creepy enough on his own, but those friends of his look like they've come straight from a serial-killer convention.'

'I didn't think he even *had* any friends,' I say.

They all turn to look at me, like they'd forgotten I was even there. There's a moment of hesitation, and then one by one – first Dominic, then Fi, and finally Shelley – they all start laughing. I feel bad at first – that wasn't supposed to be an insult. But a second later, I join in on the sniggering.

'He could have just rounded them up off the street, to be fair,' says Dominic. 'This town is full of weirdos.'

'Tell me about it,' says Fi. 'Sometimes I feel like I'm living in a horror film. You know, where the hot girl arrives in some creepy old village and slowly realises the entire place is a giant Satanic cult.'

'At least that would be interesting,' says Dominic. 'I'd take a killer cult over the actual Ashcross residents any day.'

'Same here,' says Shelley. 'They might actually be doing us a favour by killing us. At least that way, we wouldn't have to live in this shithole any more.'

The three of them burst out laughing again, until Maeve cuts them off with a conspicuous sip of coffee. 'True, the place is no New York or Paris,' she says. 'But it's not *that* bad. You just have to try and make the most of it, rather than sitting around complaining. And don't forget the reason we moved here in the first place. We'd never be able to afford an office this big – with our own fully-equipped in-house laboratory – back in Dublin.'

'Of course…' mumbles Shelley. 'I wasn't actually *complaining*.'

'And on that note,' says Maeve. 'I think it's time for us to be getting back to work. Speaking of which – Marcus, I still need to show you how to fill out the quarterly feedback report. Are you free now?'

Everybody stands up and loads their tiny cups into the dishwasher, then files back to their own respective desks. Maeve follows me over to mine, taking a seat in Noelle's empty chair. At first, her proximity makes me nervous. Like she's a landmine that could explode at any moment. But she's surprisingly patient as she explains the report. It's a simple task, requiring nothing more than copying and pasting a few figures into a spreadsheet, but when I send her the finished product a half hour later, she still responds with a *great work*. She comes over to explain several other things throughout the course of the morning, and at a certain point, I even start popping over to her desk and initiating conversations myself.

Despite having probably the most productive day of my life, I still have a million items on my to-do list by the time half-five rolls around. I watch as the office begins to empty out – people shutting down computers, pulling on coats, and waving to each other from across the room. Usually, I'd be rushing to join them, desperate to get out of the front door as soon as possible. But not today. Today, the only thing that matters is work. I pop in my headphones, select a *deep concentration* playlist, and try my best to block out the commotion around me.

The playlist does the trick. Next thing I know, the clock on my computer reads *19:23*, and Maeve is calling my name from across the room. I pull my headphones out and look around at the sea of empty desks. The two of us are the only ones still here.

'I hope you're not planning on pulling an all-nighter,' she says, sipping at another tiny coffee cup.

'I don't have too much more to do. Just a couple awkward complaints to respond to.'

'I'm sure they can wait until tomorrow. Why don't you head home and enjoy the rest of the evening? You'll burn yourself out otherwise.'

'Are you sure? I don't mind doing it now.'

'It's fine. Probably best to make a move sooner rather than later anyway. JD leaves at half-seven, and it's a pain resetting the alarm system if you go out after him. I'd already have left myself, only I have Pilates this evening, and I'm waiting for Shelley and Fi to meet me here so we can all drive over together.'

'Alright, cool.' I save a draft of the email I was working on and start shutting down my computer. I have no idea how to reset the alarm system, and I get the impression Maeve would rather not have to explain it to me. 'I'll see you tomorrow then. Have a good evening.'

'You too.'

JD gives me a wave as I pass through reception. I'm too tired to start second-guessing him again, so I go ahead and wave right back.

'Have a good one, boss,' he says, with another one of his winks.

I guess we really are on the same side now.

It's only when I'm out on the street that I suddenly realise how hungry I am. I haven't eaten anything since lunchtime, and that was just a soggy supermarket sandwich. Maybe I'll treat myself to a nice takeaway. I deserve it, after all, considering how hard I've been working. The only question is which carb-based option I should choose from the local Chinese.

I weigh the possibilities back and forth the entire walk home, eventually settling on the humble three-in-one of chips, rice, and curry sauce. I'm so busy drooling with anticipation, I don't even notice the other figure lurking in the foyer of the apartment building. It's only when the lift opens up and I catch her reflection in the mirror that I suddenly realise I'm not alone. Noelle stands frozen against the far wall, dressed in a long black trench coat. Tucked under one arm is a bulging brown envelope. And plastered across her face, a look of total mortification.

I turn around slowly, jamming my finger into the *open door* button. A million different emotions race through my mind. Guilt. Fear. Fury. I open my mouth to speak, then close it again. There are so many questions I want to ask, so many reasons I want to give, I have no idea where to even begin. Noelle does the same thing, clearing her throat and stepping forward, then hesitating and retreating back to the wall. This continues for several seconds – the two of us gulping air like goldfish, trapped in the glass bowl of the foyer.

And then, without warning, the tension breaks. She cracks a smile, rolls her eyes. *What a pair of eejits*, the gesture says. *Would we ever cop on to ourselves?*

'Sorry,' I begin, letting my shoulders relax. 'I know this is kind of weird, but—'

And then, I stop. Bile rises up in my stomach. Because I've just noticed something I hadn't seen before.

Her t-shirt.

It didn't register at first, peeking out over the lapels of her trench coat. But there's no mistaking that black and white design.

A UFO, hovering over a child's drawing of Ireland. Underneath, hidden by the folds of fabric, I know there are six simple words. *I BELIEVE IN THE ASHCROSS ALIEN.*

I take my finger off the button, letting the lift doors slide closed. Noelle calls out for me to wait, to give her a chance to explain. But I ignore her pleas.

I can't believe I almost fell for it. I can't believe I was actually going to *apologise*. She's not sorry for what she's done. Not ashamed or embarrassed or suffering from even a single ounce of remorse.

So why the hell should I be?

Nineteen

The next few weeks pass by in a blur of late nights and lunch breaks spent eating at my desk. I stagger home each evening, barely enough energy to shovel down a microwaved ready meal before passing out fully clothed on the couch. This routine forms so quickly, so seamlessly, that soon I can't even remember what it felt like not to be exhausted. But despite the darkening circles under my eyes, there's something comforting about this constant go, go, go. Like I'm pouring so much time and energy into work, I've got none left over to worry about anything else. Like as long as things are going well at the office, there's no need to slow down and wonder what the point of all this is.

The one downside to this new-found productivity is that it doesn't leave much time for play. But it's not like my social life is particularly thrilling right now anyway. Some more of Sean's relatives have come to stay at his aunt's house, and he's busy doing family stuff most evenings. I only run into Noelle once more – in the car park outside our building – and this time, neither one of us bothers to say hello. Kevin's protests grow larger and larger, swamping the footpath with his army of followers, until one day, the entire entourage disappears. A rumour swirls around the office that they've all killed themselves in some mass ritual suicide. But according to JD, the local priest showed up one morning and told them all Kevin was talking nonsense.

One Friday morning – three weeks after Noelle was fired – I find myself once again having coffee with Maeve and co in the kitchen. It's become a sort of daily ritual now – a gentle way to ease yourself into the current of each new morning. The five of us sit in a loose circle around the creaky wooden table. Shelley and Fi are chatting away about the latest episode of *Ireland's Most Notorious Killers*, their voices quivering with delight as they recount the details of some grisly murder. Dominic does his best to look interested, nodding along and stroking his chin, while Maeve just stares up at the ceiling with a glazed-over expression.

'Oh my God, that reminds me!' says Shelley, slapping her palm onto the table. 'JD said the weirdest thing to me last night.'

'Weirder than usual?' asks Dominic. 'That guy gives me the creeps.'

'Tell me about it,' says Shelley.

'Here now,' frowns Fi. 'He's not that bad. At least you can have a laugh with JD. Unlike Kevin, who was about as much fun as a coma patient at a Christmas party.'

'At least Kevin was kind of hot though,' says Shelley. 'JD looks like he's made out of salami.'

Fi shrugs, raising an eyebrow. 'I wouldn't mind a slice of that in my sandwich.'

'For God's sake!' splutters Shelley, choking on a mouthful of coffee. 'Don't be so disgusting.'

'It's not disgusting,' says Fi.

'It is so! The only reason you even fancy him in the first place is that he looks like your dad.'

'*Enough!*' snaps Maeve, making the two of them jump. 'What did he say?' she demands, glaring at Shelley.

'What did who say?'

'JD. What did he say to you last night?'

'Oh, right... He asked me if I wanted him to walk me to my car. Apparently, there've been a few attempted break-ins lately, and he said it wasn't safe for me to go down to the car park alone. I was like, *thanks, but no thanks. I'll take my chances.*'

Dominic lets out a low whistle. 'Jesus Christ, what a creeper. I wonder what he'd have done if you'd said yes.'

'He wouldn't have done anything!' says Fi. 'Only walk you to your car. And where's the harm in that?'

'Why don't you let him walk *you* out, then?' says Shelley.

'Fine. I will.'

'Great. We'll be seeing you on the next episode of *Ireland's Most Notorious Killers* so.'

'Yeah, you'll be seeing me give a teary-eyed interview as I talk about my friend Shelley who was brutally murdered in the car park. If only she'd let the sexy security guard walk her to her car.'

'Whatever,' huffs Shelley, rolling her eyes. 'He's not going to be walking any of us to our cars tonight anyway. Not unless you're planning on drink-driving again after Friday night cocktails.'

A sudden silence descends on the table. Fi nudges Shelley in the ribs, nodding over in my direction, while Dominic picks up his phone and pretends to be texting. Clearly, they've all made plans together for this evening. And I wasn't invited. I take a sip of coffee, pretending I haven't realised what's going on. The taste is still slightly bitter, but I'm starting to get used to it.

After several awkward seconds, Dominic clears his throat and sets down his phone. 'Right, yeah… I forgot to mention, Marcus, but we're heading up to Galway for a few drinks this evening. Just the four of us. You should come along if you're free.'

'Eh…' I glance around the table, trying to gauge the others' reactions. Coffee in the kitchen is one thing, but invite-only drinks would put us firmly into friend territory. Do they really want me there, or is Dominic just being polite? Shelley and Fi avoid making eye contact, but Maeve gives me a reassuring smile.

'Good idea,' she says. 'You should definitely join us.'

'Alright, sure. Sounds great.'

We assemble around Maeve's desk at the end of the day. The girls have all touched up their makeup at some point, while Dominic has swapped his lab coat for a tight-fitting blazer, complete with paisley pocket square. I suddenly feel underdressed, my shapeless shirt and school-uniform slacks sticking out like a sore thumb. If only they'd given me more notice, I could have worn something more appropriate. Although, thinking over the contents of my wardrobe, I have no idea what that would have been. All my shirts came in supermarket multi-packs, and I've never owned a pocket square in my life.

We squeeze into a six-seater taxi and head straight for Galway. After a cramped ride through the countryside, the winding, narrow roads gradually give way to smooth suburban sprawl, and then the lights and noise of the chaotic city centre. We pull up outside a crowded bar, where the bouncer immediately waves us in. The place is a million times nicer than anywhere you'd find in Ashcross – all plush leather couches and polished glass surfaces, with a cocktail menu starting in the double digits. It's a million times busier too, with various groups of after-work drinkers jostling for space around the candlelit tables. The five of us squeeze into a booth in the corner, where I end up pressed uncomfortably between Dominic and Shelley.

'Nice place,' I say, my voice barely audible over the booming of the speakers.

'It's alright,' shrugs Dominic. 'But have you ever been to Meat Street? Now *there's* a nice place.'

'Been *where*?' I ask, assuming I've misheard him. *Meat Street* sounds like a men-only leather bar.

'*MEAT. STREET.* It's this amazing steak restaurant just across the road. Maeve and I go there for our anniversary every year.'

'Oh, no… I'll have to check it out.'

Before he can say anything else, Maeve stands up and announces the first round is on her. Everybody else puts in orders for silly-sounding cocktails, so I go ahead and do the same, asking for a *North Atlantic Iceberg*.

The conversation remains stilted while Maeve is at the bar, everybody struggling to make small talk over the blaring of the music. But things start to pick up once she returns with the drinks. The bartender hasn't skimped on the alcohol, and soon everybody is shedding their inhibitions and shouting at the top of their lungs. As usual, the primary topic of conversation is other people from the office. Shelly, Fi, and Dominic prove themselves to be ever-flowing fonts of gossip, with pregnancies, divorces, and dodgy online romances all dissected with sadistic delight.

After a few more rounds, the spotlight turns onto present company. Nobody dares take a dig at Maeve, and Dominic, by association, escapes largely unscathed. But there's plenty of tittering over Fi's ex, who's just been in court for punching a police horse, as well as a series of impotence-themed jokes about the older American tech executive who Shelley is *sort-of-but-not-really* seeing whenever she's back in Dublin.

'How about you, Marcus?' asks Dominic, giving me a nudge. A slight slur has crept into his words, his pocket square drooping down like a wilted flower. 'Are you seeing anyone?'

'Eh…' I've been lurking on the edge of the conversation, trying to stay involved without saying anything too incriminating. But I can't see the harm in telling them about Sean. 'I have been out on a few dates with this one guy. Nothing's official yet, but it seems to be going well.'

'Oh my God!' squeals Fi. 'That's adorable. How did the two of yous meet?'

Next thing I know, I'm launching off into the entire Sean story, from our unlikely online meeting to the tragically romantic prospect of him having to go back to America. Of course, I do leave out a few key details, like the fight he almost started at the pub, and the phone call in the disabled bathroom when we discussed the nature and origins of Maeve's assholery.

'Good for you,' says Dominic, as I conclude the story. 'Get stuck in while you're young and single! It's all downhill once somebody locks you down.'

Maeve shoots him a dirty look, then turns towards me with a supportive smile. 'It's great you've found someone in Ashcross,' she says.

'And even greater that he's not actually *from* Ashcross,' adds Shelley. 'All the local men are pigs.'

Maeve turns to glare at her, picking up an empty glass and shaking the ice cubes in her face.

'I just got a round!' protests Shelley. But the look in Maeve's eyes makes it clear she's in no mood for excuses. With a huff, Shelley stands up and trudges over to the bar.

'Anyway,' says Maeve, rolling her eyes. 'I hope things work out for the two of you. You deserve to be happy.'

'Thanks,' I reply, surprised to hear her getting so personal.

'And I hope you stay at WellCat for a long, long time.' She slides around the side of the table and into Shelley's empty seat. I can smell the cocktails on her breath now – a mix of hard liquor and sickly-sweet fruit juice. 'To be honest, now that Noelle's gone, we'd be lost without you.'

'Well, no need to worry about that. I'm not going anywhere.'

'That's great. So great. You've been doing such good work lately.'

'Thank you,' I mumble, trying not to blush. She's complimented me before, but never quite so strenuously.

'You know, I've actually been thinking we might not need to replace Noelle.'

'Not replace Noelle? But how would that work?'

She turns to look directly at me. There's a sudden lucidity in her eyes, like all the alcohol has evaporated from her system. 'In a way, you'd replace her. You've already been covering the bulk of her responsibilities, and I'm sure you could pick the rest up easily enough. Of course, it would mean another little bump in your workload. But that's something we could discuss at your two-year salary review.'

It takes a moment for her words to sink in. I'm too tipsy to be certain, but I'm pretty sure this is a good thing. 'You mean like a promotion?'

'Sure…in a sense. Your job title would remain the same, along with your salary. But you could certainly think of it as an *unofficial* promotion, if that's something you'd be interested in?'

The cocktails must be making me giddy, because suddenly it takes all my strength not to burst out laughing. A promotion! *Unofficial*, sure…but a promotion all the same! 'Yeah, that's definitely something I'd be interested in.'

'Brilliant. Let's put something in the diary for Monday to iron out the details.'

Shelley has just returned from the bar with a fresh tray of drinks. Maeve snatches up one of the glasses and thrusts it into the air. 'In the meantime, a toast to our new arrangement!'

I pick up a glass of my own and clink it against hers.

'Cheers!' I cry, downing the contents in one go.

Twenty

I manage to sleep off the worst of the hangover, drooling into my pillow until well after noon. It's only when the pressure on my bladder gets too much to bear that I finally crawl out of bed and into the bathroom. As I sit down on the toilet, flinching at the cold sting of the seat, that old familiar fear comes creeping back to haunt me. I did something embarrassing last night, didn't I? Something so stomach-turningly shameful I can never show my face at the office again?

I run through a mental playback of the evening – from the cocktails, to the late-night chipper, to the return taxi journey from Galway – but nothing particularly mortifying comes to mind. The only memory that makes me cringe a little is spending sixty euro on a single round of drinks. But everybody else had already taken their turn, so it's not like I could have refused. And besides, this wasn't just any old night out on the town. I was networking with colleagues. Investing in my future. And would you look at that? It's already paying off. Maeve said she was going to promote me!

Pride swells inside me, dulling the edges of my hangover. I've never been promoted before. And to be honest, I sort of just assumed I never would be. I thought that was the kind of thing that only happened to successful people. Go-getters and risk-takers. Team players with passion and enthusiasm. And I've never been any of those things. I've never even been close...

Until now.

I wish my old manager Liam could see this. That would wipe the smile off his baldy little face. Tell me I haven't got what it takes? That there's no fire in my engine? Well guess what, Liam? I'm burning bright now. Hotter than the surface of the motherfucking sun. So maybe the problem was never really me. Maybe it was *you* all along. *You're* the one who was too thick to see my true potential. *You're* the one who was holding me down. But now I'm somewhere people actually appreciate me. And I'm going all the way to the top.

This calls for a celebration. Something decadent to mark the occasion. I flush the toilet, hitch up my underwear, and stagger excitedly into the bedroom. After rummaging around through the pockets of my trousers, I eventually locate my phone amongst the folds of the duvet. I scroll through my recent conversations, open up the one with Mam, and begin typing out a message.

Hey, guess what happened at work yesterday...

Oh God, she replies. *You're not in trouble again, are you? Because Granny is back in hospital with her heart, and I don't think she could handle the shock.*

No, I'm not in trouble! For Christ's sake.

Oh. What is it then?

I'm being promoted!

There's an awkward pause, like she's waiting for a *gotcha*.

Seriously? she replies at last.

Yes, seriously.

That's brilliant. I can't wait to tell Granny. She'll never believe it!

I close down the conversation, rolling my eyes. That wasn't quite the reaction I was hoping for. But maybe I should have known better than to turn to my parents. Maybe this is the sort of situation that requires peer-to-peer support.

With a tap of my finger, I open up my Facebook page. I haven't posted a status in over six months – not since I got fired from my last job and Neil broke up with me. But this is exactly the sort of news that deserves to be shared. *That feeling when you've just been promoted*, I type, accompanied by a gif of a dancing cat.

The post gets thirteen likes within the first five minutes. Not bad for somebody who's been out of the game as long as I have. Amongst the people offering their congratulations are college friends, distant cousins, and even a great aunt in Australia who I could have sworn was dead. The only person missing is Neil. I can see he's online, which means he must have read the post. But I guess he can't bring himself to like it. Can't admit he was wrong, and letting me go was a mistake.

I watch the likes flow in for a few more minutes, then close down the page. Virtual praise is all well and good, but it's no substitute for the real thing. What I need now is something physical.

Hey there, I text Sean. *Are you free tomorrow evening?*

I can be, he replies. *Did you want to meet up?*

I was thinking we could maybe go out for dinner? My boss just told me I'm getting a promotion, so I need to celebrate!

Congrats! Dinner sounds great. Is there anywhere in particular you wanted to go?

I pause to consider this, thinking over the options in Ashcross. But the only proper restaurant just got closed down due to a rat infestation. The Chinese takeaway has a bench you can eat on, but that feels a little cheap. I want somewhere fancy. Somewhere with real napkins and waiters in aprons with curly little moustaches.

And then I remember something Dominic said last night.

There's this steak place called Meat Street that's supposed to be amazing, I text Sean. *It's up in Galway, if you don't mind a taxi ride?*

His next reply takes several minutes to arrive. I pass the time by checking to see if Neil has liked my status yet.

He hasn't.

Sorry man, says Sean. *I've just had a look at the menu, and I'm afraid it's a little out of my price range. I still haven't found a job yet, so I'm on a pretty tight budget…*

Don't worry, I'll cover you. I want the evening to be special!

Thanks, but shouldn't I be the one treating you? Why don't I come over to your place and whip you up something instead?

I sigh, visions of Meat Street fading from my mind. But I suppose I should be grateful. It's nice of him to cook.

Sure, I reply. *Sounds great. Need me to pick anything up?*

I'll take care of the food, if you can grab some booze. See you tomorrow!

The rest of Saturday is spent nursing my hangover. I lie in bed with a box of cereal, watching rerun after rerun of old nineties sitcoms. Sunday morning, I wake up with a long list of chores to complete before Sean comes over. Put on a load of laundry. Clean up the apartment. And most important of all, pick up the drinks for this evening. I could just pop out to the local newsagents for a bottle of whatever, but I feel like the occasion calls for something special. Something with a touch of class. I sit down at my desk, open up my laptop, and run a quick search for *off-licences in Ashcross*.

The initial results are less than impressive. *Beer 4 Less. Drink and Drive-Thru. Cans, Cans, Cans!* But then, at the bottom of the list, something slightly more promising. *World's End Wines.* Sounds about as fancy as you can hope for in a town like Ashcross. I put the address into my phone, pull on a smelly old hoody, and set off into town without a moment's delay.

After battling my way through a legion of old ladies on their way to Mass, I arrive at a deserted side-street I've never noticed before. *World's End Wines* is a dusty little hole in the wall with floor to ceiling shelves and handwritten prices on curling, yellow paper. The old man at the counter ignores my arrival, so I go ahead and show myself over to the red wine section. The bottles are lined up from most expensive at the top to cheapest at the bottom. I scan my eyes down towards the floor, searching for that perfect balance between quality and affordability. Five euro feels cheap, but ten is just extravagant... And then I spot it. Seven euro fifty, reduced from twelve. Perfect! I pick up two bottles, and then on second thought, grab a third. I know it's a work night, but you can't celebrate sober.

I pay for the booze and head back out into the street. Now that I've got what I came for, I allow myself a little time to browse the neighbouring shops. Most of them are closed – either boarded up for good, or simply not open on Sundays. The only other place that appears to be doing business is a men's formalwear store with a *75% off everything* sign hanging in the window. On a table underneath, resplendent with every colour of the rainbow, sits a shimmering display of pocket squares.

I step inside, hypnotised, and begin thumbing through the fabrics. They're all so smooth and silky. So bold and self-assured. I've never had notions of wearing one before, but maybe this is a sign that it's time for a change. I reach out for a green and gold paisley, but then decide against it. It's too similar to the one Dominic was wearing on Friday. Instead, I pick out a breezy sky blue with bright white polka dots (which on closer inspection turn out to be fluffy little clouds). I fold it over, and over again, then hold it up to my chest. It looks good. Respectable, even. Like the badge of a true professional.

I pay for the pocket square, plus a discounted blazer, then head straight back to the apartment. I have just enough time to pick the dirty underwear up off the floor and take a quick shower before Sean is due to arrive. But of course, he doesn't actually show up on time. I sit at the kitchen table, watching wax drip down the freshly-lit candlesticks, and get more and more impatient as the minutes tick by. Just as I'm on the verge of sending him a passive-aggressive text, the doorbell finally rings out in the hallway. I buzz him into the building and wait for him to come up in the lift.

'Sorry I'm late,' he says, stepping in through the door. 'You wouldn't believe how hard it is to find coconut milk in this town…. Nice jacket, by the way.'

'No worries. And thanks.' I've changed into my brand-new blazer – complete with sky blue pocket square – to set the tone for the evening. I try not to let myself get too disappointed when I see he's just in his usual jeans and t-shirt.

He shows himself into the kitchen and dumps a canvas bag full of groceries onto the table. 'Congrats again on the promotion, by the way. I take it that means things are going better at work?'

'Much better, yeah. Thanks again for listening to me rant the other day. It really helped me get my head back into the game.'

'My pleasure,' he grins, unpacking the food. There's a bag of lentils, a couple sweet potatoes, and an assortment of multicoloured tins and sachets.

'So… what are you making?' I ask.

'My speciality. Sweet potato and coconut curry!'

'Oh, wow…' A far cry from Meat Street, it must be said. But I try my best to be gracious. 'Sounds lovely.'

'I know it doesn't look like much, but trust me, it's delicious. And cheap, too. Which is a major bonus when you're as broke as I am.'

I shuffle out of his way as he begins chopping vegetables and go to fill up two glasses of wine. 'Are you still struggling with the job hunt, by the way?' I ask. 'Because I've been getting along much better with Maeve lately, so I could probably put in a good word for you at WellCat.'

He pauses, knife halfway through an onion. 'Thanks, but I don't think that will be necessary any more.'

'You mean you've found something else?'

'Sort of…'

'In Ashcross?'

'Yeah. I mean, technically it's up in the city. Galway, right? My aunt pulled some strings for me at the hospital where she works.'

'That's brilliant! What's the job?'

'Oh, you know…' He resumes chopping the onion, pausing to wipe at his watering eyes. 'Nothing too exciting. Just some mindless admin.'

'Hey, that's better than nothing. Especially if it keeps you here in Ashcross.' I hand him a glass of wine and go in for a *cheers*. 'You should have told me earlier. We could have made it a double celebration.'

'Sorry, I thought I mentioned it on the phone.'

'No, you just said you were broke. Because you hadn't found a job yet…'

'Oh.' The chopping gets louder as he moves from the onion to a sweet potato. 'I must have meant I hadn't *started* yet, so I'm still on a budget for the time being.'

'Fair enough. And when do you start?'

'Next week. Or the week after. I'm not sure yet.'

'Do you think you'll stay on at your aunt's house? Or maybe try to find your own place closer to Galway?'

'I don't know. I haven't really thought about it…' He downs the contents of his glass, then goes to fill up another. 'Anyway, let's get back to celebrating the real news. Your promotion!'

The curry turns out to be much tastier than I was expecting – rich and creamy, with just the right kick of chilli. Once dinner's been cleared away and the dishes stacked in the sink, we curl up on the sofa to watch a film. Sean selects some random horror flick from the list of online options. It's total trash – something about a little girl getting possessed by the ghost of Stalin and indoctrinating her kindergarten into communism – but the cheap jump scares provide the perfect pretext for a bit of cuddling. The petting gets heavier and heavier as the film progresses, and the second the credits roll, we're standing up and undressing each other as we stumble into the bedroom.

Twenty minutes later, we lie tangled in a sweaty heap on the bedsheets.

'Damn,' yawns Sean, burrowing down deeper into the pillows. His hair hangs limply over his forehead, making him look even more dishevelled than usual. 'I'm beat.'

'Same here,' I mumble, matching his yawn. 'I feel like I've just run a marathon.'

'Well, you'd better rest up. Round Two is coming in the morning!'

He rolls over to tickle me, but I push him away. 'I'm not sure if I'll have time to hang out in the morning...' I mumble. 'I've got a meeting with Maeve first thing, and I need to get to the office early to prepare.'

'Oh.' He lowers his eyes, like a puppy who's just been kicked. 'Okay then.'

'But we should do this again another day.'

'Sure, yeah. Totally...' He sits up on the side of the bed, turning his back to me. 'Would you mind if I still crashed here tonight? It's just that I kind of assumed that's what would be happening, and it's a little late to go walking back to my aunt's place.'

'Of course, yeah. I'll be getting up around seven, but you can sleep in and show yourself out later.'

'Alright, thanks.'

An awkward silence follows. I know I should say something to try and comfort him, but my eyelids are already drooping closed.

'Do I need to lock up or anything on the way out?' he asks.

'Just pull the door behind you. And press the button in the foyer to get out of the building.'

'What if I need to get out and come back in? For a smoke break or something.'

'I didn't know you smoked.'

'I don't usually, but sometimes I like to wake and bake. Especially when I'm staying somewhere unfamiliar.'

'Fair enough,' I yawn. 'There's a spare set of keys on the hall table.'

He says something else after this, but I don't quite catch it. My senses are already switching off, my body shutting itself down. Somewhere in the back of my mind, I'm aware I shouldn't sleep yet. I still need to brush my teeth and clean up after the sex. But it's too late. I'm already slipping away...

Something wakes me in the middle of the night. A noise on the street outside, or maybe just a bad dream. I turn over to check on Sean, wondering if he's awake too. But there's no sign of him.

The clock on the bedside table reads 02:37. He must have gotten up to go to the bathroom. Or maybe downstairs for a smoke. That must be what woke me in the first place.

With a yawn, I roll over and close my eyes. Nothing to worry about here. Everything is perfectly fine.

Twenty one

The bed is still empty when I wake up the next morning. I pat the spot where Sean was sleeping, checking for any signs of warmth. But the sheets are ice cold.

'Hello?' I call out, climbing to my feet. 'Sean?'

But there's no answer.

I trudge towards the kitchen, figuring he might have got up early to make breakfast. But there's no sign of him there. I check the bathroom, the lounge, and then the bedroom again. And that's when I discover the message waiting on my phone.

Hey man, sorry for disappearing. Had to get back to my aunt's place before she realised I was out all night.

I sigh, typing out a *no problem*. To be honest, I am a little offended that he left without saying goodbye. But now's not the time to go picking a fight. Today is promotion day, which means there's only one thing that matters. Putting my best foot forward for the meeting with Maeve.

I set out for the office at exactly eight, pocket square poking proudly from my brand-new blazer. For the first time since I arrived in Ashcross, it's actually a nice day. Sunlight blazes down from a perfect blue sky, bleaching away the town's grime. Everybody on the street has stripped down to shorts and t-shirts, with several of the pastier specimens already displaying the first signs of sunburn. I tug at the collar of my shirt, feeling a bead of sweat trickle down my back. Maybe this blazer wasn't such a bright idea after all.

JD is standing just inside the door as I approach the office. His shirtsleeves are rolled up to his bony elbows, his tie hanging in a limp loop over one shoulder. I wave at him through the glass, but he doesn't return the greeting. It's only when I get a little closer that I can make out the murderous scowl on his face.

I go to take my keycard from my wallet, wondering what's got him in such a grim mood. But it's not in its usual slot. I flip through the rest of the contents – bank cards, expired condoms, my proof of age for buying booze – but the keycard is nowhere to be seen. It must have fallen out of my pocket at some point. Probably while Sean and I were tearing each other's clothes off last night. I'll have to check the bedroom floor when I get home this evening.

'Hey, I think I forgot my keycard,' I say, looking back up at JD.

But he doesn't seem to hear me through the glass.

'I SAID I THINK I FORGOT MY KEYCARD!'

This time he does react, but not in a particularly helpful way. He shoves a finger up his nose, rolls it around from side to side, then produces a glistening blob of yellow-green snot. After examining his catch for several seconds, he flicks it at the window and wanders back over to his desk.

'COME ON!' I call after him, banging on the glass. 'ARE YOU GOING TO LET ME IN OR WHAT?'

But there's still no response. He picks up the phone and begins dialling a number, giving no indication whatsoever that he's aware of my presence. After muttering a few words into the receiver, he hangs up the phone and returns to his magazine. I try one last round of banging, smacking the glass so hard I'm afraid it's going to shatter. But he just keeps reading.

I curse him under my breath, beginning to lose patience. Does he think this is funny? Is he five fucking years old? The sun is rising higher and higher, increasing the flow of sweat down my back. I glance up and down the road, searching for another staff member I can tailgate in behind. But there's nobody in sight.

Just as I'm about to begin another round of knocking, Maeve emerges from the corridor. She's dressed in her usual dark blue suit, a pair of designer sunglasses tucked on top of her head. I let out a sigh of relief when I see her. No way JD will keep up his childish antics in front of the boss. I give the door one last knock – politely this time – and wait for him to come let me in.

But it still doesn't happen. JD remains seated at his desk, while Maeve strides over towards the door.

'Sorry!' I blurt out, as the glass swings open. 'I forgot my keycard.'

'Did you now?'

'I must have left it at home.'

'Hmmm. Isn't that interesting?' Her voice is cold as ice,

sucking the heat from the morning and making me shiver.

'Sorry. I'll make sure it doesn't happen again.'

'That's not good enough, Marcus. You know you're supposed to carry that card with you at all times.'

I wince, taken aback by the strength of her reaction. Who knew a forgotten keycard would be such a big deal? 'I can go home and get it now if you want?'

She pulls the sunglasses down over her eyes, obscuring her expression. 'Yes, I think you should go home. The only question is whether you'll be coming back.'

'Sorry... What?' I stutter. 'Why wouldn't I be coming back?'

'Because, Marcus, unless you come up with a very good explanation for what's going on here, you won't be a WellCat employee much longer.'

I stare up at my reflection in her sunglasses. Even in the darkened miniature, I can make out the look of total bewilderment on my face. 'I don't understand... What are you talking about?'

'Don't play dumb with me, Marcus. You know exactly what I'm referring to.'

'But I haven't done anything! I just forgot my key card...'

She snorts, folding her arms across her chest. 'Come on. You really expect me to believe you had nothing to do with the little break-in last night?'

'Break-in?' Shit. 'You mean there was another one?'

'Yes. There was *another one*.'

My reflection frowns back at me, wide-eyed and panicked. Could this have something to do with Noelle and the alien girl? Or was Kevin lying when he said he didn't need to get back inside the lab?' 'Do you have any idea who it was?' I ask her.

'Not yet. The cowards kept their faces covered. But the Guards will have them identified soon enough. So you might as well go ahead and tell me now – which one were you? The cow? The goat? Or the little piggy?'

'The *what*?' I groan. 'I don't know what that means! But if there was a break-in, it had nothing to do with me. I swear!'

She lifts the sunglasses up so I can get a clear view of her eyes rolling. 'Oh really? Then explain why they used your keycard to buzz into the building?'

'My keycard? But I don't know where it is. I mean, I haven't seen it since Friday. I thought I left it at home, but maybe I dropped it somewhere else. Like the bar in Galway. A burglar could have picked it up!'

'So, let me get this straight. You're telling me the card fell out of your pocket, and some opportunistic criminal just happened to stumble across it and decide to break into this office?'

'Maybe... I don't know how burglars operate. But it definitely wasn't me!'

She sighs, like this is the most tedious conversation she's ever been forced to endure. 'The problem is, this wasn't just any old burglary. The alarm system activated as soon as the perpetrators entered the building. If they were only after valuables, they could have just grabbed a few computers and run. But they didn't do that. Instead, they marched themselves straight down to the basement. To the laboratory. Because they were after one thing, and one thing only... Future Fish.'

My heart sinks. Of course this wasn't a regular burglary. Nothing in this town is ever that simple.

'Unfortunately for them,' she continues, 'the Guards arrived before they managed to get through the laboratory door. They slipped out the emergency exit and scattered into the night, like a bunch of frightened rats. But they won't get away that easily. The DNA samples they left behind are already being analysed by a specialist forensics team. And I'd bet my left foot that the trail leads back to Miss Meow.'

'Hang on!' I say, hope sparking in the darkness. 'Wouldn't that prove my innocence? If none of the DNA matches mine? I can provide a sample if you want. Blood, urine…anything!'

'You can keep your bodily fluids to yourself. Even if you weren't there on the night, how can I be sure you weren't involved? You could have given them your card, told them where the laboratory was located, then sat back with your feet up while they did all the dirty work.'

'But that's not what happened, I swear! Maybe the Guards can get the CCTV footage from the bar. They can see whoever picked up the card, and track them down, and then—'

'*Enough*,' she hisses. 'If that's the best excuse you can come up with, there's no point in wasting any more of our time.'

The world around us suddenly goes quiet. The ocean, the seagulls, the cars on the street – all the sounds of life in Ashcross, fading away into nothing. Like Maeve and I are floating through space. Just the two of us, alone in an infinite void. 'So, that's it then?' I ask. 'You're firing me?'

For just one second, I think I see the shadow of a doubt crossing her face. But it must just be a trick of the light. When she speaks again, her voice is firm with resolve. 'Yes,' she says. 'We're letting you go. Now wait here.'

She steps back inside, leaving me alone on the footpath. A few other staff members are starting to arrive now. One of them – a friendly older woman from HR – smiles and waves at me as she passes. But all I can do is blink stupidly in her direction. My mind has gone blank, unable to function. Like it's refusing to process what Maeve has just said. I stare up at the sun, sweat dripping down my forehead, and tell myself everything will be fine once she comes back outside.

She reappears a few minutes later, clutching a giant cardboard box in both arms. JD springs up from his desk to hold the door open for her.

'Here,' she says, thrusting the box into my chest. 'These are your things. Make sure it's all there before you go. Anything you leave behind will be binned.'

My arms shoot out automatically, taking hold of the box. Inside is a jumble of loose paper, chewed-up pens, and a half-eaten packet of rice cakes I was planning on finishing for breakfast. I give the sides a shake, hoping I might uncover something helpful. But nothing in the box can save me right now.

'Hang on…' I say, looking back up at Maeve. 'What about my promotion?'

She frowns, tucking her chin in towards her neck. '*Promotion*? What promotion?'

'The one you mentioned on Friday. We were supposed to talk about it this morning.'

'Oh, that. I thought I made it clear that wasn't a promotion. Not that it matters now anyway. You'll find written notice of your dismissal among the contents of that box. Needless to say, you're no longer welcome on the premises.'

She turns around, stepping past JD and into reception.

'Wait,' I say, adjusting my grip on the box. 'Please. You have to believe me.'

She sighs, glancing back over her shoulder. 'The only thing I *have* to do is look out for the best interests of this company. And that means removing any security threats.'

'But... I thought we were friends?'

'So did I, Marcus. But I'm not the one who went and betrayed the company.'

She turns back around and continues inside. JD shuts the door behind her, grinning and giving me the finger through the glass. It's only when I turn around to avoid him that I notice Dominic, Shelley and Fi standing a few metres down the footpath. I have no idea how long they've been there, or how much they've heard. But judging by the looks on their faces, they haven't missed a single humiliating detail. Shelley and Fi are whispering and laughing, while Dominic just shakes his head in disappointment. I hurry past them, too shell-shocked to say anything, and don't look back as I leave the office behind me.

I wander home in a daze, sunlight blazing down onto the back of my neck. All around me, people are laughing and playing, making the most of this rare burst of summer. An elderly couple lounge arm-in-arm on a bench. A little boy screams with delight as the waves chase him up and down the beach. And a teenaged girl – clearly mitching off school – giggles hysterically as she wipes ice cream off her boyfriend's nose.

These shameless displays of contentment only dig the knife

in deeper. At least the last time this happened – that grey winter morning in Dublin when I was fired from my first job – everybody else was miserable too. The bitter wind biting at their faces, the freezing slush seeping into their socks. But this time around, they're all having the perfect day. Enjoying their own little slice of paradise. The only person stuck in hell right now is me.

I shift the cardboard box from one arm to the other as I walk. I have no idea why I'm even bothering to keep it. It's not like it has any value, sentimental or otherwise. But the resolve required to make a decision right now – even one as simple as throwing out a boxload of junk – is totally beyond me. I'm not even sure when I decided to head home. I could just as easily have walked into the pub to drown my sorrows. Or walked into the ocean to drown myself.

The box is light, but awkward to hold up, and my arms are on fire by the time I reach the apartment. I dump it down on the hallway floor, sighing with relief as I stretch my aching muscles. But the satisfaction is short-lived. Because I have no idea what I'm supposed to do next. Getting home was the only goal I had in mind. The one thing that kept me going after Maeve left me on the footpath. But now that I'm here, it no longer feels like a destination. Just a big, empty hole with nothing to fill it.

Next thing I know, I'm kicking the box against the wall, driving my foot into the cardboard over and over. Crumpling sides, crushing staples, and ripping entire flaps clean off. The pens inside crackle, their plastic shattering, while a mug explodes into thick ceramic shards. Once the whole thing has been flattened, and there's nothing left to destroy, I collapse in a panting heap against the wall. My mind is on fire, burning with fury, but the touch of the cool plaster begins to soothe me. I close my eyes, sinking down deeper, and feel the pounding in my heart begin to slow down. Maybe I could fall asleep right here. Drift off somewhere soft and easy, where I can forget everything that's happened. And if I'm lucky, maybe never come back.

But before I have a chance to slip away, an unfamiliar noise shakes me from my reverie. A creaking sound, like footsteps on floorboards.

'Hello?' I call out, rising cautiously to my feet.

But there's no answer.

I exhale slowly, trying to remain calm. Maybe it was just my imagination. My poor battered mind losing touch with reality. But then I hear it again. A long, aching *creak* on the other side of the kitchen door.

'...Hello? Is somebody there?'

I tiptoe towards the kitchen, grasping for a rational explanation. The noise can't be coming from the neighbours – this entire top floor is empty, as is the one below. But maybe it's just a mouse. Or a leaking tap. No need to panic just yet. I push the door open as slowly as possible, revealing the long kitchen counter...the cupboards on the far wall...and the hulking figure at the head of the table.

I flinch, nearly jumping out of my skin. And then I let out a relieved little laugh. Because it's not an intruder after all. It's just Sean.

'Jesus Christ,' I grin, taking a seat in the chair opposite him. 'You scared the shit out of me.'

'Sorry,' he replies. 'I wasn't expecting you home so soon.'

'Yeah, well, neither was I. But everything's gone to shit today.'

'Did something happen at work?' he asks, in an oddly robotic voice.

'I don't want to talk about it…' I mumble, staring at the floor. The wound is still too fresh to go poking and prodding at it.

'You got in trouble, didn't you?'

'…I guess you could say that.'

'You got *fired*, didn't you?'

I nod slowly, feeling my face turn red. I guess there's no point trying to hide it.

'I'm sorry to hear that, Mark.'

'It's not your fault.'

'It was because of the keycard, wasn't it?'

I nod again, feeling my eyes begin to mist up. And then my spine suddenly stiffens. 'Hang on,' I say, looking back up. 'How did you know that? And what are you still doing here, by the way? I thought you were heading back to…'

My voice trails off, fading into silence. Because I've just realised the answer to my own question. All the pieces clicking together, like some nightmarish jigsaw puzzle. The missing keycard. Sean's disappearance last night. The break-in at the office…

'…It was you, wasn't it? You stole my keycard.'

'I'm sorry,' he replies, lowering his eyes. 'I never meant to hurt you.'

'You're *sorry*?' I laugh, the full absurdity of the situation beginning to sink in. 'Jesus Christ, you really are one of those alien freaks, aren't you? I should have realised. Should have known this was too good to be true.'

'*Alien freaks*? Don't be ridiculous. You've got it all wrong.'

'What, then? Please don't tell me you're a Catholic, because I've already had more than enough of that particular brand of rejection.'

'Catholic?' he laughs. 'I don't think we could have done the things we did last night if I was a Catholic. Not without a trip to Confession afterwards, anyway. And trust me, there's no way I'm repenting for the time we had.'

'This isn't funny!' I hiss, slamming my hands down onto the table. 'If it wasn't aliens, and it wasn't demons, then what the hell was it? You must have had some reason for breaking in.'

'Of course we had a reason...' He throws back his shoulders, puffing out his chest. 'We were trying to rescue the fish.'

'*Fish?* What fish!?'

'The Future Fish fish.'

'Oh...'

Right. I'd almost forgotten about those stupid Friends of the Fish people. It's been so long since their last email, I assumed they'd got bored and moved on to harassing somebody else. But I guess they don't give up that easily.

'Hang on,' I say, a fresh shot of fear coursing through my system. 'You said *we* had a reason. Not *I*... That means there's more than one of you, doesn't it?'

He stares down at the table, avoiding my eyes. 'You're going to be okay, Mark. Just don't panic. This will all be over soon.'

'Wait! What are you talking about? What's going on!?'

Another floorboard creaks behind me. I try to turn around, to see who's there. But it's already too late. A pair of hands clamps down on my shoulders, holding me in place.

And then everything goes black.

Twenty Two

The following seconds are pure chaos. A blindfold covers my eyes, the coarse fabric chafing against my face. I reach up to pull it off, but a pair of hands grabs my arms and forces them down to my sides. I thrash about, desperate to shake off this unseen assailant. But it's no good. They've got me pinned down. And then something starts winding itself around my shoulders. Round and round it goes, moving down to cover my elbows, my stomach, my legs. Pulling me tighter and tighter against the chair, until every muscle is immobilised.

That's when I start screaming. First at my attacker – telling them to get the hell off me. And then, when that doesn't work, I try calling out into the ether – desperately begging for help, hoping that somebody out there might hear me. But I already know there's no point. This entire floor is empty, as is the one below. I might as well be lying at the bottom of the ocean, calling up to passing ships on the surface.

The chair suddenly tilts backwards, and I brace myself for a fall. But the motion pauses half-way down. I hover for a moment in mid-air, and then the wooden legs start screeching across the kitchen floor. Somebody must be pulling me, dragging the chair over towards the lounge. There's a bump as the legs cross the threshold, followed by a swooping semi-circular motion, and then a sudden stop. The chair is slowly set back upright. I hear voices whispering, curtains being drawn. And then the room goes quiet.

For a few seconds, everything is perfectly still. Like the eye of the storm.

And then somebody rips the blindfold off my head. The lounge is dark and gloomy, all the lights switched off and the sun shut out behind the curtains. Sitting opposite me, on another one of the kitchen chairs, is a tall, shadowy figure dressed all in black. A shiver runs down my spine as I try to focus on his face. Even through the darkness, I can tell there's something wrong with it. The ears are too long and pointed, the nose too flat and round. For a second, I wonder if my eyes are playing tricks on me. But then I realise it's a mask. A rubber pig mask.

Another shiver as Maeve's words outside the office replay in my mind. *Which one were you? The cow? The goat? Or the little piggy?*

'Hello Mark,' says the figure, his pig-mouth remaining perfectly still. 'So nice of you to join us.'

His accent is similar to Sean's, only without the laid-back drawl. In one hand, he holds a long, rounded object, tapping it up and down against the palm of the other. I squint, struggling to make out the shape in the darkness. And then I wish I hadn't.

It's a baseball bat. This maniac has got a fucking baseball bat!

I try to push myself back, to get out of striking range. But I'm still completely paralysed. Looking down, I discover layers and layers of duct tape wound around my body.

'HELP!' I scream. 'PLEASE, SOMEBODY HELP ME!'

'Shut your mouth,' hisses Pig. 'Or we'll have to tape that up too.'

'Just take it easy, Mark,' says Sean. 'Everything's going to be okay.'

I hadn't even noticed him before, hiding in the shadows behind Pig. He slouches forward on the couch, a rubber goat mask dangling between his fingers. I do as he tells me, closing my mouth and trying to hold down my panic. But then I remember he's not on my side any more. He was never on my side to begin with.

'HELP ME! I'M IN APARTMENT SIX ONE SIX! SOME MASK-WEARING WEIRDOS HAVE GOT ME ALL TIED UP!'

Pig grunts and clicks his fingers. Another figure, whose presence I wasn't aware of, comes scuttling out from behind me. This one appears to be a woman, long blonde hair spilling out from beneath her cow mask. In her hands is the largest roll of duct tape I've ever seen.

'Don't even think about biting,' she says, in a vaguely Russian accent.

She peels off a generous length of tape and reaches out for my face. I pull my head back and to the side, desperate to escape the sticky strip. But there's only so far I can go. After a brief, pointless struggle, she succeeds in sealing up my mouth. She winds the roll around my head for good measure, then smooths down the loose end with a firm slap.

I fire off a string of curses as she returns to her station behind me. But the only sound that escapes the tape is a limp, lifeless whimper.

'Much better,' says Pig. 'Now, if you're done whining like a little bitch, maybe we can finally get down to business.'

He drags the chair closer, drawing his face up just inches from mine. The stench of rubber and bad breath floods my nostrils. Through the mouth hole of his mask, I can just make out the ends of a greasy black moustache. No wonder they chose Sean rather than this guy for the role of seducer...

'Don't be frightened,' he says, in the soothing tone of a serial killer. 'We're not going to hurt you...unless you give us a good reason to.'

'We're not going to hurt him *full stop*,' says Sean.

'Shut your mouth,' growls Pig, glancing back over his shoulder. 'We tried your sexy spy routine, and it got us nowhere. So now we're doing things my way.'

'If you don't like it, you can leave,' adds Cow.

Sean grunts and shakes his head, but he doesn't say anything else. Clearly, the other two are further up the pecking order than he is.

'As I was saying,' continues Pig, 'before I was so rudely interrupted... We don't want to hurt you. And as long as you cooperate, we won't have to. That sounds reasonable, right?'

I roll my eyes, not wanting to give him the satisfaction of

playing along with his little tough-guy act. But then he starts tapping the baseball bat up and down again. 'Mmmhmm,' I mumble, the sound spluttering out through the tape.

'Excellent. Now I'm sure you're wondering what exactly you can do to help us. But before we get into that, allow me to give you a proper introduction...' He pauses for dramatic effect, and I resist the urge for another eye roll. 'We're Friends of the Fish, an underground animal liberation movement dedicated to the emancipation of our piscine cousins. We rescue fish from farms, aquariums, and all other sites of abuse. Why? Because fish are people too!'

'Fish are people too!' echoes Cow, her voice swelling with passion.

'Fish are people too...' mumbles Sean, slouching down further on the couch.

'We've had WellCat on our radar for years,' says Pig. 'Ever since you massacred those innocent salmon on your failed farm. We were the ones who launched the campaign against you, recruiting hundreds of kind-hearted activists to our cause. The movement may have quieted down for a while, but when we heard about Future Fish, we realised this was the perfect opportunity to start it back up. We won't let you get away with your sick experiments – breeding an army of GMO Franken-fish for you to torture and exploit. We'll rescue those poor creatures from your laboratory, whatever it takes.'

I shake my head, trying to explain that this is all total nonsense. But Pig isn't listening.

'The only problem,' he says, 'is that you've got the place locked up tighter than a nun's panties. We thought borrowing your keycard would be enough to get us inside, but it turns out we were mistaken. It turns out we also need a code...'

My eyes widen. So *that's* what this is all about? They want the code to the lab, and they think I can give it to them! I try to open my mouth, to explain that they've got the wrong person. But the duct tape has still got me gagged.

'So,' concludes Pig, lifting the baseball bat onto his shoulder. 'Are you going to be a good boy and give us what we need? Or are we going to have to force it out of you?'

Cow's fingers dance across the back of my head. She rips the duct tape off in one smooth motion, taking several clumps of hair with it.

'I don't know any codes,' I gasp, wincing at the stinging pain in my scalp. 'You've got the wrong person.'

'Bullshit!' grunts Pig.

'I swear. I'm just a minimum-wage Customer Service Assistant. What goes on in the lab has nothing to do with me.'

'And how do we know you're telling the truth?' He leans forward, until his rubber snout is practically tickling my nose. As I stare into the blackened nostrils, I can't help wondering where you'd even get a mask like that. It's too Uncanny Valley for a school play, but not quite horrific enough for Halloween. Must be some weird fetish thing.

'Because I have no reason to lie,' I say. 'I don't give a shit if you break in again. The company just fired me, so it's not like I'm feeling particularly loyal right now.'

He hesitates, pitching a look over at Cow. 'Even if that's true,' he continues, 'there must be some way you could get the code. Phone up a colleague and ask them to tell you. Log into the computer system and figure out where the passwords are stored… I'm sure you can come up with something.'

I shake my head, beginning to lose patience. 'Didn't you hear what I just said? I don't work there any more. I don't *have* any colleagues. Because the three of you decided to break in with my keycard and get me fired. If you were planning on kidnapping me, you really should have done that first. Because there's literally no way I can get you dumbasses the code now.'

'Watch your mouth,' snarls Pig, hitting me with a hot spray of spittle. 'And I hope for your sake that's not true. After all, there's not much reason for us to keep you alive if you can't deliver that code.'

A fresh tremor of fear rumbles through me. I glance over at Sean, hoping for another intervention. But he's just playing around with his goat mask again. Meanwhile, Cow has emerged from behind me, strutting over to Pig and whispering something in his ear. I can't make out what they're saying, but I can tell from the way Pig is nodding that I'm not going to like it.

'Maybe you just need some time to think it over,' he says. 'I bet a few hours in that chair would help jog your memory. Or a few days, if that's what it takes. Without food. Without water. Without toilet privileges. We'll leave your mouth open, so you can let us know if you have any bright ideas. But don't even think about screaming, or we'll shut you up for good. Understood?'

I remain silent, eyes fixed on Sean. But he still won't look at me.

'I'll take that as a *yes*,' says Pig, following my gaze over towards the couch. 'And to make things easier for you, we'll even help block out any distractions.'

Cow steps towards me, holding the blindfold out in front of her. And then everything goes black again.

All sense of time dissolves in the darkness. The only indication of the hours passing, of day advancing on towards night, is a growing stiffness in my neck and shoulders. I hear voices murmuring, feet pacing, and doors slamming shut. But nobody speaks to me, and I speak to nobody. At one point, my phone starts vibrating in my pocket. I strain against the tape, trying to slip a hand down and reach it. But I can't move a muscle. After a few seconds, the ringing stops, and silence settles back over the room.

As the adrenaline wears off, the full weight of the situation begins to sink in. Pig and co. can't keep me locked up here forever – sooner or later, one way or another, this will have to end. And there are only three possible ways I can see that unfolding.

Number one – the Guards arrive and rescue me. A nice thought, but not very likely. I was ambushed inside my own home, which means there were no witnesses. And since I no longer have a job to show up for, or any friends expecting to see me, nobody is even going to notice I'm missing.

Number two – they let me go. This one seems even less likely. Besides the fact that I'll never be able to give them what they want, it would be far too risky to just turn me loose. I could march straight up to the Garda station and report everything that's happened. Pig and Cow may have kept their faces covered, but I could describe Sean in perfect detail. From the tattoos on his arms to the moles on his ass. Which leaves me with…

Number three – they kill me.

It's hard to tell if they'd really go that far. But I wouldn't put it past them to try. Pig certainly seems unhinged enough to hurt somebody, and I can't imagine Cow raising any moral concerns. Even if Sean tried to stop them, he'd be outnumbered two to one.

I wonder how they'd do it, when the time came. Bash my brains in with the baseball bat? Duct tape a plastic bag over my head? Or simply leave me here in the apartment, tied up and alone, until dehydration or deep-vein thrombosis finished me off? It's funny, but the thought of meeting such a gruesome end doesn't actually sound all that bad right now. Sure, the pain would be unpleasant. But the part that comes after – the actual *being dead* – might kind of be a relief.

After all, it's not like my future is looking particularly bright right now. My career is in ruins, my *boyfriend* is a terrorist, and as soon as next month's rent is due, my landlord is going to be evicting me. So, what am I supposed to do now? Move back in with my parents? Start another round of applications and interviews, hoping somebody out there might be desperate enough to hire me? And the best-case scenario, the only possible light at the end of the tunnel, is that I find another job and the cycle starts all over?

Well, fuck that. I've had enough. Let Pig and Cow do their worst.

I drift in and out of consciousness, drool soaking into the fabric of the blindfold. Just as I'm finally slipping off into a proper sleep, somebody rouses me with a shake of my shoulder.

'Mark, Mark? Can you hear me?'

It's Sean.

'I hear you.'

'I'm taking the blindfold off. Please don't scream.'

His hand touches my head, and light floods back into the world. I squint at the sudden brightness, surprised it's already morning. But then I realise the light is coming from the ceiling. The sliver of sky outside the curtains is pitch-black.

'What time is it?' I groan, feeling like I've just stepped off a transatlantic flight.

'Nearly one am. I've been waiting for the others to leave me alone on the nightshift so I could talk to you properly.' He sits down in the chair opposite, smiling sheepishly as he fiddles around with the blindfold.

I glare back at him. Without Pig and Cow around to make him look like the Good Cop, all my resentment has suddenly come rushing back. 'I thought they were your friends. Why couldn't you talk to me in front of them?'

'They're not my friends. Or at least, Magda isn't. Carl used to be...'

'Well, they're clearly psychopaths, whoever they are.'

He sighs. 'This isn't how it was supposed to be. We're meant to be a non-violent organisation, opposed to all forms of captivity – including human. But Carl is desperate to recapture the glory days of the first anti-WellCat campaign. And ever since he started dating Magda, she's been egging him on to do crazier and crazier things. She's the one who convinced him to kidnap you, so we could try and get the code for the lab.'

'But I don't know the stupid code. I swear!'

'I believe you,' he says. 'You just need to sit tight, and the others will come around eventually.'

'Why don't you just let me go, before they get back? You said they're gone for the night, right?'

'I wish I could,' he sighs. 'But Magda would kill me if she found out I untied you. And there's no way they'd believe you escaped by yourself. I could get you a glass of water though? Or something to eat? Maybe massage your muscles, if you're starting to get cramps?'

I turn my head, looking as far away from him as my neck will allow. 'I don't want anything from you.'

'Please. Let me help. I really do care about you, you know...' He scoots his chair over to the side, positioning himself back into my line of sight. I immediately jerk my head up towards the ceiling.

'How can you say that?' I ask, neck muscles straining. 'Our entire relationship has been a lie. All that stuff about visiting family and taking a gap year in Ashcross was just a cover story so you could get your hands on Future Fish, wasn't it? Do you even have an aunt?'

He shakes his head.

'Jesus Christ!'

'Listen, Mark. It's true I was playing a role at the beginning. But after all the time we spent together, my feelings started getting real. How could they not, with a guy as amazing as you?'

'Yeah right. I should have known somebody like you would never really be interested in me. You're a nine out of ten, and I'm a five at best.'

'What if I like fives? I've spent my entire life surrounded by tens. Every asshole in LA is an actor, a model, a *social media influencer*. Do you have any idea how tedious those people can be? What a bunch of desperate try-hards they all are? It's refreshing to meet somebody like you. Somebody who's comfortable with their own averageness. Who doesn't try to be anything special.'

'So you like me because I'm mediocre? Gee, thanks Sean. That makes me feel so much better.'

'No, that's not what I meant! I was just—'

A knock at the front door cuts him off mid-sentence.

'Who's that?' he asks, forehead scrunching.

'How the hell should I know? Probably your stupid friends coming back to torture me some more.'

'No. They're not due back till morning. And besides, they've got your spare key. They wouldn't need to knock.'

'Well, maybe they forgot it. It's not like I'm expecting any guests at one o'clock in the morning.'

Another round of knocking, louder this time.

'Alright,' he whispers, tiptoeing towards the hallway. 'I'll go take a look. You wait here. And don't move a muscle.'

'Sure,' I reply, glancing down at the layers of duct tape covering my body. 'I'll try not to.'

Twenty Three

I cock my ear towards the front door, struggling to work out who the late-night caller could be. Sean seemed pretty convinced that it wasn't Cow or Pig, but who else would come knocking at one o'clock in the morning? A fast-food delivery driver with the wrong address? A shit-faced businessman who can't remember which floor he lives on? Or just a disgruntled neighbour, come to complain about all the noise? Maybe I should start screaming again. Hope that whoever's out there gets suspicious enough to call the Guards.

I listen carefully, waiting for the sound of the door clicking open. But before I can start calling for help, I hear Sean let out a startled grunt. A female voice mutters something in response. I can't make out what she's saying, but I'm pretty sure it's not Cow. Sean starts to reply, his voice swelling with indignation.

But then he stops abruptly. There's a tense silence, followed by more muttering back and forth, and then several sets of footsteps moving up the hallway.

Sean re-enters the room a few seconds later. He moves slowly, hands folded on top of his head. This strikes me as an odd way to be walking, until I see the barrel of a rifle follow him through the doorway. It's a rusty old thing – the sort farmers use to scare off foxes – but still perfectly capable of blowing somebody's brains out. I hold my breath as the person with their finger on the trigger emerges into view.

It's a mousy-haired girl, dressed in a baggy grey hoodie and laddered black leggings. I recognise her straightaway. The girl from the alien video. But what the hell is she doing in my apartment? And why is she pointing a rifle at Sean?

As if on cue, a second figure comes waltzing in behind her. And this one needs no introduction.

'Noelle!'

'Jesus Christ, Mark!' Her eyes widen as she takes in the duct tape holding me to the chair. 'Are you alright?'

'I'm fine,' I laugh, giddy with relief. 'Just a little bit stiff.'

'Let's get this shite off you, so.'

She hurries over and starts unpeeling the tape from my arms. The skin underneath is red and raw, but it feels good to regain some movement. 'Thank you,' I mumble, still trying to process her arrival. 'But what are you even doing here? It's one o'clock in the morning…'

'I was just coming up to borrow some sugar.'

'Really?'

'No, you eejit! I'm here to rescue you.'

'But…how did you know? I shouted as loud as I could, but I didn't think anybody would hear me.'

'I didn't hear a thing. But I did spot some suspicious-looking characters taking the lift up to the top floor…' She shoots a dirty look at Sean, who's pinned face-to-the-wall by the alien girl's rifle. 'Then Sally recognised their van in the car park. She's been staking out the office, and she'd seen them trying to break in.'

'They didn't even change their plates,' says Sally. 'Amateurs.'

'I tried ringing you to make sure you were alright,' continues Noelle. 'But you didn't pick up. That's when I started getting nervous. We decided to keep an eye out, waiting for their van to leave, then come up and check on you. And it's a good thing we did!'

I stretch out a freshly freed arm, wincing at the stony stiffness. 'Thanks. But wouldn't it have been easier just to call the Guards? You could have gotten yourselves hurt.'

Noelle hesitates, eyes flickering over towards Sally. 'We thought the situation was a bit delicate to go getting the law involved. And besides, Sally was confident she could handle this lot herself.'

'I've seen worse,' says Sally, jabbing the rifle into Sean's kidney for emphasis.

'Well, thank you either way,' I say. 'I don't know what would have happened if you hadn't arrived.'

'No worries,' says Noelle, removing the last strip of tape from my ankle. 'That's what friends are for, isn't it? You'd have done the same for me.'

I stand up slowly, my legs shaky and uncertain after being stuck in the same position for so long. Somewhere in the back of my mind, I wonder if Noelle is right. Would I really have done the same thing for her? But now's not the time for soul-searching. Noelle is already sidling over towards Sean, eyeing him up with intense curiosity.

'Any idea who this guy is?' she asks, turning towards Sally.

'Not a clue. He's no extra-terrestrial investigator though – I can tell you that much.'

'For your information-' begins Sean, glancing back over his shoulder. But Sally cuts him off with another jab of the rifle.

'Nobody asked you, you prick.'

'His name is Sean,' I sigh, cracking my neck from side to side. 'He's one of those Friends of the Fish people. The ones who sent WellCat all the angry emails.'

'Ah ha,' says Noelle, eyes lighting up. 'So they were serious after all… But how did he end up in your apartment?'

'It's a long story,' I mumble, face turning red. 'We were sort of going out for a few weeks. Or at least, I thought we were. But it turns out he was only using me to get to Future Fish.'

Noelle gives him another once-over, nodding in approval. 'I can see how he drew you in. It's not every day you encounter such a fine specimen in Ashcross.'

'Thanks lady,' says Sean, earning another dig from Sally.

'I don't get it…' she says. 'Why are a bunch of animal rights activists so interested in an extra-terrestrial specimen?'

'Because they don't think Future Fish is an alien,' I sigh, struggling to believe I'm actually having this conversation. 'They've convinced themselves it's some sort of animal experiment, and they want to get inside the lab and rescue the fish.'

Sally snorts.

'Something funny?' asks Sean, spinning around to face her.

'Sorry,' she smirks, clearly not sorry. 'It's just, even if that was true, who cares about a bunch of stupid fish?'

'Fish aren't stupid,' he growls. 'That's a myth propagated by the seafood industry.'

'Cop on, would you?' says Sally. 'I've taken shits with more intelligence than your average fish.'

He balls his hands up into fists, looking awfully brave for a man with a gun in his face. 'Why is intelligence so important, anyway? Why should that determine whether somebody lives or dies? You believe in aliens, right? So how would you feel if some super-smart species landed on Earth and starting harvesting humans? Would you be totally cool with it, since they're more intelligent than us? Would you lay down in front of their spaceship, cover yourself in barbecue sauce, and say *come on over Daddy and eat me up?* Somehow, I don't think so.'

She takes a step forward, pressing the barrel of the rifle into his forehead. 'First of all, no close encounters on record have ever involved an extra-terrestrial attempting to *eat* a person. But if an alien ever did try to mess with me, I'd shoot it right in its poxy face. Now, when's the last time you saw a fish who was armed and dangerous?'

'Here now,' says Noelle, pulling Sally gently backwards. 'This is a fascinating conversation, but I think we'd better focus on the current situation. The rest of those Fish lads could be back any moment, and we should probably be gone before that happens.'

'We still haven't decided what to do with *him*,' says Sally, scowling at Sean.

'Good point,' says Noelle. 'What do you think, Mark? Is it safe to let him go?'

I shrug my shoulders, not wanting to get involved. My feelings towards Sean are already complicated enough without having to decide whether he gets kneecapped.

'We can't just turn him loose,' says Sally. 'He could call for backup and have those other wankers on our tail before we're even out the door.'

'I wouldn't do that,' says Sean, holding his head up high. 'Not that I give a damn what happens to *you*. But I don't want to put Mark in any more danger.'

Sally lets out another snort. 'As if we're just going to take your word for it. How thick do you think we are?'

'I'm not asking you to just *take my word for it*.' He brushes the rifle aside and walks over to the bookcase, where the roll of duct tape lies waiting. 'You can tie me to the chair. That way you won't have to worry about me pulling any funny business. And the others won't blame me for letting Mark escape. I can say there were two of you. And you had a gun. There was nothing I could do.'

Sally's eyes narrow, but Noelle nods her approval. 'Sounds reasonable to me. As long as we can do it quickly.'

'We just need to make it look convincing,' says Sean. 'Like there was some sort of struggle.'

He grabs the cushions off the couch and begins tossing them over his shoulder. One knocks a picture frame clean off the wall, while another hits Noelle square in the face. He picks up a lamp next, rolling its weight around in the palm of his hand, then hurls it full force against the coffee table. A million shards of glass explode across the room.

'Jesus Christ!' I shout, shielding my eyes. 'What the hell are you doing? I *would* like to get my deposit on this place back, you know.'

'Sorry,' he says, with a sheepish smile. And then, turning towards Sally: 'I need you to hit me.'

She blinks. 'Sorry, what?'

'I said, I need you to hit me. In the face, ideally. I don't want them thinking I went down without a fight.'

She pauses to consider this, then shrugs and tucks the gun under one arm. 'If you insist…'

Her knuckles launch directly into his eye socket, connecting with a bone-shattering *crack*. He winces, doubling over in pain, then pulls himself slowly back upright. 'Once more,' he groans. 'In the mouth this time.'

She takes the rifle in both hands, spinning it around a hundred and eighty degrees, then thrusts the butt into his teeth.

'Fucking hell!' he cries, raising a hand to his lips. His fingers come away with a hot, red stain. 'Now, for the finishing touch, any chance you could fire off a few rounds? Not at me, obviously. But into the wall or something? Just to prove there really was a gun.'

'Hang on!' I say. 'You can't seriously—'

But it's too late. She swings the barrel of the rifle up towards the ceiling, squeezes one eye shut, and then…

BOOM!

A cloud of smoke and debris engulfs the room. I cough, waving a hand in front of my face, and stare up in horror as the dust begins to settle. A jagged black hole runs clean through the ceiling.

I'm never getting that deposit back.

'Alrighty,' says Sean, surveying his work. 'I think that should do it. The only thing left now is getting me tied down to that chair.'

He offers the duct tape to Sally, but she recoils from his touch. 'Not a chance. It's one thing smacking you around a bit, but there's no way I'm getting all up close and personal like that. Somebody else can do it.'

He turns towards Noelle, licking a sticky strand of blood from between his lips.

'Maybe you should do it,' she whispers, nudging me in the ribs. 'Probably easiest that way.'

'I don't want to get all up close and personal with him either!'

'Come on,' she says, with an unsubtle wink. 'Surely the two of yous have already crossed that bridge?'

'Oh, you'd better believe we've crossed it,' says Sean, puffing his chest out like a horny pigeon. 'East to West and West to East, if you know what I mean.'

'Good for you,' says Noelle. 'You've got to enjoy it while you're young. Men my age just don't have the stamina any more.'

'Jesus Christ!' I groan, surprised they haven't started high-fiving. 'Fine. I'll do it. Just shut up, the pair of you.'

Sean grins and tosses me the tape. I pull a long, snakelike strip loose as he strides over to the chair and assumes the position. With a silent prayer that this will all be over quickly, I bend over and start in on his right forearm. Round and round winds the tape, covering his tattoos up one by one.

'Hey,' he whispers, as I move across to the left arm. 'Is it just me, or is this kind of hot?'

I ignore him, pulling the tape a little tighter. Once I've finished his arms, I move down to his stomach, his thighs, and finally his ankles.

'There,' I say, standing back up. 'All done.'

He strains his arms against the tape, and then his legs. 'Feels good. No way am I getting out of this.'

'Brilliant,' says Noelle, clapping her hands. 'If that's everything, we should probably be getting a move on.'

'Fine by me,' says Sally, snatching the duct tape from my hands and marching straight out the door.

I listen as her footsteps disappear down the hallway, then turn uncertainly towards Noelle. It's still not clear where they're going. Or whether I'm invited...

'Come on,' she says, reading my mind. 'It's not safe for you to stay here. And not safe in my flat any more either. We'll head over to Sally's place and lie low while we figure out our next move.'

I nod. Sally's place sounds about as comforting as the Seventh Circle of Hell, but it's not like I have any better ideas.

'Probably best you call in sick to work tomorrow, too,' says Noelle. 'You don't want those gobshites showing up at the office and causing any more trouble.'

'No need to worry about that,' I tell her. 'I don't have a job to call in to any more. Maeve fired me after they used my keycard to break in.'

'Jesus Christ... I'm sorry.'

'It's fine,' I shrug. 'It doesn't matter any more.'

'Alright, well, we should probably get going.' She glances

over at Sean, who's been shamelessly eavesdropping on our conversation. 'I'll give you a few minutes to tie up any loose ends. We'll be down in the foyer when you're ready.'

I watch her shuffle out of the room, pulling a pack of cigarettes from her pocket, then turn around to face Sean.

'So,' he says, with a melodramatic sigh. 'I suppose this is goodbye.'

I roll my eyes, not wanting to dignify his nonsense with a response. But something about the sight of him tied to that chair – all bruised and battered and by himself – begins to soften the edges of my resentment.

'You're sure you'll be alright?' I ask, lowering myself onto the arm of the sofa.

'I'll be fine. I've just got to sit back and relax until the others arrive.'

'But what if they don't come back? You could be stuck in that chair forever.'

'Don't worry. They'll be here at eight am sharp. Magda is a stickler for punctuality.'

'What if something goes wrong though? Like they crash their car, or the Guards finally catch up with them?'

He smiles, flashing me a row of blood-stained teeth. 'How about this? I'll send you a text message once I'm free. That way you won't have to worry about me all day.'

'I'm not worried,' I mutter, staring up at the hole in the ceiling so he can't see me blush. 'I just don't want somebody dying in my apartment.'

'Of course not. You wouldn't want me haunting you for all eternity.'

I laugh, despite myself, and glance back down at his gory grin. 'Anyway...' I say. 'I should really get going.'

'Wait, Mark. Before you go...' His expression suddenly changes, the smile fading into something sadder. 'I really am sorry, you know. For lying to you. For getting you fired. For everything...'

I stare into his eyes, trying to untangle my own twisted feelings. But I have no idea where to even begin. The knot is pulled too tight.

'Goodbye Sean.'

Twenty four

Noelle's bright red sports car carries us high into the hills, leaving the feeble lights of Ashcross far behind us. Just as the dashboard clock flashes 02:30, she turns off the main road and onto a winding, tree-lined drive. The headlights twist and turn through the undergrowth, picking out strange shapes in the shadows. I stare out of the back window, too tired to make conversation, and begin to wonder what exactly this safehouse of Sally's is going to look like. An abandoned warehouse, accessible only through a hole in a barbed-wire fence? Or some unlicensed pub with a secret staircase underneath the bar? As we clear the trees, emerging onto a lonely, windswept clifftop, our destination finally looms up before us…

And it's a cottage. A cosy little hideaway, complete with thatched roof and whitewashed walls. Like something straight out of a postcard. Nestled amongst the flowerbeds and ornamental shrubberies is an engraved stone reading: *Our Lady of Hope – Bed and Breakfast.*

'*This* is the place?' I ask, trying not to laugh.

'Why?' says Sally from the passenger seat. 'You got a problem?'

'No, no. It's just, I wasn't expecting something quite so... quaint.'

She unbuckles her seatbelt and glares back at me. 'You're welcome to leave if you don't like it. You could probably make it back to town by sunrise if you hurried. Just try not to get yourself kidnapped again along the way.'

'Come on,' groans Noelle, popping open her door. 'Let's just get inside.'

We trudge across the car park in single file, our footsteps crunching on the loose gravel. Sally pauses in front of the *Céad Míle Fáilte* doormat and presses her ear to the letterbox.

'Sounds like the coast is clear,' she whispers. 'But in case we do run into anybody, let me do the talking.'

The door opens onto a small foyer lined with fake flowers and sightseeing pamphlets. The lights are all switched on, but there's no sign of any staff on duty. Instead, a life-sized portrait of the Virgin Mary hangs above the desk, like an immaculately-conceived receptionist waiting to check us in. I can't help thinking of Kevin when I see her. It's been weeks since we last spoke, and I suddenly realise how much I've been missing him.

Sally leads us past the desk and down a narrow, twisting corridor. She pauses outside room thirteen, bending over to peep through the keyhole before unlocking the door.

Inside is an explosion of pink, like somebody's just butchered an entire flock of flamingos. The two twin beds, the armchair in the corner – even the toilet bowl in the en suite bathroom – every single surface is the same hideous shade.

'Here we are,' says Noelle.'Home sweet home.'

'It's, eh…lovely,' I lie, hoping to make up for my previous insult. But Sally just rolls her eyes and drops down onto one of the beds.

Noelle tosses her handbag onto the other duvet, leaving me to claim the armchair in the corner. The cushions are made of some glossy faux velvet that makes me shudder as soon as I sit down. I slide my phone out of my pocket, half-hoping to find a message from Sean. But the screen is blank. My inbox is empty. I set the phone down with a sigh and try to rearrange the cushions into a vaguely comfortable position.

When I look back up, Noelle has changed into a pair of fluffy flannel pyjamas. She positions herself in front of the mirror and begins applying a thick layer of night cream. It's funny seeing her like this – so relaxed and unguarded. So different from the Noelle I knew at work. All of a sudden, the guilt I've been forcing down comes bursting back to the surface.

'I… I'm sorry, by the way.'

'What's that?' she says, raising an eyebrow in the mirror.

'I said, I'm sorry. For what happened back at the office. For ratting you out to Maeve.'

'Ah, *that*.' She tries to laugh it off, but she can't hide the twinge of emotion from her freshly moisturised face.'Don't worry about it. It's water under the bridge.'

'But what I did was awful… I betrayed you. Stabbed you in the back.'

'Look,' she sighs, turning around to face me. 'You were in a difficult position, I get that. And I've worked with Maeve long enough to know she has a knack for bringing out the worst in people.'

'It wasn't just Maeve, though. It was me. I let the bullshit get into my head. I let it turn me into an asshole. I thought they were my friends – Maeve and the others. But she never gave a shit about me. I was just another cog in her machine. And as soon as I stopped being useful, she tossed me out without a second thought.' I pause, holding back a wave of hot, angry tears. 'Meanwhile, I treated you like dirt, but you were still there when I needed you. You've been a true friend, and I've been a terrible one. And there's no way I can ever make it up to you.'

'Ah, Mark,' she says, getting a little teary-eyed herself. 'You're not a bad friend. Sure, you were acting like a bit of an eejit back there, but everybody makes mistakes. You don't need to do anything to make it up to me.'

'Are you sure?'

'Of course I am!'

'Alright,' I sniff, a little bit of weight lifting off my shoulders. 'Thank you. And sorry again.'

Noelle smiles and turns back to the mirror. I pick up my phone, about to check again for a message from Sean. But before I can wake up the screen, Sally clears her throat from the far side of the room. She's been so quiet since we got here, I'd almost forgotten she was there.

'Actually,' she says, glaring over at me. 'There is one thing you could do to make it up to her.'

'No,' says Noelle. 'Not now. We've all had a long enough night already. Let's save the scheming for tomorrow.'

'And *why* have we had such a long night?' asks Sally. 'Because we've been busy saving Mark's skin, that's why. Paying us back for our trouble is the least he could do.'

'Come on. I told you not to try and drag him into this. It's too dangerous.'

'So what? Didn't we put ourselves in danger rescuing him? We could use an extra pair of hands. And I'd feel a lot better about him hanging around if he had a little dirt on his.'

'He'd never agree to it. Especially not the current plan. Mark's not like us.'

Sally snorts. 'He's a coward, you mean?'

'I never said that.'

'Eh…hello?' I say, feeling the blood rush to my cheeks. 'I'm right here, you know.'

Sally rolls her eyes, standing up and storming off into the bathroom. Noelle flinches as the door slams shut behind her.

'Sorry about that,' she sighs. 'She means well, but she sometimes has a bit of a one-track mind.'

'It's fine,' I shrug. 'I don't care what she thinks. But aren't you at least going to tell me what the two of you are planning?'

She hesitates, glancing over at the bathroom door. The splashing of the shower has just started up on the other side. 'It's a little complicated. But basically, what we're trying to do is get back inside the lab so Sally can record some footage for her next video. What little I got last time wasn't much use to her.'

'And she wants me to help you break in?'

She nods. 'It's a three-person job, she reckons. And there's nobody else we can ask.'

I hesitate, shifting around in the armchair. As annoying as Sally is, she did have a point earlier. I do owe Noelle for rescuing me. Not to mention ratting her out to Maeve...

'Alright, fine. I'll help you.'

Her eyes widen. 'You will?'

'Sure, why not? But I do it on one condition.'

'And what's that?'

'You tell me why *you're* doing this. Why you'd throw your job away just to help some random crazy. I know you don't actually believe in any of that alien bullshit.'

She sits down on the bed, lips twitching into a grin. 'I wouldn't say I *don't* believe in it. I mean, you should hear Sally when she gets going. She's got this whole spiel about how there are billions and billions of planets out there, so when you think about it, it's actually more unlikely that there *wouldn't* be other forms of intelligent life.'

'Come on,' I say. 'Cut the crap. How did the two of you even get in touch in the first place?'

'Alright,' she sighs, reaching down for her handbag at the foot of the bed. 'I suppose you have a right to know, if you're seriously considering helping us.'

Her hand disappears inside the purse, re-emerging a moment later with an ornate silver picture frame. It's the photo of her mother. The one she used to keep on her desk.

'That's her,' she says, pointing at the mask-wearing nurse in the background. 'That's Sally.'

'Oh...'

I stare down at the photo, feeling like a fool. It was sitting right in front of me the entire time.

'She was Mam's carer. Not the main one, mind you, but she covered whenever Lisa wasn't available. We never really spoke much at the time. She can be a little prickly, as I'm sure you've picked up, and I usually tried to leave her a wide berth. But still, you develop a certain sort of bond in those situations. Sharing the responsibility for somebody else's pain. Knowing she was there for Mam when I couldn't be. We were a team of sorts, passing the baton back and forth.

'After Mam passed away, we didn't keep in touch. I went months without even thinking about her. But when I saw her pop up in that video, it was like somebody slapping me across the face. I had no idea she was into all that conspiracy theory stuff. I thought she was just your average angsty teenager who spent too much time online. But for some reason, I felt compelled to reach out to her. To make sure she was alright. That she wasn't going to end up homeless or anything after she talked about quitting her job. Of course, she remembered me right away. Remembered I worked at WellCat, too, and it wasn't long until she started pestering me for help.

'I said no at first. All her talk about aliens and spaceships meant nothing to me. But then I started thinking, *why the hell not?* It's not like I cared about losing the job. I'd been looking for an excuse to get out of Ashcross anyway. Waiting for somebody to come along and give me a push... Hunting aliens with a teenager wasn't quite what I'd been imagining, but I figured, hey, maybe it could be fun. At least I'd get to piss Maeve off one last time on my way out.'

'*Fun?*' I groan. 'I don't think that's quite the word I'd use.'

'You know what I mean. At least I'm getting out and doing

something with my life, instead of sitting around in the office all day. I was never really happy in that place. And I'm pretty sure you weren't either.'

I sigh, massaging my fingers into my aching skull. She might be onto something. But I'm too tired to think about it right now. 'Look, whatever your reasons are, it doesn't matter. I still want to help you.'

'I appreciate the offer,' she says. 'I really do. But I'm not sure that's such a good idea. If things go badly – which they easily might – you could end up in serious trouble.'

'So what? I've already lost my job. There's nothing more Maeve can do to me.'

'It's not just Maeve you need to worry about though. The stakes are higher this time around. You could get yourself hurt. Maybe even end up in prison.'

'*Prison?*' At first, I think she's joking. But there's no sign of the usual twinkle in her eye. 'Would they really lock you up, just for sneaking into the office? I mean, you're only going to record another video, right? It's not like we'd be stealing anything. Or hurting anybody.'

'We wouldn't *actually* be hurting anybody, no. But we might have to—'

The bathroom door slams open, making both of us jump. Sally steps out in a fluffy white bathrobe, her hair dripping dark patches onto the bright pink carpet.

'Everything alright?' she asks, shooting me a suspicious glance.

'Grand, yeah,' says Noelle. 'We were just having a little chat.'

'About what?'

'Here,' says Noelle, jumping up from the bed. 'If we're going to stay up all night gossiping, we might as well put on some tea.'

She shuffles over to the coffee table and switches on the kettle. Sally and I watch on in silence as she carefully brews three cups of tea. She moves slowly, methodically, like an actor in an instructional video. It's only when she's handed each of us a mug, sat down on the bed, stood back up to add a little more milk, and then sat down again, that I realise she's been stalling.

'So…' she says, clearing her throat. 'Mark was just saying he might be interested in helping us out after all.'

Sally's eyes flicker over in my direction. Her expression remains blank. 'Go on.'

'I told him I wasn't sure if that was such a good idea. Especially considering we've had to resort to Plan B…'

Sally shrugs, taking a sip of her tea. 'Maybe you're right. If you don't think he could handle it.'

'Hang on,' I say, looking back and forth between the pair of them. 'Aren't you at least going to tell me what this Plan B is?'

Noelle glances over at Sally, who gives her a nod. 'To put things into context,' she begins, 'we've been having similar issues to Sean and his friends. With unlocking the door to the lab, I mean. I managed to sweet-talk the original code out of JD, but I'm sure Maeve will have changed it since then.'

'It's the same issue with the alarm code,' adds Sally. 'Those fish fuckers might be happy to smash and grab before the Guards show up, but recording quality footage takes time. We need to make sure we can disarm the system before we go inside.'

I nod, letting this all sink in.

'We considered various different options,' continues Noelle. 'Calling the company who installed the door and asking if there was a way to disable it. Bribing Susan from Accounting to get the codes for us. But none of those plans panned out. In the end, the only option left was…' She pauses, giving Sally another nervous glance, '…asking Maeve to let us in herself.'

'Wait, what!?' I snort. 'No offence, but that's a terrible idea. Maeve is never going to just *let you in*.'

'Not of her own free will, maybe,' says Sally. 'But we have ways of making her cooperate.'

'Oh yeah, like what?'

She reaches under her mattress and pulls out the rusty metal length of the rifle. 'Like *this*.'

'You can't be serious…' I groan, setting down my teacup. Maybe it's just the late-night caffeine, but I suddenly feel like I'm about to throw up.

Noelle sighs. 'Like I said, it wasn't my first choice. But it's the only option we've got left.'

'So what, you're just going to charge into the office, guns blazing, and threaten to shoot her if she doesn't let you into the lab?'

'Nobody's going to be *charging in* anywhere,' says Sally. 'Maeve is always the last person to leave in the evening. All we have to do is catch her on her way out – preferably in the car park, where it's nice and dark – and politely explain the situation.'

'And if she refuses to play along? What then?'

Sally shrugs. 'That would be a very stupid move on her part.'

'Jesus Christ,' I mutter, turning back to Noelle. 'This is all sounding hauntingly familiar. You're talking about doing the exact same thing Sean and his scumbag friends did to me. Are we really going to stoop to their level? I thought we were better than that...'

'I never claimed to be better than them,' says Sally. 'Just smarter.'

'We're not really going to hurt her,' says Noelle. 'Just give her a little scare.'

I close my eyes, burying my head in my hands. What the hell have I gotten myself into?'...This isn't right. Maeve might be an asshole, but not even she deserves this.'

'It's not too late to drop out,' says Sally, slurping the dregs from her cup. 'If you're going to be such a pussy about it, maybe we'd be better off without you.'

'Who said anything about dropping out?' I snap. 'I offered to help you, and that offer still stands. But there must be a better way. One that doesn't involve threatening to kill people.'

'Nothing's set in stone,' says Noelle. 'If you've got any other ideas, we're all ears.'

I stare up at the ceiling, trying to picture the hallway outside the lab. 'If we can't get the code, maybe there's some other way to get through the door? Like picking the lock, or battering the whole thing down?'

Noelle shakes her head. 'Not possible, even if we were pros. Maeve spent thousands of euro having that thing installed. It's indestructible.'

'*Great idea*,' says Sally. 'If only we'd thought of it sooner.'

I ignore her, racking my brain for another idea. 'How about a fire escape? Or a window we could climb in through?'

'Nothing like that in the lab,' says Noelle. 'At least, not as far as I'm aware. And nobody knows the building better than I do. Except maybe Maeve.'

'This is a waste of time,' says Sally. 'Let's cut the bullshit and get back to Plan B.'

But I barely even register what she's just said. Because I've just thought of somebody else who knows the building better than Noelle. Somebody who said something interesting during our last conversation. The one on the street corner outside the office, when he was shouting into his megaphone…

Besides, even if I did want to get back in, I wouldn't go through the front door. I wouldn't go through any doors at all.

'I think I have an idea.'

Twenty five

We go to meet Kevin first thing in the morning. Sally refuses to come along at first, saying she wouldn't be caught dead working with a Jesus freak, but Noelle manages to convince her eventually. A little creative persuasion is also required for Kevin. When I first ring up, he tells me he's going bowling with Sister Rose, and he couldn't possibly cancel on such short notice. But once I mention being fired – including a cryptic comment about how it's shown me a *whole new side* to Maeve – he agrees to meet me at the Black Cat café.

Noelle drives us down through the hills and back into town. It was too dark to make out much of the scenery last night, but now we find ourselves sailing through a sea of purple heather. Smooth, wind-bleached stones line the road, which is empty of any other cars or pedestrians. The only sign of life at all is the occasional group of sheep floating past like fluffy white clouds.

My phone buzzes with an incoming text message as we reach the outskirts of town. At first I assume it's Kevin, letting me know he's arrived at the café. But it turns out to be Sean.

Hey man, just letting you know that I'm safe and sound. The others arrived this morning and untied me. They were pissed you got away, but they have no idea I helped you :)

I shove the phone back into my pocket, suppressing a grin. I'm glad he's alive, I guess. But I'll be damned if I give him the satisfaction of an instantaneous reply.

But then, a few seconds later, another message arrives. And this one is too ominous just to ignore.

Listen, I need to see you ASAP. You and your friends are in danger.

'So, eh…Sean just texted me,' I announce to the front of the car.

'Oh yeah?' says Noelle. 'Tell him I say hi.'

'You might be able to tell him yourself. He's asking to meet up again. Says we're in some sort of danger.'

'No way,' grunts Sally. 'What sort of simpletons does he take us for? Just ignore him.'

'I don't know,' says Noelle, glancing back in the rear-view mirror. 'Did he mention what exactly this danger was?'

'No. But I can ask him.'

Hey, I'm a little busy at the moment, I text back. *What's going on?*

He replies immediately. I read the message out loud.

Can't talk about it over the phone. You never know who could be listening in… Let's just say the situation is about to BLOW UP.

'Oh my God,' says Noelle. 'You don't think they're planning to bomb the office, do you?' She sounds delighted.

'No way,' snorts Sally. 'That sleazy Yank hasn't got the balls for something like that. He's just bluffing. Trying to trick you into meeting up again so he can squeeze more information out of you.'

'I don't know…' I say, thinking back to my encounter with Pig and Cow. 'You haven't met his friends. The two of them make Sean look well-adjusted by comparison. A bombing would probably be right up their alley.'

'Mark might be right,' says Noelle. 'If there's any chance Sean is telling the truth, surely we should at least hear him out?'

'Fine,' grumbles Sally. 'We'll give him a chance. But he meets us alone. Somewhere public, with plenty of witnesses. Any sign of his idiot friends and we abort the mission immediately.'

'Why don't we ask him to come to the café?' says Noelle. 'We could talk to him after we're done with Kevin. Kill two birds with one stone.'

'Not a bad idea,' nods Sally. And then, with an evil grin into the back seat: 'Good thing I brought my rifle.'

The café is practically empty when we arrive. Kevin sits alone at a table in the corner, dressed in a retro green bowling shirt. His blonde beard has continued growing, moving on from *dishevelled artist* and entering *homeless meth head* territory. He stands up and waves when he sees me walk in, then frowns and sits back down when Sally and Noelle follow.

'Eh…hi there,' I say, as we join him at the table. 'Thanks for agreeing to meet us.'

'I didn't realise there'd be an *us*,' he says, eyeing Sally up suspiciously.

'Sorry, yeah, I forgot to mention Noelle was coming. And this is Sally, Noelle's…niece.'

'I know who she is,' he replies. 'I've seen her videos.'

'Thanks for watching!' says Sally. 'I hope you enjoyed them.' She hits him with a sickly-sweet smile, the likes of which I've never seen from her before.

'Well I didn't,' says Kevin. 'I thought they were at best childish, at worst an outright mockery of God's plan.'

I wince, expecting Sally to flip the table on him. But all she does is laugh nervously and run her hands along the greasy length of her ponytail.

'I don't mean to sound rude,' he continues, turning back towards me. 'But what's she doing here? I thought you wanted to talk about Maeve.'

'I do want to talk about her. But Sally and Noelle are also interested in Future Fish. So I thought maybe we could all put our heads together.'

He sighs, like his day is already shaping up to be a profound disappointment. 'Please don't tell me you've gotten yourself caught up in all this alien hysteria, Mark. I expected better from you. And *you*…' He turns towards Noelle. 'Well, this is exactly the sort of thing I would have expected from you.'

Noelle grins, apparently taking this as a compliment. But I can't bear the disapproval in Kevin's eyes. 'It's not like that! I'm just helping Noelle. And she's just helping Sally. And I was hoping, maybe, you could help me.'

His eyes narrow behind his glasses. 'Help you with what, exactly?'

I take a deep breath. This isn't quite how I'd imagined the conversation going. 'Well, we're sort of trying to get into the lab. But it's tricky, obviously, since none of us actually work there any more. We can't just go waltzing in through the front door... But I remembered you mentioning you might know another way in. A way that didn't involve any doors, I think you said?'

He shakes his head, eyes hardening with indignation. 'So that's what this is all about? You don't really have anything to tell me about Maeve. You're just using me for blueprints to the office.'

'No, no, you've got it all wrong!' I splutter. 'I still want to help you. But I thought we could all work together. Like, you tell us how to get inside, and we tell you if we come across anything... demonic.'

'I don't think so, Mark. Father Marsh is already refusing to take me seriously. He's chased off all my supporters, and even threatened to have me excommunicated. How do you think he'd react if he found out I'd cast my lot in with a bunch of conspiracy theorists?' He stands up and starts pulling on his coat. 'I'm sorry, but I think I should go. Coming here was clearly a mistake.'

'Wait!' says Sally, grabbing hold of his sleeve. 'Please, don't leave. We have more in common than you might think. Just because somebody believes in life on other planets doesn't mean they can't also believe in Jesus.'

I study her expression, wondering what sort of game she's playing. No way she'd ever be this nice to somebody simply out of the goodness of her heart. It's only when I spot the blush blooming in her cheeks that it finally hits me...

Sally fancies Kevin!

My first reaction is to laugh. I can hardly blame her for that one. But when I see him soften under her touch, sitting back down and mumbling something about not being so quick to judge, I suddenly want to scream. What if he fancies her back? What if she succeeds where I failed? I don't think I could bear it if the two of them ended up together. Getting married. Having children. Fully embracing the heterosexual lifestyle.

Luckily, Sally doesn't know how to quit when she's ahead.

'You know,' she says. 'Some people believe Jesus himself was an extra-terrestrial. One of the so-called Nordic types from Venus.'

'Christ give me strength,' groans Kevin. 'I've heard enough.'

He stands up and storms off towards the exit. Sally calls after him, begging him to come back, but he acts like he hasn't heard her. Just as he's reaching out for the door handle, another figure comes barrelling in from the opposite direction. It takes me a second to recognise him, with his bruised and swollen face. But there's no mistaking that signature swagger.

It's Sean.

He snaps at Kevin, telling him to watch where he's going, then scans his eyes around from table to table.

'Hey babe,' he calls, waving over to me from across the room. Kevin stands frozen in the doorway, watching him stride across the floor and kiss me on the cheek.

'Stop!' I squeal, squirming away from him. 'Not in front of Kevin.'

'Kevin? Who the hell is Kevin?'

I point over at the bewildered figure by the doorway. 'That's

Kevin.'

'Oh.' He looks him slowly up and down, like a feral cat sizing up its rival. 'I take it he's another one of those alien freaks?'

'I am not!' says Kevin, stepping back towards the table.

'What are you then?'

'I'm a Catholic. A follower of Jesus Christ and His Holy Church.'

'Ew, Jesus. Gross...' Sean glances across the table at Noelle and Sally. 'And speaking of weirdos, I didn't realise you'd be bringing the entire entourage with you.'

'Just sit down and shut up,' I groan. 'We'll deal with you in a minute.'

He shrugs, taking a seat in Kevin's empty chair. Noelle smiles and waves at him, but Sally just grunts and crosses her arms.

'Nice to see you too,' he taunts her.

'Don't even talk to me.'

'Or what? You'll start pointing a gun in my face again?'

'A gun?' says Kevin, turning even paler than usual. 'What in God's name are you lot playing at?'

'Don't worry,' says Sally, reverting back to friendly mode. 'It's not a *real* gun. Just an old hunting rifle I borrowed off my dad.'

Kevin swallows down a lump in his throat, not looking particularly reassured.

'Guns are the least of your worries now anyways,' says Sean.

'Of course,' says Noelle. 'You mentioned something about an...*explosive* situation?'

'You can't be serious...' groans Kevin, collapsing into a chair at the neighbouring table.

'That's what I came to talk to Mark about,' nods Sean. 'But the rest of you all being here wasn't part of the deal.'

'Just get on with it,' I beg. 'I'm going to tell them everything you say anyway.'

'Okay, okay…' He pauses, clearly enjoying the attention. 'No big surprise, but my comrades weren't too happy with their latest plan being foiled.'

'Hang on,' says Kevin. 'Who are your comrades? And while we're at it, who are *you?*'

'I'm Mark's boyfriend.'

'You are not!' I groan.

'Okay, fine. I'm Mark's lover.'

I bury my face in my hands, too mortified to even look at Kevin.

'I'm also a member of an underground animal liberation movement called Friends of the Fish. We specialise in the rescue and rehabilitation of abused and neglected sea creatures. Or at least, we did… Things have been getting kind of weird lately.'

'Of course,' says Kevin, taking this all surprisingly well. 'And you said your comrades were unhappy?'

Sean nods. 'They're pissed off that their plans to get inside the WellCat lab keep failing. And it's starting to make them desperate. So desperate, in fact, that they've decided to blow the whole thing to hell.'

'I knew it!' grins Noelle, slapping her thigh.

'This isn't a good thing,' hisses Sally. 'What if they blow the place up before we have a chance to get inside? They could destroy the specimen, as well as all the evidence.'

'True,' says Noelle, slumping down in her chair. 'They could also blow it up while we're still inside. Which would make for some interesting footage, but would also, you know…kill us all.'

'Maybe I should clarify,' continues Sean. 'They're not planning on nuking the entire building. Just a tiny little controlled explosion to knock the door off its hinges. And they'll do it at night, when the place is empty. So I wouldn't worry about them hurting anybody. Other than themselves, anyway.'

'That's not so bad,' nods Noelle.

'It's not so *good* either,' says Sally. 'They could still end up damaging something important. And besides…' She turns reluctantly towards Sean. 'I thought they were trying to rescue these so-called fish. Wouldn't there be a risk of the explosion killing them? The heat alone could turn their tanks into chowder.'

'That's what I'm afraid of,' says Sean. 'They insist they know what they're doing, but neither of them has any experience with explosives. I don't think Magda even cares what happens to the fish. All she wants to do is make a statement. Get her name in the papers. But I can't have something like that on my conscience if it goes wrong. That's why I've decided to strike out on my own.'

'You mean you're splitting up with your pals?' asks Noelle.

He nods. 'My best chance to save the fish now is to get into the lab before they do.'

'But how are you planning on getting inside?' Noelle presses. 'You'll have even less of a chance flying solo.'

'Well, actually…' He glances around the table, mouth curling into a mischievous smile. 'I was kind of hoping you guys could help me.'

Sally snorts. 'Help you? Why the hell would we do that?'

'In exchange for the bomb information, obviously.'

'Isn't it a bit late to be making deals?' she asks. 'You've already told us everything we need to know.'

'Have I though? Because I can't recall telling you *when* they were going to strike. And until you agree to help me, I'm not going to.'

Sally snarls, reaching down for her suspiciously large and rifle-shaped handbag. But before she can produce the weapon, Noelle leans over and whispers in her ear. 'Maybe it wouldn't be such a bad idea letting him come along. He can look around for his fish while we record our footage. No reason we'd have to get in each other's way.'

'I don't trust him,' says Sally. 'This could still be a trap. What if he delivers us straight into the clutches of his gobshite friends?'

'That's a risk we're just going to have to take,' says Noelle. 'If they really are planning on blowing up the lab, we need to know when. And besides…' She glances over in my direction. 'I wouldn't worry about him hurting us. He's clearly got the hots for Mark.'

'Seriously?' I groan, kicking out at her under the table. But she dodges the blow, and my toe stubs painfully against the leg of her chair.

'Fine,' grunts Sally. 'He can come. But on two conditions. One, he follows my orders. And two, he doesn't get to touch the gun.' She reaches down and pats her purse for emphasis.

'Fine by me,' shrugs Sean. 'I wouldn't want to touch that tetanus-riddled piece of junk anyway.'

'Excellent,' says Noelle. 'So tell us, how much time do we have? When are they planning to drop the bomb?'

He squints up at the ceiling, like he's struggling to work out a complicated equation. 'Not much time, actually. They're going to do it tonight. At midnight.'

'Fucking hell!' says Sally. 'That's cutting it a bit close. We'll only have the one chance this evening to catch Maeve in the car park. If we fuck that up, we're screwed!'

'More like zero chances,' sighs Noelle. 'Today is Tuesday – Maeve's Pilates night. She always heads straight to the sports centre with Fiona and Michelle. There'll be too many of them for us to make our move.'

Sally's eyes go wide, pupils dilating with panic. She rounds on Sean like a vengeful spirit. 'Are you sure it's tonight? Absolutely *one hundred percent* sure? Maybe you're getting mixed up with that stupid American date system!'

'I'm sure,' he shrugs.

'Fuck!' she groans. 'Fuck, fuck, fuck! What the hell are we supposed to do now?'

But nobody responds.

I wait a few seconds, hoping somebody else will speak up, then turn reluctantly towards Kevin. He's been lingering on the edge of the conversation, not saying much since the bomb talk began. I was hoping not to have to put him on the spot again. Especially after he nearly did a runner last time. But at this stage, it doesn't look like there's any other option.

'So,' I say, clearing my throat. 'This is why I was hoping you might be able to tell us about that other way into the lab…'

Sally's eyes light up, but Kevin remains impassive. He stares out of the window, squinting at the golden morning light. The day looks set to be another scorcher.

'Please, Kevin,' says Noelle. 'We're in a tight spot. We need your help.'

'*Please*,' echoes Sally, laying a hand on his arm. 'You're the only one with the inside knowledge.'

Even Sean joins in, leaning across the table and slapping him on the back. 'Come on, man. What would Jesus do?'

He hesitates for a few more seconds, lips twitching in silent prayer. And then, with a world-weary sigh, he scoots his chair in closer to the table. 'Fine,' he says. 'You're clearly all going to get yourselves killed if I don't help you. And that wouldn't be very Christian of me. But I do it on one condition...'

'Whatever you want!' wheezes Sally.

'I go into the laboratory with you. And I get to look around first. Maybe I can still rustle up some evidence of Maeve's possession to help convince Father Marsh. Like an occult grimoire. Or some Satanic power symbol.'

'Of course,' says Noelle. 'The more the merrier.'

'We can all drive there together!' adds Sally.

'Not so fast,' says Sean, holding up a hand. 'You still haven't told us what this secret entrance actually is.'

Kevin pauses, fixing him with a steely stare. For a second, I'm afraid he might be reconsidering his offer. But then he shakes his head and sighs again. 'The vents,' he says. 'We go in through the vents.'

'Vents?' frowns Noelle. 'You mean the ones in the car park?'

'Exactly. You can reach them by climbing up on top of the bin. Unscrew the cover, and the opening is just big enough to crawl inside. They run the entire length of the building, through the basement and up to the ground floor. No need to worry about codes or keys or any of that nonsense.'

Noelle nods, looking impressed. 'I had no idea.'

'Neither did I, until last year. Remember when there was that mysterious smell in the office?'

'Christ, how could I forget? It was like a dead body had been stashed underneath the floorboards.'

'Well in a way, it had. One of the stray cats climbed inside the vents and never made it back out. Its body was rotting, the smell diffusing throughout the entire building. Maeve made me crawl through and clean it up myself. She said we couldn't hire a professional because she didn't want word getting out that a cat had died on the premises.'

Noelle nods slowly, biting her lip. 'You know, this might actually work. But if Maeve already knows you can get in that way, are you sure she hasn't sealed the vents up?'

'Pretty sure. I never mentioned how deep they went, and she never brought them up again after the cat incident.'

'I don't like the sound of *pretty sure*,' says Sean. 'What if you're wrong, and we miss our only opportunity to get inside?'

'I trust Kevin,' says Sally. 'If he says it will work, then there's nothing to worry about.'

'It is risky,' admits Noelle. 'But it's the only plan we've got... I say we give it a try.' She slaps her hand down onto the middle of the table, glancing around at the rest of us.

'I'm in!' says Sally, placing her palm on top of Noelle's.

'As am I...obviously,' says Kevin, sliding his fingers over Sally's.

'Fine,' grunts Sean, adding his hand onto the stack. 'I guess I am too.'

They all turn to look at me.

'Eh...'

I can think of a million reasons why this is a bad idea. Besides somebody getting shot or blown to pieces, we could all end up stuck inside those vents. Scalded by a cloud of steam. Eaten alive by feral cats… But I know there's no point arguing. The others will only laugh off my objections. Or worse, go ahead without me.

I know it's crazy, but a part of me actually wants to go along with them. To see how this all ends. I still don't believe Future Fish is anything strange or mystical, or that it will provide the answers to any of our questions. But these four people are the only connections I have left in Ashcross. Friends, rivals, sort-of boyfriends. And if they're all going into the lab together, then – fuck it – I'm going in too.

'Alright,' I say, sliding my hand across the table. 'I'm in.'

Twenty six

The five of us pile into Noelle's car and head straight back to the B&B. Over the course of the next few hours, the tiny twin room is transformed into a sophisticated centre of espionage. Maps are plotted and pinned to the wall, timetables drawn up, and individual tasks assigned. Every minute detail is taken into consideration, from the latest statistics on local traffic to the average crawling speed of the group. When all the different graphs and diagrams start to get confusing, Noelle compiles everything into a single multicoloured Gantt chart.

'Maeve made me go on a *project management* course last year,' she grins, holding the finished product up for inspection. 'I thought it was a load of bollocks at the time, but it turns out it's actually quite useful!'

I stay out of it for the most part, having nothing useful to contribute. Kevin and Noelle know the office far better than I do, and Sean and Sally both seem to have an alarming amount of experience infiltrating buildings.

As I sit back in the armchair, watching everybody work, I can't help noticing how different the atmosphere is from a day at the office. How everybody in the room looks focused and content. Because unlike the office, nobody is forcing them to be here. They've chosen this position for themselves. And sure, their reasons might be misguided. They might be ill-informed, or even outright insane. But they're still theirs, and nobody else's. And that's got to count for something, right?

We leave the B&B at exactly nine twenty-five. The plan is to arrive at the office for ten, by which time everybody should be long gone – including Maeve, who'll be busy sweating it out at Pilates – leaving us a two-hour window before Pig and Cow are due to arrive. We make a quick pitstop at Kevin's house to borrow a few items from his parents' shed – a screwdriver, an assortment of bright yellow gardening gloves, and a shiny metal nine iron. These are tossed into Sally's oversized purse, along with the rifle, the duct tape, and a set of hot pink balaclavas Noelle fashioned from the B&B pillowcases.

It's just getting dark when we reach the town centre, the last drops of sunset draining down into the ocean. We leave the car parked a few blocks up the road – far from the scene of the crime – and cover the remaining distance on foot. The streets are quiet, but not deserted, and a handful of figures drift by in the twilight. I keep my head down as we pass them, trying to act inconspicuous, and hope nobody notices the arsenal of weapons sticking out of Sally's bag.

The lights in the office are all switched off – no sign of any late-night stragglers. As per the plan, Noelle and I linger on the corner to keep watch while the others head down to the car park to unscrew the vent. It's only when I see them slipping on their balaclavas and gloves, like a team of makeshift supervillains, that it finally hits me. *This is actually happening. The five of us are about to break into the lab.*

Holy fuck.

'Smoke?' asks Noelle, sensing my anxiety. We've left our faces uncovered for now, to avoid attracting attention from passers-by.

'Eh...' I know I shouldn't, but... 'Fuck it. Yes please.'

She lights us both up and takes a long, slow drag. 'So... Nerves getting to you?'

'A little bit, yeah. How about you?'

'No way,' she grins. 'I can't wait to get inside.'

I take a drag of my own, then immediately start coughing. I'd forgotten how horrible cigarettes are.

Noelle laughs, nudging me in the side. And then a more serious expression begins creeping over her face. 'By the way,' she says, 'have you thought about what you're going to do with yourself when all this is over? Probably head back to Dublin, I suppose?'

'I don't know,' I sigh, forcing down a lungful of smoke. 'I'm not ready to go back home just yet, but I can't see what other option I have. I thought helping you and Sally would buy me a few more days to think about it. But things have moved faster than I was expecting...'

'Fair enough,' she nods. 'Things *have* escalated quickly.'

'How about you?' I ask. 'What are you going to do after Sally's investigation is finished and she doesn't need your help any more?'

She hesitates, exhaling a thick cloud of smoke. 'I was thinking I might head back to Galway with her. She's keen to keep the momentum up with her channel and jump straight into the next project. And I figured I might as well carry on helping her.'

I stub my cigarette out against the wall, only half-smoked. All this talk of endings is starting to get me down. 'Sounds like you've got it all figured out.'

'You know,' she says, in a delicate tone, 'you could always come along with us. I'm sure Sally wouldn't mind.'

'Thanks,' I sigh, rubbing at the ash mark on the wall. Part of me was hoping she'd say that. But another part knows it would never work. 'But I don't think Sally would be too happy with me tagging along. And besides, it wouldn't feel right. I still don't believe in any of that alien stuff.'

'Alright,' she shrugs. 'It's up to you. But you can always change your mind later.'

Before either of us can say anything else, my phone starts ringing in my pocket. I pull it out with shaking fingers, already knowing what I'm going to see on screen. *Sean calling.*

'We're in,' he says, hanging up immediately after.

All thoughts of tomorrow disappear from my mind, drowned out by the deafening roar of adrenaline. We suit up in our gloves and balaclavas, take one last look around to make sure nobody is watching, then follow the others down the ramp to the dimly-lit car park.

It takes me a second to work out who's who with their faces covered. But the one propping a giant metal grille against the wall must be Sally – you can tell from the fact she's a good foot shorter than everybody else. And the one sitting on top of the bin, a stray cat in his arms, could only be Sean – he's removed one of his gloves, revealing several inches of tattooed forearm. Which means the figure crouching in the open mouth of the vent, half hidden by shadow, must be Kevin.

'All clear out front?' asks Sally, wiping sweat from underneath her balaclava.

'All good,' says Noelle. 'Nobody paid us any mind.'

'Great,' says Sally. 'Let's film a few quick soundbites before we head inside.'

Noelle pulls her phone from her pocket and starts pointing it at Sally, leaving me to approach the vent on my own. The bin underneath is taller than I remembered – a metre and a half of smooth, green plastic.

'Come on,' says Sean, setting the cat aside and holding out a hand. 'I'll help you up.'

I grip the edge of the lid in both hands and begin pulling myself upwards. I only manage to get a few inches off the ground, but it's enough for Sean to hook his arms under mine and start dragging me up beside him. After several seconds of kicking and flailing, accompanied by an awkward chorus of mutual grunting, I finally manage to get both legs over the edge.

'Thanks,' I pant, climbing to my feet. The plastic buckles under our combined weight, and I have to lean an arm on his shoulder to keep myself steady.

Directly in front of us looms the mouth of the vent. A gaping black hole leading God knows where. I peer inside, struggling to make out any shape to the darkness. But all I can see is Kevin's hunched-over shoulders. He crawls forward a few metres, beckoning with a gloved hand for me to follow.

Slowly, reluctantly, I stick my head inside. The space is even tighter than it looks, and I have to wriggle forward on my elbows to make room for my knees. I've never been particularly claustrophobic, but something about the dark, airless tunnel makes me feel like I'm being buried alive. I freeze a few feet in, unable to go any further, until Sean climbs in behind me and forces me forward. Noelle grunts behind Sean, and then Sally's voice echoes up along the walls.

'We're all in.'

'Alright,' Kevin calls back. 'Let's get a move on.'

We start crawling properly now. Progress is slow, the narrow space leaving little room to manoeuvre, and my knees begin to ache from the hard, metal floor. It gets hotter and hotter the deeper we go, until I'm so slick with sweat that I pull off my balaclava and tuck it into my belt. Everybody is too busy huffing and puffing to speak, except for Kevin, who calls out *left* or *right* whenever we come to a fork in the path.

After what feels like an eternity in this sticky underworld, Kevin comes to a sudden stop in front of me. 'This is it,' he says, pulling his phone from his pocket and directing the torch beam onto the floor.

In the bottom of the vent is a large metal grille, identical to the one Sally was carrying outside. We've passed over several of them already, but it was always too dark to see what was on the other side. I have no idea how Kevin knows this is the right one.

In the neon glare of the phone, I see him reach into his pocket and produce the screwdriver. He presses it into the top-right corner of the grille and begins twisting. After a few seconds, he moves onto another corner, then another, and another. There's a loud metallic crash, and a gust of cool air rushes up into the vent.

'Now for the fun part,' he says.

With a little squeezing and squirming, he manages to turn himself around a hundred and eighty degrees. He shoves the phone back into his pocket, extinguishing what little light was left in the world. Through the darkness, I can just make out the shape of his body slipping down into the freshly opened hole.

There's a thud below, followed by a faint groan. And then total silence.

'Kevin?' I call down. 'Are you alright?'

'I'm grand,' he replies. 'Just landed a little funny. Hang on a second and I'll get the lights.'

I hear footsteps crossing the floor, followed by a switch flicking. Blinding white light floods the room below. I peer down into the gap, blinking away the brightness, and see Kevin waving up at me from a row of metal desks.

'It's not as high as it looks,' he says. 'Just lower yourself down and let go. You'll be grand.'

'Sure,' I mumble. 'If you say so…'

I turn myself around and begin backing up towards the hole. Sean, now facing me, gives me a yellow-gloved thumbs up. I lower one leg into the air, followed by the other, resting all my weight down onto my stomach. From here, I let gravity do its work, pulling me slowly downwards until only my elbows remain inside the vent. I hang there for a few seconds, half-in and half-out, until my feeble upper body strength gives out and I crash down onto the desk below.

Miraculously, I land on my feet. The impact reverberates painfully through my ankles, but other than that, I appear to be uninjured.

'Watch out!' calls Sean, dangling his own legs down.

I step aside as he drops onto the desk beside me. He lands on his haunches, crouching down like a cat, then slowly straightens back up.

'So this is it?' he says, spinning around to survey the room. 'The infamous WellCat laboratory.'

'This is it,' I reply, remembering it's my first time on the inside too. I did catch a brief glimpse through the doorway when I followed Noelle down on that fateful afternoon, but all I saw then was a few glass jars.

Now that I have a chance to look around properly, I can't help feeling a little disappointed. It's not exactly the Gothic torture chamber I'd been imagining. Just a tidy, spacious room, dominated by two long workbenches running like an equals sign down the centre. A variety of equipment lines the desks – microscopes, mixers, and several machines I've never seen before – alongside the multi-coloured jars I noticed last time. Across one wall is a row of heavy-duty metal lockers. Across the other, a massive bookcase stuffed with folders and ledgers. Nothing strange or sinister is immediately apparent.

Sean and I climb down off the desk just as Noelle plops out of the vent. She lands on her feet, but can't find her balance, and ends up tipping backwards onto her bum. As she lies giggling on the desk, Sally drops down gracefully beside her. She immediately pulls the rifle from her purse and begins scanning its barrel around the room.

'Is this it?' she demands, from behind her balaclava. 'Where's Future Fish?'

'Good question,' says Sean, plucking the golf club from her purse.

Noelle sits up and stops laughing. For a few seconds, nobody says a word. We all peer around the room, each person searching for their own version of an answer. And then Kevin points a gloved finger at the corner opposite the door.

'There.'

A long, rectangular mass lies hidden beneath a black cloth. Like a coffin draped in a shroud.

'What is it?' asks Noelle, sounding genuinely uncertain for the first time all day.

'Probably a freezer,' says Sally. 'To keep the specimen fresh.'

'Looks more like a water tank,' says Sean. 'Crammed full of fish.'

'Or an altar,' adds Kevin. 'A monument to blasphemy.'

The three of them advance slowly towards the shape, pausing in a semi-circle before it. After a moment of reverential silence, Kevin reaches a gloved hand out and grips the edge of the sheet. The whole room holds its breath as his arm hovers in mid-air. And then, like a magician delivering his grand finale, he whips the cloth off in one fluid movement.

Underneath is a metal box. Its sides are smooth and featureless, its lid held shut with a heavy-duty padlock.

Sean exhales loudly, prodding the box with his nine iron. 'Well that was an anti-climax.'

'Not necessarily,' says Kevin, tugging at the padlock. 'This just proves it's something dangerous. Something Maeve doesn't want anybody to see... We need to get the lock off.'

'Leave it to me,' says Sean, shoving him aside. He raises the golf club over one shoulder, wiggling his hips from side to side, then swings it full force against the lock. There's a toe-curling screech of metal on metal, but the blow doesn't even make a dent. He repeats the process several times – screech! screech! screech! – until he's bent over double, struggling to catch his breath.

'This is getting us nowhere,' says Sally, pulling him out of the way. 'Why don't I just shoot the stupid thing off?'

'Careful!' says Noelle, filming the entire scene on her phone. 'What if the bullet ricochets off? It could take your eye out.'

Sally shrugs, raising the rifle. 'You only need one eye anyway.'

I turn away, clamping my hands over my ears, and brace myself for the roar of the gunshot.

But another sound arrives first. The click of a lock releasing, followed by the smooth sweep of a door opening.

And then a voice. Loud and clear and full of fury.

'Marcus! What in God's name do you think you're doing?'

Twenty seven

My heart nearly stops when Maeve walks through the door. In place of her usual blazer and slacks, she wears a neon orange tracksuit with matching headband. This casual getup only makes the murderous look on her face all the more terrifying. Her eyes linger on mine for several seconds, before moving on to take in the rest of the room. A fresh wave of panic washes over me as I realise I'm the only one who's removed my pink balaclava.

'Jesus Christ,' she mutters, shaking her head. 'That's Noelle Fitzgerald, isn't it? And Kevin O'Mahoney too?'

Kevin lifts a hand to wave, but Sally smacks it back down. Nobody says a word.

'You've got ten seconds to explain what the hell you're doing here,' says Maeve, 'before I call the Guards and have you all arrested.'

Sally steps forward, the rifle held discreetly behind her back. 'And who exactly put you in charge?'

'Excuse me?' says Maeve, matching her advance. 'I'm the CEO of this company, and you're trespassing on our property. So if you think I'm going to be intimidated by a bunch of costume-wearing clowns, you've got another thing coming.'

Sally snorts, revealing the rifle. 'Intimidated now?'

A brief cloud of fear passes over Maeve's face, before burning up in the heat of her fury. 'Who sent you here?' she demands. 'Miss Meow?'

'What did you call me?' growls Sally.

'Don't mind her,' says Noelle. 'She thinks we're spies from a rival company.'

'*As if,*' groans Sally. 'God, she really is as annoying as you made her out to be. Assuming this is Maeve, and not some other bitch with a stick up her arse.'

'That's Maeve, alright,' says Noelle. 'She must have decided to skip Pilates.'

Maeve rolls her eyes, gesturing down at the tangerine tracksuit. 'Does it look like I skipped Pilates? The class finished an hour ago. I was just popping by to pick up some paperwork when I heard a noise coming from the basement. I assumed one of those mangy cats must have gotten in again, since no burglar would be stupid enough to make such a racket.'

'Who are you calling *stupid*?' asks Sally, pressing the barrel of the rifle into Maeve's stomach.

'Come on now,' says Kevin, putting a hand on her shoulder. 'Let's not do anything we might regret.'

Sally glares at Maeve for another moment, then huffs and

lowers the gun. 'Fine. But we need to make sure she doesn't pull a runner. You' – she nods over at Sean, who's still holding on to the nine iron – 'go stand guard beside her. If she moves a single digit towards the door, give her a whack of that golf club.'

'No way,' says Sean. 'I'm staying right next to this box.'

Sally rolls her eyes through her balaclava. 'For fuck's sake. Give the club to Mark, then. He can watch her while we deal with the box.'

Sean shrugs and tosses the golf club at my feet. I bend over to pick it up, feeling my hands begin to tremble. I've never hit anybody in my life. And surely Maeve must know I wouldn't have the guts to start now. If she calls my bluff and makes a run for the door, there's nothing I could do to stop her.

But it's too late for objections. The others have already turned their attention back towards the box. They remove their balaclavas one by one, the prospect of remaining anonymous having gone out the window.

'Right,' says Sally. 'Where were we? Oh yeah, I was just about to blow a hole through this stupid lock.'

'Wait!' says Maeve, holding out a hand. 'Don't open the box. Let's just take a second to talk this through.'

But nobody is listening to her any more. They're all too focused on the padlock, debating the best spot to aim the bullet.

She rounds on me next, a hint of desperation creeping into her eyes. 'Listen, Marcus, you have to stop them. Is it money you're after? Because whatever Miss Meow is offering, I'll double it!'

I ignore her, doing my best to avoid eye contact. I can't let her see that I'm shitting bricks.

'Come on,' she whispers, positioning her face in front of mine. 'You don't want to end up in prison, do you? Because that's exactly where those idiots are headed. But if you help me out, I'll make sure the Guards go easy on you. Just don't let them open that box.'

But it's too late. The others have reached a consensus on the far side of the room. Sally raises the rifle... Aims...

BOOM!

Maeve groans as a plume of smoke spreads across the room. The others cough and splutter, holding their balaclavas over their mouths. When the air finally clears, all that remains of the padlock is a mangled hunk of metal. Kevin kicks it aside, reaching a gloved hand towards the latch.

'This is it,' he says, grabbing hold of the lid. 'Everybody ready?'

Sally and Sean nod on either side of him, like a devil on each shoulder. Noelle gives a thumbs up from behind the camera of her phone.

'Right, so. Here we go...'

In that instant, everything flashes before my eyes. All the events of the last few weeks, leading one after another towards this moment. Stepping off the bus on my first day in Ashcross. Maeve warning me to stay out of the lab. Sally's alien video, Kevin's possession story, Sean and his friends proclaiming fish are people too. Each new twist, chaotic but unrelenting. Like a current you don't realise has got hold of you until it's already too late.

The lid crashes back against the wall, and Kevin, Sean, and Sally lean forward one by one.

A few seconds pass in perfect silence.

And then all three of them bend over and stick their arms into the box. I stand up on my tippy-toes, trying to see what's inside, but they're blocking my view with their backs. There's a rush of rustling as they rifle through the box's contents, and then a wave of empty cans spills out over the edge.

'What the fuck?' says Sally, standing back up. 'It's just a giant recycling bin filled with empty tins.'

Kevin removes his glasses and wipes them on the corner of his shirt, while Sean frantically digs down deeper in the box. 'I don't get it…' he grunts. 'Where's Future Fish?'

'I think this *is* Future Fish,' says Noelle, bending down to pick up one of the fallen cans.

I lean forward, squinting at the bright yellow label. But it's too far away for me to make out what it says.

'But how can that be?' asks Kevin, turning over an identical tin. 'They're not even made by WellCat… They're Miss Meow's Tuna Tsunami.'

'I think that's the point,' says Noelle. 'They must be stealing the recipe. Trying to pass it off as their own.'

'You mean they're scooping out the Tuna Tsunami and putting it into WellCat tins?' asks Kevin.

'No,' says Noelle. 'That would be too messy. They're probably just analysing the ingredients. Trying to reverse engineer the composition so they can reproduce it.'

'Oh,' says Kevin, his shoulders sagging. 'I see…'

Sally raises up her rifle and rounds on Maeve. 'Is this supposed to be funny?' she roars. 'Where's the fucking alien?'

Maeve blinks at her, bewildered, and then begins to smirk. 'Jesus Christ. You really aren't from Miss Meow, are you? You're just a bunch of raving lunatics.'

But Sally doesn't respond. Instead, she drops the gun onto the desk and presses her shaking hands down either side of it. Sean, meanwhile, has started stamping on the fallen cans, while Kevin has produced a set of rosary beads and begun to pray.

Maeve continues grinning, like the whole thing is a scene from a sitcom. And in a way, I can't say I blame her. There is something absurd about the sight of them. Three fully-grown adults on the verge of a breakdown, and all over some stupid tins of cat food…

But no matter how ridiculous they might look, I can't bring myself to laugh. Because I know this must be a crushing blow for them. My own disappointment is palpable enough, and I never took Future Fish seriously to begin with. But the three of them were true believers. They've dedicated their hearts and souls to the cause. Left behind jobs, friends, and families. Sacrificed it all to get inside the lab. And now that they're here – now that they've finally made it – it turns out they were wrong all along. There's nothing behind the curtain. Nothing to fight against. Nothing to rescue. Nothing to expose. Just a bunch of empty cans rolling around in a box.

The only person who seems unfazed is Noelle. She picks up another can, turning it over with a look of detached curiosity. 'Was it worth it?' she asks, raising an eyebrow at Maeve. 'All the secrecy, all the security, all the people you fired… Just so nobody would find out you were stealing your rival's recipe?'

Maeve stiffens, holding her head up high. 'You don't understand. The company has been in the red ever since the recession hit. If things don't turn around for us soon, we're sunk.

That's why we need Future Fish to be a success.'

Noelle shrugs, as if to say she doesn't necessarily disagree.

'But launching a product into this market is a nightmare,' continues Maeve. 'Nobody wants to take a chance on something new. They just want the same old trash they've bought a million times before. No matter what exotic recipe we formulated, no matter how much we splashed out on top-end ingredients, focus groups kept choosing Tuna Tsunami over Future Fish.'

'That must have driven you crazy,' grins Noelle.

'It was humiliating. Seeing our premium product outperformed by that bottom-shelf trash… But then one day, there was a mix-up at the test centre. The focus group coordinator accidentally put a Future Fish label onto a can of Tuna Tsunami. And the participants went wild for it. They said it smelled just like Tuna Tsunami, and the texture was the same too. They were sure their cats would love it. The feedback forms showed a thirty per cent spike in purchase intent, putting us on track to overtake Miss Meow within six months. And I thought to myself, could it really be that simple? Is that all we need to do? Copy the recipe, make a couple of tiny tweaks, and if anybody asks, say we came up with it ourselves.'

'Never mind the ethical considerations, eh?' adds Noelle.

'It's not like I had a choice,' says Maeve, clenching her jaw. 'I did what I had to do to save the company. So go ahead and judge me all you want. You would have done the same thing in my position.'

'Maybe,' says Noelle. 'But I wouldn't have been stupid enough to leave the evidence laying around for anybody to find.'

'What were we supposed to do?' snaps Maeve. 'Toss a hundred

Miss Meow cans into the bin and hope nobody noticed? We had to store them down here until we had a chance to destroy them. That's why I cracked down so hard on that idiot Valentina. We couldn't risk word getting out about Future Fish before we'd had a chance to cover our tracks. Miss Meow would sue us into oblivion if they found out what we were doing.'

'True,' nods Noelle. 'It'd be enough to sink the whole company...' She smiles at this thought, then turns back to Sally. 'Here now,' she says, putting a hand on her shoulder.'I know this isn't what we were hoping for, but it's not the end of the world.'

Sally mumbles something in response, but I don't quite catch it. Because Maeve has started whispering in my ear again.

'Listen Marcus, it's not too late. All you've got to do is look the other way and let me slip through that door...'

I shuffle a few inches away from her, tightening my grip on the golf club.

'Alright, alright,' she croons. 'I know what you want... As well as putting in a good word with the Guards, how about I also reinstate your old position? I'll even throw in that promotion we were talking about. You'd like that, wouldn't you?'

My eyes swivel slowly in her direction. I know I shouldn't listen. Shouldn't let her get inside my head. But what if she's serious about giving me my job back? I thought my career was over. Dead and buried and never coming back. And I'd accepted that. Even begun to make peace with it. But a chance to pick up where I left off would change everything. 'Even if I wanted to help you,' I say, choosing my words carefully, 'how do I know I can trust you? That you won't go back on your word as soon as this is over?'

'I swear,' she hisses, gripping hold of my arm. 'Ask yourself who you really trust – me, or this lot?' She gestures over at the others, who are still wallowing in despair.

'So this whole time,' mumbles Kevin, 'we've been barking up the wrong tree. Future Fish is just a façade. A smokescreen for a Miss Meow product.'

'Hang on…' says Sean, suddenly perking up. 'That means these Miss Meow people must be the ones who are actually carrying out the animal experiments!'

Sally's eyes go wide, the colour returning to her cheeks. 'You mean they're the ones who are holding the alien specimen.'

'Maeve's not the source of all this evil,' nods Kevin. 'She's just another victim. The real demonic influence must be coming from Miss Meow.'

'Where can we find these sickos?' asks Sean. 'I mean, where's the Miss Meow office?'

'Somewhere in Dublin,' says Noelle. 'Out in the Docklands, I think.'

'Brilliant,' says Sally. 'It won't take us long to get there, so.'

'And there'll be plenty of priests nearby,' adds Kevin. 'In case we need an exorcist.'

I stare at each of them in turn, my jaw dropping open. They can't be serious, can they? Just two minutes ago, they were all in a state of shock. Struggling to reckon with the loss of everything they believed in. On the verge of a full-blown existential crisis. But now they're acting like nothing's happened. They're picking themselves back up. Dusting themselves off. Already planning the next phase of their madcap adventures.

'Think very carefully,' says Maeve, her fingers digging like talons into my arm. 'You don't want to end up like the rest of those idiots, do you?'

'Eh...'

I close my eyes, imagining what it would be like to go back to the office. To sit down at my desk each morning and switch on my laptop. To wade through the mire of emails and meetings, feeling my life drain away one day at a time. And suddenly, I want to hit something. I want to smash that mental office into a million little pieces. Because Noelle is right. I was never really happy there. And no matter how hard I might try to convince myself, I know I'll never believe in any of it.

I open my eyes, turning back towards the others, who are already planning their assault on the Miss Meow office. And a dull rumble of longing rises up from my stomach. Because they may be crazy – there's no denying that – but at least they've got a little fire in their engines. Their lives may be going nowhere, but at least they're taking the scenic route. I know I'll never be like them. I'll never believe in any of their conspiracy theories. But maybe that doesn't matter. Maybe believing isn't the point.

'Actually,' I say, snatching my hand away from Maeve. 'I think I want to end up exactly like them.'

Everything after that is a blur. Maeve's entire demeanour changes in a heartbeat, the desperate pleading replaced by something harder and meaner. She spins around and lunges for the door, propelling herself forward with a feral roar. I reach out and grab hold of her tracksuit hood just in time, yanking her back inside and knocking us both off our feet. A brief, vicious struggle ensues, until Sally breaks it up with a warning shot from her rifle. All the fight goes out of Maeve then. She puts her hands up in the air, fury cooling into sullen hatred, and refuses to acknowledge anything that follows.

After a heated debate about the best way to deal with her – Sally advocating for execution, while Sean suggests taking her hostage, and Kevin pleads for a non-violent solution – Noelle eventually convinces them to leave her tied up in the lab. 'It won't kill her to spend the night here,' she reasons. 'And by the time anybody finds her, we'll already be long gone.'

Sally and Sean set to work with the duct tape, wrapping her up from head to toe. She remains perfectly still, making no attempt to resist, and stares up at the ceiling like she's bored out of her mind. They heave her mummified body across the floor, laying it down lengthways in the can-filled sarcophagus. Kevin goes to place the lid on top of her, but Noelle catches hold of his hand.

'Hang on,' she says, holding her phone up for a photo. 'It's like Maeve said, Miss Meow would sue her into oblivion if they found out she was ripping them off.'

'You bitter old hag!' screeches Maeve, finally awakening from her stupor. She thrashes around in the box, desperately trying to break loose, but the duct tape cocoon holds her tight. 'It's not enough for you to humiliate me, but now you want to destroy the entire company too?'

'Pretty much,' shrugs Noelle.

'It's not just me and Dominic you'll be ruining, it's all our staff too! Shelley will have to go back to being an escort if she loses her job. And Fi's ketamine habit will spiral out of control. Not to mention what JD's parole officer will do if she finds out he's not in full-time employment any more!'

Noelle grins, that old familiar twinkle shining in her eyes. She blows Maeve a kiss, then slams the lid of the box down with a deafening *crash*.

And then it's all over. The only thing left to do is make our getaway.

We file out of the lab and up the stairs to the ground floor. Maeve has left the lights on, flooding the hallway with their fluorescent glow. For a few seconds, it almost feels like an ordinary evening. Like the events of the last few days have been nothing but a dream. But there are no waves goodbye from colleagues. No *have a good night* or *take it easy*. And definitely no *see you tomorrow*. Because I know now with absolute certainty that I'll never be coming back.

The alarm system has been deactivated, allowing us to stroll nonchalantly out of the front door. We pause outside, making sure the coast is clear, then hurry up the road towards Noelle's waiting car. Nobody says a word as we walk. The night is hot and muggy, with a thick bank of clouds rolling in from the ocean. Somewhere in the distance, thunder is rumbling.

It's only when we're safely inside the car that I finally pipe up with the inevitable question.

'So…what happens next?'

'I don't know about the rest of you lot,' says Sally from the passenger seat, 'but I'm heading straight to Dublin to find the real Future Fish.'

'Same here,' says Kevin, on my right.

'Me too,' nods Sean, on my left.

'In that case,' says Noelle. 'It's probably best that we all stick together. Maeve will have the Guards on our tail as soon as she's out of that box, and we've got a better chance of evading them if we pool our resources.'

Sally hesitates, eyeing Sean and me with suspicion. But then she shrugs and rolls her eyes. 'Fine,' she grunts. 'I suppose they've been useful so far. I can get us a fresh car in Galway, in case they try to track your licence plate.'

Kevin nods slowly, letting this all sink in. 'I've got an auntie in Clontarf we could stay with. A good Catholic woman. She'd never rat us out, even if the Guards came knocking.'

'And I've got a couple fake passports we could use,' adds Sean. 'In case we get ID'd anywhere. We'll just need to swap you guys' photos in for my friends.'

'Jesus Christ,' says Noelle, spinning around in the driver seat. 'Your friends! Weren't they planning on blowing the place up tonight? They could kill Maeve. Or worse, set her free before we've had a chance to escape.'

'Oh yeah...' yawns Sean. 'I'll message them now.' And then, with a sleepy smile: 'Magda will lose her shit when she finds out I got inside the lab before her. She'll probably end up dumping Carl over this.'

'Great,' says Noelle. 'That's sorted, so.' She settles back in her seat and switches on the engine. And then, like she's trying not to spook me, she gives me a gentle glance in the rear-view mirror. 'How about you, Mark? Will you be coming with us too?'

The others turn to look at me, all awaiting my answer.

But this time, I don't hesitate.

'Sure,' I say, grinning at Noelle. 'It's not like I've got anything better to do. Might as well come along for the ride.'

'Brilliant,' she beams. 'Something tells me this is going to be a wild one.'

She pulls out of the parking spot and skids around the corner. We cruise down Main Street and up into the hills, leaving the grey world of Ashcross behind us forever.

My stay here hasn't worked out exactly the way I was planning. I figured I'd keep my head down for a year or two – just long enough for it to look good on my CV – then move back home for the next phase of my career. Never in a million years did I imagine myself ending up like this. Throwing my career into the bin and setting it on fire behind me. Returning to Dublin with a gang of unhinged criminals. On the verge of becoming unhinged myself… I can only imagine what everybody back home would say. The looks of horror on their faces if they could see me now. But the funny thing is, right now, in this moment, I feel happier than I have felt in a long, long time.

And so, as the first bolts of lightning dance across the horizon, I feel a slow smile spread across my face. Sally and Noelle chat away in the front seat, discussing the latest spate of crop circles in County Mayo. Kevin flicks through a *Book of Daily Prayer* on my right, while Sean dozes off with his head on my left shoulder. As we pass under a faded billboard reading *Goodbye from Ashcross*, I feel the first bittersweet stirrings of nostalgia.

The town wasn't as bad as I expected after all.

Acknowledgements

Thank you to everybody who supported me on the long journey of writing *Future Fish*. To Kristin, who read an extremely messy first draft and provided invaluable feedback and encouragement. To Rachel, who read a slightly less messy later draft and provided expert technical advice. To Ali, Amy, Carolyn, Hannah, Jack, Jodie, Luke, Nadine, Noel, Paul, Ralph, Ruth, and everybody else who shared their feedback or support. Thanks also to everybody in the Camden writers' group for providing camaraderie along the way, and to Quinn's for providing all the pints. Thank you to the team at Lightning Books for taking a chance on *Future Fish* and helping make it the best book it could be. Finally, thank you to my parents for always supporting me in my creative endeavours, no matter how strange or silly. And thank you to Gordon, for everything.